WHAT WE CAN'T HAVE

Lessons in Life & Love

by

Selina Violet

Copyright © 2024 by Selina Violet.

All rights reserved.

No part of this publication may be reproduced, distributed, or transmitted in any form or by any means, including photocopying, recording, or other electronic or mechanical methods, without the prior written permission of the publisher, except as permitted by U.S. copyright law. For permission requests, contact Violet Publications, Inc. at https://selinaviolet.com

The story, all names, characters, and incidents portrayed in this production are fictitious. No identification with actual persons (living or deceased), places, buildings, and products is intended or should be inferred.

Book Cover ©2024 by https://100Covers.com

Illustrations ©2024 by Moonchildreams

Book Layout ©2024 by Violet Publications, Inc.

Author Photos ©2024 Wings and a Prayer Photography

What We Can't Have: Lessons in Life and Love/Selina Violet. — 1st Ed.

ISBN Paperback: 978-1-7355804-5-6

ISBN eBook EPUB: 978-1-7355804-6-3

To my boys-

You are the only names tattooed on my heart.

Not every love story is a fairytale.

-Selina Violet

What You Missed

What We Can't Have: Hollywood Hot Shots

Austin and Sydney get paired to compose an original song for their Music Composition class. They win their college talent show, and a Hollywood agent wants their song for a movie soundtrack. This opportunity leads to them moving to L.A. to work as songwriters. Life in L.A. presents challenges. Sydney gets a canine companion to combat her homesickness and loneliness. Austin drinks and carouses with women to avoid his inner demons. They rely on each other even as they fight their growing feelings for each other.

Austin's poor decisions result in an accident, hospital stay, and criminal charges. Sydney stands by him and supports him, at the expense of her own identity. While Austin is in rehab, Sydney realizes how far she's strayed from her own goals and ambitions to keep Austin afloat. Three years in L.A. culminate in an Oscar win for their song. They have a night of passion and Sydney leaves to chase her own dreams.

Content Warning

This book contains material that may not be suitable for everyone. It contains, among other issues:

- alcoholism
- sexual assault (off page)/PTSD
- pregnancy and infant death
- fatphobia
- explicit sex

Closed Door Option

For those who prefer a closed door romance, follow these reading instructions:

- Skip Chapter Three and Chapter Twenty-Four
- Skip any section following a scene break identified by flames.

Please note that there are one-off sexual comments included in the main body of the story.

Spotify Playlists

Austin and Sydney have distinctly different musical preferences. They each compiled a list of some of their favorite tunes. Enjoy them!

Cowboys & Cowgirls - Austin's Playlist

Happy Tunes & Smooth Grooves - Sydney's Playlist

Table of Contents

1. SYDNEY – REVELATION — 1
2. AUSTIN – CULINARY EXPERIMENT — 7
3. SYDNEY – RAGING HORMONES — 13
4. AUSTIN – CHANGE OF PLANS — 19
5. SYDNEY – UNEXPECTED REUNION — 23
6. AUSTIN – TAKING THE BAIT — 27
7. SYDNEY – ALPACA FARMERS — 31

Fullpage image — 40

8. VINNIE – FIRESIDE CHAT — 41
9. SYDNEY – HEARING A HEARTBEAT — 45
10. AUSTIN – FOOD FOR THOUGHT — 51
11. SYDNEY – TWINS CHECKUP — 55
12. AUSTIN – STROKE OF LUCK — 61
13. SYDNEY – LABOR DAY — 65
14. VINNIE – ZOEY ARRIVES — 73
15. SYDNEY – AT THE PARK — 77
16. VINNIE – PLANTING THE SEEDS — 83
17. SYDNEY – PREGNANT IN NYC — 85

Fullpage image — 91

18. AUSTIN – SHOW BUSINESS BLUES — 93

19. SYDNEY – NESTING ASSISTANCE	101
20. AUSTIN – SECRET DATE	107
Fullpage image	111
21. CHEYENNE – CATCHING FEELINGS	113
22. SYDNEY – BABY SHOWER	117
23. AUSTIN – FINAL ROUND	123
Fullpage image	128
24. CHEYENNE – NAKED FUN	129
25. SYDNEY – HAPPY BIRTH DAY	133
Fullpage image	141
26. SYDNEY – MOTHERHOOD	143
27. AUSTIN – TAKING A MEETING	153
28. VINNIE – FRESH PERSPECTIVE	163
29. SYDNEY – BISTRO 501	167
30. VINNIE – CONFESSION	173
31. AUSTIN – TEAMWORK	177
32. VINNIE – NEXT LEVEL	181
33. SYDNEY – BED AND BREAKFAST	185
34. CHEYENNE – THAT ONE TIME	191
35. AUSTIN – THE WHOLE TRUTH	195
36. SYDNEY – SURPRISE PARTY	197
Fullpage image	202
37. AUSTIN – GRAND OPENING	203
Fullpage image	206
38. CHEYENNE – A HUNDRED ROSES	207
39. SYDNEY – AN INVITATION	213
40. CHEYENNE – VEGAS, BABY	217
Fullpage image	222

41. AUSTIN – MELODY	223
Fullpage image	230
42. VINNIE – CHANGES	231
43. AUSTIN – TAKING A BREAK	235
44. AUSTIN – ONE GOOD PUNCH	239
45. CHEYENNE – CALLING IT QUITS	241
46. AUSTIN – WAKE UP CALL	251
47. AUSTIN – ALIGNING THE STARS	257
48. VINNIE – SYDNEY'S CONFESSION	263
49. SYDNEY – VOWS	267
Fullpage image	273
50. AUSTIN – UNINVITED GUEST	275
51. VINNIE-HONEYMOON SUITE	279
52. CHEYENNE – FORMULATING A PLAN	283
53. AUSTIN – THE NEXT PHASE	285
54. CHEYENNE – RE-IGNITING THE FLAME	289
55. SYDNEY – REALITY BITES	293
Acknowledgements	297
About the author	299
Endnotes	301

ONE

SYDNEY - REVELATION

The lightbulb came on in my head. "Shit! Mother trucker! Damn! Damn! Damn!" I checked my mirror and plowed across three lanes of interstate to make it to the Scenic Overlook ramp. My truck sped up the incline. I found a spot in the back of the parking lot, jammed into neutral, and pulled the emergency brake—my stream of expletives flowing the whole time. "Cheese and rice! Crap on a cracker! Son of a biscuit! Fuck! Fuck!"

Samson regarded me from the passenger seat with one eye open and the other still committed to his nap. I had to check my phone. I opened the calendar and scanned through the past six weeks, eight weeks. There, in black and white. The date I was dreading. In the midst of the chaos and excitement for the Oscars, I'd missed my notification to change my birth control ring.

I peered at Samson. "I think I'm in deep dog do-do, no offense." He gazed his cocoa eye at me and closed it again. "Yeah, no worries. I'll figure it out. You go back to sleep, buddy. So glad we had this chat."

It could just be stress. You've been under so much pressure from Austin being in rehab and getting ready for the Oscars.

But in my gut, I knew I was fooling myself. I was pregnant. I didn't want to say the word out loud. As if not saying it would erase the predicament I found myself in right now.

Samson perked his snout up as I opened the door. "Stay here, buddy. I won't be long." I strolled up the path to the overlook. The lush mountains in the distance appeared covered with broccoli florets. Down in the valley, miniature boats floated on the river. The sun warmed my freckles as I stood on the overlook, trying to force my brain to stop short circuiting.

Taking the long way back around the edge of the parking lot, I passed some tiny buttercup flowers sprouting up through the concrete. Samson took a quick stroll around the pet area and watered a few trees. Before I put the truck in gear, I texted Abby.

> Can you call me after work? No hurry.

I needed a little time to figure out how to tell her about my stupidity. It still barely registered in my brain. My original plan for tonight had been to camp out under the stars, but now a hot shower and some guilty pleasure TV from a hotel bed sounded better.

Two more hours tearing up the asphalt, then I called it quits for the evening. I ordered Chinese take-out and picked up some M&M'S®, strawberry milk and a pregnancy test at CVS. Once ensconced in our hotel room, I kicked off my sandals and tossed my suitcase onto the bed. Samson had his own tote bag with his necessities and I opened that first, pulling out his food dishes. I poured tap water into his bowl and scooped out a can of wet food then stood back to keep safe. Sam takes treats gently from my hand, but he's a ferocious hurricane in front of his food bowl.

I propped up some pillows against the headboard and sank into them with the remote in my hand. *Oh yeah, hotel was* definitely *the right choice.* I settled on watching *Pretty Woman* for the umpteenth time while lingering over my Chinese feast. I've eaten lots of mediocre meals on the road, but Chinese never disappoints. It's like David said in *The Lost Boys*: *How could a billion Chinese people be wrong?*[1] They're not.

The test sat on the counter in the bathroom, but I wasn't quite ready yet. Shower first, definitely.

I cleared away my duck sauce packets and fortune cookie wrappers while I ran the hot water. Dirty clothes into a corner, step into the steam.... *Ahhh. Bliss.* Camping meant not showering every day, so I savored every single second of naked warmth. After scrubbing and shampooing, I pulled up the plug and let the water fill the tub. I sank into the wet blanket and closed my eyes. With me being a plus-size woman, tubs did not accommodate my body the way they did when I was a kid and pretended to be a mermaid swimming in the ocean.

I reheated the water twice before emerging from my watery cocoon. All four towels lay scattered about the floor as I brushed out my wet curls. I smoothed some conditioner into them, hoping to keep the frizz to a minimum. My silky nightgown clung to my skin. When I'm camping in a tent, I don't bother changing my clothes for sleeping.

As I approached the bed to snuggle under the covers, my phone rang. Abby. The moment of truth. I took a deep breath and answered.

"Hi, Sissy! What's going on?" she chirped.

"Just living it up with my glamorous life on the road."

She laughed. "You signed up for this. No one said you had to do this forever, silly goose."

"I am enjoying it. But I stopped at a hotel tonight and stood under the hot shower forever. I almost didn't get out."

"Tell me what you've been up to today."

I thought for a moment. "I drove today. Yesterday, I tooled around Hungry Horse Dam, and now I'm heading to the Badlands."

She sighed. "I sure do wish I could be with you. I bet you're seeing some amazing things."

"I am. I can't stop taking pictures, although none of them compared to seeing these places with my own eyes. My dreams have been so vivid when I'm sleeping in the fresh air." I paused, trying to find my courage. "There might be another reason, though."

"What other reason? Did you take one of those rocks you're not supposed to take from the desert? You know that's asking for bad juju."

"No, not exactly." *Just say it.* "I think I'm pregnant."

Radio silence came from the other end of the line. I waited for a beat. "Abby?"

She rallied. "Yeah, Sissy. I'm still here. I'm speechless, and that isn't an easy task. Are you sure about this? Did you take a pregnancy test?"

"In all of the excitement over the Oscars, I neglected to swap my birth control ring for a fresh one. That was over eight weeks ago. I bought a test at CVS today but I'm afraid to take it."

"Oh goodness! I'd be afraid, too. I'm so sorry you're all alone right now. Why don't you take the test now? I'll stay on the phone with you."

"Okay. Thanks, Abby." I went into the bathroom and read the instructions. "I'm going to put the phone on the counter and put you on speaker. I need both hands." I completed all of the steps and laid the stick face down on the counter. "Can you time me for ten minutes? Then we will have the results."

Abby jabbered on about her work and a new boyfriend she had started dating, but all I heard was my heart pounding in my ears. My mind kept replaying that day on my calendar, trying to figure out how I managed to forget something so important. That's when I remembered.

Jason. The day he attacked me in the sound booth. Tori, Venus, Daisy and I went to the beach and held a pizza and margarita party at my townhouse to take our minds off that terrible event. My phone alert went off somewhere in the middle of it all so I missed it. I didn't tell Marcus about the attack because I didn't want to ruin the Oscars, and Austin couldn't try to murder Jason from rehab.

"Sissy? Sissy!" Abby shouted. "Time's up. Are you ready? I'm right here for you."

I flipped over the test to reveal my fate. "Oh shit. Wonder what Mom will say about this."

"Oh, Sydney. I wish I could hug you right now. I love you and will support you no matter what."

I stared at the word *Pregnant* in the test window. Relief washed over me, knowing my suspicions were correct, which was probably hella weird. There was no relief about the new problems on my hands.

"Is it Marcus?" Abby interrupted my thoughts.

"What? What do you mean?"

"Is Marcus the father? I don't mean to pry, but you two are dating? Were dating? I mean, it doesn't matter to me. God, Abby, shut your mouth," she reprimanded herself.

"It's not like that. I don't know who the father is. I feel like I'm in a warped Twilight Zone version of *Mamma Mia*."

"I don't follow."

"I think I had protected sex with Marcus on Oscar night. Did I? I don't know, I blew it with the birth control, I just don't know when I blew it. Then three days later I had sex with Austin, still not aware of my birth control snafu. Ending up pregnant was not part of my plan. Now what do I do?" I burst into tears. It was too much for one pregnant woman to take. I shuffled out of the bathroom, crawled under the sheets, and cried myself to sleep.

Journal Entry

Finding out I'm pregnant wasn't what I had envisioned for my extended road trip. When I woke up the next morning, I put my hands on my abdomen and thought about the life growing inside me. I've never contemplated what it means to be a mother, and I never had a romantic relationship where that idea or conversation came into play. I only have my own mother as an example, and it isn't what I want for my own child. I still can't quite wrap my head around the idea that I'm going to be responsible for another living being other than Samson.

I don't want to stop traveling yet. If my calculations are correct, I'm about six to eight weeks along. It gives me a little time before I start showing and need to think about a safe place to land to have my baby.

My baby. But not just my baby. I suppose I will need to wait until s/he is born to tackle that dilemma.

There's no such thing as a clean break, is there?

Two
Austin - Culinary Experiment

Every day hurt. My entire life, I spent so much time and energy keeping everyone at a distance, protecting myself and them from me. From my brokenness. But I screwed up. Sydney snuck through my fortress walls and stole my heart.

Even though I wanted to respect her wishes, at the same time I wanted to find her and tell her she was wrong. The more time passed, the more foolish it grew to pursue her. How could I explain why I waited so long to respond? To choose her. To try and change her mind.

This is how almost four months went by without realizing it. My brain short-circuited every morning in the shower and every night as I tried to fall asleep, trying to make sense of it all. The rest of my days went by in a blur of songwriting and poker games. Once or twice a week I ventured out to a club to find a hookup. Tourists minimized my chances of an awkward second meeting with any of them, or God forbid, the possibility of starting a relationship.

The one smart thing I did right after Sydney left was post ads for roommates. The two spare bedrooms upstairs became home to a couple of aspiring actors, Avery and Dale. They waited tables at an upscale restaurant while they auditioned for their big break. Sydney's room stayed empty because I couldn't bring myself to rent it. On some level, I probably held out hope she might return. Besides, I lived rent free already with my two roommates.

At the last poker night, I got an idea in my head and couldn't shake it. Being an established songwriter fulfilled me, but I wanted to cement my place here in a more permanent way. As we were cashing out at the end of the game, I posed a question to the boys.

"I know we all love pizza and snacks, but I want to try something different next time. Can I ask you to be test subjects for me? I've been experimenting with a recipe at home and would love for you to try it. It's a pulled pork sandwich."

Murmurs buzzed around the table. Derek was the first to speak. "Where have you been hiding this talent? We could handle a pulled pork sandwich or ten."

"Second that," Jack replied.

"Voting for myself and Andy, I think we're all in." Tyler gestured around the table. "It's settled. The cowboy is bringing the grub next week." He scowled at Austin from under his eyebrows. "And shame on you for holding out on us for so long."

Everyone laughed, and my excitement grew about my plans.

Since poker was on Tuesday this week, I told Venus I would be working from home today. Working on getting my smoker on, that is. When I bought it, I wanted to put it on the deck, but we would've lost our morning coffee corner. It sat in the belly of the garage and I pulled it out to the driveway when I had a slab of meat to roast. Having a live, hungry audience to give feedback on my recipe gave me the courage to go all out. I spent all day nursing my babies, checking temperatures, marinade and tenderness.

When I finished, I put them on the kitchen counter to rest. The aroma of spices and meat made my mouth water. Thank goodness Samson wasn't here to drool over them and beg me with his chocolate-brown orbs. And there she was again. Sydney. Dancing around the kitchen and singing with her spatula microphone while she mixed cookie dough in her grandma's Kitchen Aid mixer.

Get her out of your head. Cowboy Up, Austin. You have other things to think about right now.

I loaded up the car with paper products and the rolls I purchased from the bakery. Everything needed to be just right. The meat rested in a thermos container to keep it warm. The last piece of the puzzle was my favorite grilling shirt that said: *Once you put my meat in your mouth, you're going to swallow.* Hilarious.

Derek came out of the garage to greet me. We clasped hands and side-bumped each other.

"Hey brother! You need help with the food?" he asked.

"There's a box with the rolls in the back seat. I'll grab the precious cargo."

Derek inhaled. "Oh. My. God. My nose just had an orgasm. I can't wait to devour whatever's in that cooler."

I laughed. "This gastro-joygasm took all day. Everyone better like it."

Derek smiled. "Five hungry men? How could you go wrong? You bet I'm going to swallow. Cool shirt. Glad my kids can't read yet."

"Oh shit! I can turn it inside out..." My cheeks flushed and he started laughing.

"I'm just busting your nuts. It's all good."

The food table already had drinks and chips on it. I put the rolls in a basket and set the thermos container next to it. Then I added bottles of ketchup, mustard, relish, and a small container of chopped onions next to it. Chinet plates and a generous stack of napkins completed my offering.

Derek smacked me on the shoulder. "Look at this fancy spread. This beats pizza any day. But I'm still going to take your money, man."

"Keep telling yourself that. Your money from last week is still in my wallet."

"Ouch! You know how to make a guy feel loved."

Once Jack, Andy and Tyler arrived, we wasted no time digging into the sandwiches. The only sounds around the table were the moans of approval and the smacking of lips and fingers. Occasionally, someone came up for air and offered up their accolades. It was difficult to keep my head from swelling with the compliments. I kicked back and absorbed it all.

"Question for y'all: Would you buy this from a food truck?" They mulled it over and all started talking at once.

Jack spoke up. "I'm not an adventurous eater, but I do like pulled pork. This is something I might try from a food truck."

"Count me in! I would chase a food truck around town for pulled pork this outstanding," Andy gushed.

"Are you quitting your job to start a food truck?" Tyler asked.

"Wait! Is this what you're up to? Going to leave the glamourous record industry to sling spiced slabs of meat?" Derek gaped at me.

"Okay, okay. Don't get your panties in a twist. Let me explain." I waited for them to shut up. "I want to open a restaurant, but I don't have enough startup capital. Establishing a food truck would serve two purposes. First, it would help me build up a nest egg. Second, I would use it to perfect my restaurant menu staples based on customer feedback. Hang out at the touristy locations on the weekends and rake in the dough for my seed money. It would also come in handy at fairs and other events as a mobile venue for promotional purposes."

I scanned the faces around the table, waiting for a response. Everyone seemed to have lost the ability to speak. "Well? Give it to me straight."

Andy coughed. "The sandwiches are next level tasty! You won't have any issues unloading them at the beach or at the Walk of Fame. Hangry tourists are always easy bait. But do you know what your competition will be like?"

"That's a valid question. I'm going to do some research before I decide to use my savings for anything foolish. My goal tonight was to test the food first. Taking a couple of business classes to familiarize myself with all of the behind-the-scenes stuff will help, too."

Derek interjected. "It sounds like you're being methodical and not jumping into this. I'm excited to see what you do. But right now, I'm more excited about taking my money back out of your wallet. Let's play some poker, shall we? Tip the chef extra on your way out."

"Seriously man, thanks for the tasty grub," Tyler added. "Who's cooking next? I vote the loser gets to be the chef next week."

"Now that sounds like a fantastic idea," Jack interjected. "Why didn't we think of this before now? Derek better hope his cooking is better than his card playing."

We played a few rounds, and the subject turned to office gossip. I didn't often have any dirt to dish, but I liked hearing conspiracy theories.

Jack started. "Hey! Guess who I saw over the weekend at the hardware store?" Everyone shook their heads. "Jason Cooper. I had no idea he took his talents down the street."

Everyone murmured. I knew why that asshole sexual harasser didn't work with us anymore. Guys like that give the rest of us a bad name. It's one thing to have consensual fun with a woman, but I can't understand that objectifying, predatory mentality; it's just sick. When Sydney told me he tried to rape her, I was murderous. He didn't want to run into me anywhere, believe me. While I was in rehab, he stopped coming to poker nights. I remained silent as the conversation continued.

"I asked him how it was going and why he left. He started acting nervous and said he shouldn't talk to me. He muttered something about a lawyer and walked away. It was the strangest thing."

Tyler laid his cards face down on the table. "I fold. I heard he got fired for sexual harassment." Bingo. "I stopped Tori in the hall one day and tried to ask her about it. She wrote in her notebook *I can't talk about that* and walked away."

My curiosity got the better of me. "How long ago did this happen?"

Jack glanced up over his glasses, counting. "It was around the same time as the Oscars, which is why it got swept under the rug." He put his hand down. "I'm out."

"Oh hell, I'm out, too. Who brought these cards anyway?" Andy complained.

It was down to me and Derek. "I call."

Derek checked his hand. "I call and raise you ten."

He couldn't beat me with the cards I held, but my head wasn't in the game anymore. "I fold."

Derek's mouth flew open. "You mean I won? Woo hoo!" He did a little victory dance. He raked in the chips with a huge grin on his face. My three aces for a full house got swept back into the deck. It was worth it, seeing how happy he was. He deserved it.

Three
Sydney - Raging Hormones
(explicit chapter)

My revelation did not deter me from continuing with my road trip. On a video call with my PCP, she prescribed prenatal vitamins and encouraged me to schedule regular exams throughout my pregnancy. At this stage, my breasts were tender and my nipples were on alert 24/7. My hormones were making me crazy like back when Danny and I first started having sex, but the more I masturbated, the hornier I became.

When I couldn't control myself any longer, I put on a low-cut t-shirt over a black lacy pushup bra that highlighted my swollen breasts. Then, I squeezed my expanding stomach and ass into a thong and my favorite cutoffs. The zipper barely closed, and the button was a challenge. Too much eye makeup, bright red lipstick and perfume rounded out my best sexy/slutty vibe.

At the bar, I chose a stool left of the center but with a decent view of the stage. The band finished their sound check, and the local crowd came in as couples and small groups. The bartender got a hefty tip to keep my cranberry vodkas (Sprite only) coming. Now all I had to do was find the right sucker, make that *stud*, to rock my world for a night.

It didn't take long. The bass player flirted with me from the stage as I sipped my drink and twirled on my stool. The band's cover songs were on par, and I started reminiscing about the good ol' days when I was a kid. The bartender came over with another drink for me. My eyes widened.

"From the gentleman on the end. You won't mind if I charge him full price, will you?" He winked at me.

"Of course not."

I raised my glass in thanks and he raised his bottle of beer in return. He got down from his stool and approached me. His hairline was receding, but he had a friendly smile. This wasn't a deal-breaker, I had to remind myself—he's only someone to fill the void for a horny pregnant woman. He was close-shaven and lean. I could go for that.

"Hi, beautiful. I'm Corey. I've never seen you here before."

"That's because I haven't been here before." I pursed my lips and lowered my voice. "Can I tell you a secret, Corey?"

He nodded.

"I broke up with my boyfriend. He would go out with his buddies all the time and leave me at home alone. It wasn't fair and I decided I wasn't putting up with it anymore. So here I am. Looking for a man who will treat me right." I looked up at him from under my heavily mascara'd lashes. "Are you that kind of man, Corey?"

"If there's one thing I know how to do, it's to keep my woman happy."

"And satisfied?"

"Yes, ma'am. And satisfied."

I licked my lips, leaned in next to his ear and whispered, "Would you like to show me now?" My tongue touched his earlobe, and his body shivered. That's when I knew I had him. "Let's go back to my hotel room. I'm getting wet thinking about it."

I dug through my purse and found my spare card key. "Room 723. Wait here ten minutes before following me." It took me every ounce of strength not to sprint out the door. Once in my room, I peeled off my shorts and t-shirt. The handful of cheap candles I bought at the dollar store provided enough lighting, and I pulled up my "SXXY SONGS" mix on my phone. Lying on my stomach to camouflage its size, propped up on my elbows to highlight my thong, I waited.

Corey knocked on the door and slid his key card in to enter the room. "Wow," he breathed as he came towards me. "I wasn't sure if someone was punking me or not. You look scrumptious."

I turned my head and looked at him over my shoulder. "That's the plan, stud. Why don't you ditch those clothes and come over here?"

"Yes, ma'am." He took my cue and was naked in less than ten seconds. His six-foot frame was toned and muscular and he reminded me a little of Robert Downy, Jr. as his dark brown eyes caught the light of the candle flames. "Where should I begin?"

"Why don't you start with your tongue and work your way from there?"

He grabbed me by the ankles and yanked me towards the end of the bed.

I gasped. "Oh, Corey! What are you going to do to me?"

His hand connected with my bare left cheek. "Turn you inside out with pleasure until you scream my name." He knelt at the foot of the bed and put his hands on my ass. He kissed on top of the tiny swatch of fabric covering my vagina, then pulled my thong to one side and began his exploration. His tongue licked up one side of my ass and down the other. "Mmm. It's so sexy when a woman has hair down here."

I moaned.

"Yes, lover. Tell me what you like. Do you want some more?"

"Yes. More." My hormones were already raging, and I didn't want it to be over in two minutes.

He yanked my panties down to my knees. "Can you toss me a couple of those pillows?"

I grabbed one at a time and tossed them backwards. He piled them together, then flipped me over on top of them. I wasn't ready, and I let out a little squeal.

With one eyebrow cocked, he licked his lips. "That's right. Keep it up. I'm going to make you cum so hard." He threw my panties to the side and trailed his eyes up and down my body. "God, you're gorgeous." He reached up my torso and took my breasts in his hands, still bound by my lacy bra. "Real breasts! I'll be back for them." And he disappeared between my thighs.

His lips and tongue nipped and sucked at my most sensitive parts. My breathing came faster, and my moans of pleasure kept him going. "Your pussy is magnificent," he mumbled. "Do you want me to stop, or are you thirsty for more?"

"Yes! I want some more! Give it to me!" I put my hands on top of his head, but he swatted them away. "Hold onto the headboard so I can move my head." I obeyed and gripped the rungs. I began to buck up and down.

"Oh Corey! Yes! Yes lover! Right there! Oh yes! I'm cumming!" I squealed and shook while his tongue worked its magic on my swollen clitoris. The waves of pleasure subsided and I lay on the mattress, panting.

He came up on the bed beside me and lay on his back. His penis stood at attention, and I reached over him with my hand, aiming for his hard cock, but he grabbed it before I made contact. "What do you think you're doing?" he growled.

His reaction startled me. "I was planning on returning the favor," I stammered.

He shook his head at me. "Not yet, mistress. Not yet. I'm not finished with you."

Most of the time, I was satisfied to have one orgasm out of a naked session. "I promise, I'm satisfied. What else did you have in mind?"

"For one, your breasts look hungry. They're about to pop out of your bra all by themselves. Two, I'm not finished with your pussy yet. It needs some more attention. You can help me relieve my tension once I'm finished."

He propped himself on his elbow and rolled me to my side facing away from him. His fingers unhooked my bra, and he pulled me back towards his chest. His hard dick pressed against my ass, and I ground my checks into it. I wanted him to fill up my pussy and rock my world.

He held my breast in his hand, squeezing and playing with it. He used his thumb and forefinger to tease my nipple, bringing it to a turgid point. It sent pulses to my clitoris and I squirmed underneath his grasp.

"Oh, do you like that?" He chuckled. "Come over here and I'll give you some more." He scooped me around and I found myself sitting on his stomach. His hands took both of my breasts and teased them into submission. I rocked my hips back and forth. I wanted to sit on his cock and I started to slide back towards his hips. He grabbed my waist and scolded me. "Not yet." His intense expression gave me pause, but I chose to let him have his way.

"Lean forward so I can taste them." He beckoned me with his tongue and I complied. As he teased them, I struggled to keep my wits about me. He took one of my tits in his mouth and I lost my mind. I thought I had some hot sex under my belt, but this was not the same. It might have been the one-night stand aspect, or my limited experience with different partners. Maybe he was that skilled. I didn't care. I gave in to the moment, and it was next level amazing.

I couldn't take it anymore. "I want you inside me." I gasped. "Now." He continued worshiping my breasts as though he hadn't heard me. I gave him another minute. "Corey, did you hear me? I want you. Inside me. Right now." He grasped my waist and rolled me over on my back without letting go of my breast.

"Do we need protection? I should have asked before we got started."

I licked my lips. "I'm on birth control." *Close enough*.

"Are you sure? This guy isn't daddy material, sweets."

It took everything I had not to roll my eyes. "Yes, I'm sure." *Really sure*.

My legs snaked around his hips. "I want you. Now." That first thrust always takes my breath away. Nothing else compares. My whole body hung on the brink, and I struggled to keep myself from climaxing right away.

He held himself inside me but didn't start stroking my vagina with his cock. "Squeeze your muscles. Enjoy this. I'm not going to rush to the finish line. A woman's face in the throes of passionate sex is the most amazing sight."

"Give it to me, handsome. Let me feel your cock work its magic. Make my pussy purr," I murmured, staring at him.

"Hang on, lover. This is the best part." His dick thrust inside me as I squirmed. I reached up and wrapped my arms around his neck, raising my back from the mattress. Holding my ass with both hands, he knelt back and propped me up onto his crotch.

I reached my peak and cried out. "Yes! Yes! Fuck! That's it! Come with me, lover!"

A groan escaped from his lips as his juices released inside me. I clung to his neck and squeezed my pelvic muscles around him. We stayed that way, holding on to each other. He lowered me back down to the bed, making sure I had a pillow under my head. He leaned back next to me with one arm behind his head.

"I noticed your music. Nice touch for a not-so-subtle seduction." He winked at me.

His amusement made me smile. I'd never done this type of thing before, and I didn't know if I should ask him to leave or expect him to stay. Samson was on a down stay in the bathroom, and even though he had his blanket, I was going to have to make up with him tomorrow.

Corey leaned over and kissed me on the cheek. "I don't like to overstay my welcome, so I'm going to leave you here to go to sleep. Your dog will be happier once I go."

I sat up in bed. "How did you know?"

"His water dish is under the desk."

"I'm sorry. He's my protector and would have taken your balls off without a second thought before I got to use them."

"That was mighty kind of you. Thank you for that." He pulled on his jeans and grabbed his t-shirt off the dresser. "Thank you for a fantastic time. We should do this again, but I have a feeling you're merely an apparition."

After he closed the door, I let Samson out of jail. My body fell asleep before my head hit the pillow.

When I woke up in the morning, an envelope had been pushed under my door. I picked it up and sat on the bed to read the note.

Lover,

I don't think I even caught your name last night. It was my pleasure, truly.

I don't know what that knucklehead did to you, but he will regret it later.

Corey

Journal Entry

I'm going to blame my behavior last night on my raging hormones. I don't even know who that cheap tramp was that brought a stranger back from the bar. Not that I plan to behave like that on the regular, but desperate times and all...

I didn't expect Corey's note, and it was a sweet gesture. I think we both got what we came for (pun intended). Hopefully that will keep my horny beast at bay for a few days at least. Otherwise, I may need to get a bigger belt for all my new notches, and not just my expanding uterus.

Samson usually gets a bite or two from my breakfast sandwich, but this morning he's getting an entire one all to himself. That should make up for "putting him in jail" last night. I'm off to find some more adventures on the road.

Four
Austin - Change of Plans

"I have a proposition for you." I sat down in a chair across from Venus's desk.

She looked up from her typing. "And what kind of proposition would interest me?"

"I would like to start working four days instead of five. I would put in the same amount of hours."

She nodded. "Out of curiosity, what will you be doing with this extra day each week?"

"I'm going to take a couple of business classes. Smarten myself up." I grinned at her and waited.

Venus swiveled back and forth in her chair. "I don't care if you work vampire hours in the middle of the night. It shouldn't be an issue, but I have to run it by H.R. Give me a couple of days to respond to you."

"No problem. I had one other question. Were you the one who fired Jason Cooper? Didn't he get fired for sexual harassment. He should be glad I haven't run into him."

Venus put her elbows on her desk and leaned forward. "I can't discuss that. It's still in litigation and there will be a gag order involved in the settlement. I've said more than I should already."

I stood up and turned to leave, but she stopped me in my tracks. "Let me know when I can start getting free sandwiches from your food truck."

I pivoted on my heel back towards her. "Oh. You heard about that. I wasn't trying to keep it a secret. I'm taking one step at a time."

"I'm not upset. No one keeps a secret around here. I heard the guys talking about your mouth-watering sandwiches in the coffee room. It sounds like a solid idea."

I leaned against the doorway. "I've always had a passion for cooking. Barbeque in particular. I'm hoping it leads to bigger and better things. Not that I don't love it here. I do. I'm not planning on quitting, so don't worry about me."

Venus laughed. "It's cute you think I'm concerned about you quitting. As your manager, I'll always have your back. But Sydney was special. I miss her so much. I've called her numerous times, but it goes to voicemail. She never calls back. I think she's afraid I'll try to talk her into coming back."

The second Venus said her name, my jaw locked and my heart clenched in my chest. I felt short of breath. I thought I was healing, but the Band-Aid ripped off my chest again.

Venus observed my reaction. "I'm sorry, Austin. I didn't mean to upset you."

Clearly, I hadn't built my fortress high enough. I closed my eyes and put my face back in neutral, trying to restore my emotional force field. "You didn't upset me."

"I don't mean to pry, but I have to ask. Have you talked to her at all? I miss her so much. I want to respect her boundaries, but it's killing me."

I seethed. "Her *Dear John* letter was the last communication I had. Four months ago." I stood awkwardly, unsure if I should give Venus a hug or leave the room. Finally, striding over to her desk, I commanded, "Stand up so I can give you a hug."

She looked a little startled but stood. I wrapped her in my arms and squeezed her. It felt so good to have some basic human contact, and I didn't let go. She started to wiggle and I loosened my arms as she pulled back.

"Thanks. That helps," she said and sat back down at her desk.

"I'm going to head back to the hive if there's nothing else." I was a bit rattled by my own behavior.

"I'll let you know about your request as soon as I can." She started typing again and I strode out of her office.

I set up a meeting with SCORE, an organization that pairs rookie entrepreneurs with seasoned professionals as their business mentors. There wasn't a fee for joining their program, and grant and loan options existed for those who were interested. They matched me with David Finley. His extensive knowledge of the business world, and in particular, the restaurant industry, made him a great match.

I didn't want to end up neck-deep in loans at the onset, which is why I decided a food truck made sense as a starting point. From that foundation, my profits would bankroll a full-on restaurant. David helped me formulate a business plan and steered me in the right direction for reliable vendors.

Looking for a decent used food truck proved more challenging than expected. I could afford brand new, but with the many uncertainties of small business, I didn't want to waste money. Two days ago, Derek rode with me up to Sacramento to inspect one I found on a marketplace website. We walked around it, kicked the tires, and inspected the layout inside. It had been a coffee truck, so it didn't have a grill, a critical piece of equipment for my needs.

"Hey, buddy! Would you mind letting us take it for a test drive? See how she handles? I'll give you my keys as collateral."

He handed me the keys, and Derek and I took off. It started without any issues, but I wanted to listen to the engine and how it shifted. My buddy Danny and I learned a lot about cars and how to fix them when we were in high school. Driving older-model cars forced us to figure things out on our own because paying a mechanic was not in our limited budgets. When I bought the Pinto Bean, I made sure to always have at least $300 in my dresser drawer for unexpected repairs.

"It's solid," Derek noted. "Not as bumpy as I expected."

"By the time I add a grill and a prep fridge, there won't be room for much else. I'm on the fence." I tried to remember the advice David gave me when I told him about my find. *Be one thousand percent sure before investing your money. If not, walk away. You don't want to look back and wonder what might have been if only you'd waited a little bit longer.* We took the truck back and thanked the man for his time. As we drove away, I felt confident we would find something perfect. *Patience, Austin. You will find it.*

Five

Sydney - Unexpected Reunion

After my night of satisfying sex with a stranger, I decided to try my luck again a week later. This time I was forced to wear a cute sundress because the button on my cutoffs would not close. Shit.

I'd been reading a couple of pregnancy books I picked up at a thrift store when I went in looking for shorts with elastic waists. The matronly clerk served me the stink eye at the check-out counter when she saw my reading selections. According to the experts in my new books, I was gaining weight rapidly, and I felt concerned that maybe I was gaining too much.

But I pushed those thoughts aside as I lined my eyes and lips for another evening of carnal ecstasy. This horny woman was going to howl at the moon tonight.

I made my same deal with the bartender and handed him my card to start a tab. The bar started to get busy. I took my time, scoping out the crowd. Between watching people line dancing and the tables full of people, it would be easy to find a coyote to tame.

He sniffed me out first. I left my perch to freshen up in the ladies room. When I emerged, he grabbed my wrist and pushed me up against the wall. His body pressed against mine. He whispered in my ear. "You looking for a good time, baby?" His grip and his tone were aggressive and I didn't like it. I started to hyperventilate, having flashbacks of Jason digging my face into the carpet with his knee.

I saw two other women leaving the restroom and shouted, "Hey, Angela! Don't go out on the dance floor without me!"

One of them held out her hand. "Then move your ass, sister!" I grasped it and she pulled me away from the creep. I didn't let go all the way to the dance floor.

She turned to me and mouthed over the loud music. "Are you okay?"

I shook my head. My eyes started welling up with moisture.

"Let's get you out of here. That guy is bad news." She grabbed her girlfriend and the three of us went out the side door. The fresh, cool night air woke me out of my panic. I faced my companions. "Thank you so much. He was so strong."

"Angela" put her hands on my shoulders and stared into my eyes. "Are you sober? Do you want us to call an Uber?"

I thought. "Yes, I'm sober. No, I don't need an Uber. I feel so stupid." Between the real live creep and my flashbacks from Jason, I was an emotional mess.

She disagreed. "No, not stupid. Women are stronger in numbers. Let's walk to your car so we know you're safe." They tucked me into my truck.

I rolled down the window. "Thank you, ladies. You are my angels."

"Just pay it forward. And drive safely." They waved as I drove off. Watching *Pretty Women* again sounded like a hot evening right about now.

All told, I spent almost four months on the road. The magnificent sights I had seen, hikes I had taken, swimming in crisp lake water, eating in kitschy diners and tasting food that gave my taste buds joygasms, it all melted together in my brain. I didn't want it to end, but this didn't feel like an ideal lifestyle for a single mom with an infant. Even if I did have Samson for protection.

I needed some bigger shorts again, so I scoped out Google for thrift stores. There were three nearby that looked promising. I plugged the address for the first one into Google Maps and set out to find some treasure.

At the first store, I found a super cute lamp that would be perfect in the nursery. It was a buttery yellow with cutouts of moons and stars around it. The knob turned the main lightbulb on, or the nightlight inside the base to light up the shapes.

I heard a voice behind me. "That is the cutest lamp, isn't it? I have one in pink in my baby girl's room right now. She loves how the nightlight projects the shapes on the walls."

I pivoted to face the voice. It was almost as if I'd stepped into a time warp. I was looking at a doppelgänger of my best friend from elementary school. Her silky copper hair was braided into two braids, and she smiled with her twinkly blue eyes. She was a few inches taller than me, and skinny except for her Dolly Parton-size breasts. Her name was on my lips, but she beat me to it.

"Ohmigod! Sydney Campbell, is that you?"

My mouth dropped open. "Micky? Micky Patterson? It can't be!"

"But it is." She laughed. "Although now it's Allegro. Tony and I have been married for three years." She flashed her gorgeous princess cut diamond band set in front of my face.

I held out my arms and we embraced. "It's been so long, but you look the same. I would recognize you anywhere. What are you doing here?"

"We've been living here since Tony started teaching at Purdue. The bigger question is what are you doing here? You're still in Kansas City?"

"No. I've been on the road traveling out west for several months now. I crossed to the east side of the Mississippi last week.

"That's fantastic! You're going to be around for a while, I take it?"

"I don't have any immediate plans on deck."

She checked her watch. "I'm on a short time frame today. But I want to catch up. Will you come over for dinner tomorrow if you don't have plans?"

"I can't think of anything I'd rather do. Let me give you my number." We exchanged numbers and hugged again.

"This is the best day ever!" she exclaimed. "Can't wait to see you tomorrow!" She waved as she hustled out of the store. It wasn't until that moment I realized that she was very, very pregnant.

Journal Entry

I can't believe I ran into Micky Patterson today while I was thrifting! When her family moved away from Kansas City after sixth grade, we eventually lost touch with each other. What a happy accident to run into her!

It's almost too ironic that we're both pregnant. What are the odds?

I'm excited to go to her house for dinner. Being on the road is amazing, but it can also be lonely. I love Samson, but he's not the best conversationalist, even if he is a good listener.

I didn't ask Micky how old her daughter is. I should go to a bookstore and find something to bring her as a present. I have so many fond memories of books I read when I was young. It will be difficult to narrow my selections down, but after all the time I spent working in a bookstore, I should be able to find something suitable for a young person. That's my plan.

I can hardly wait for tomorrow. It's a little like waiting for Santa.

Six
Austin - Taking the Bait
(explicit scene)

When I graduated from college, I swore I'd never have to take another pointless class, read another antiquated piece of literature, or take a meaningless test. Yet I found myself sitting in a small business seminar on Saturday morning at nine A.M. This was getting up in the middle of the night for me. My thermos brimmed with dark roast caffeination. My new blue, spiral-bound notebook and mechanical pencils lay on the table in front of me, ready to take notes.

David recommended this seminar so I registered a few weeks ago. The auditorium filled at about half capacity. Most of the people looked to be in their thirties and forties, at least a decade older than me. Ammonia filled my nostrils, and someone behind me was chewing bubblegum. It made me want a piece of grape Hubba Bubba in the worst way.

A side door at the front of the auditorium opened and a woman with candy-apple red hair crossed to the large desk in the middle. She set a laptop on the desk and dropped her hobo handbag next to it. Her bedazzled glasses sat on top of her long, hot red locks, and her smile was framed in bold red lipstick. Early thirties, maybe? She removed her black blazer and tossed it next to her purse. A black and white striped stretchy, sleeveless dress clung to her ample curves, stopping just below her knees and accentuating her round belly and upper arms. The V-neck dipped low, showing off her full breasts.

She walked around in front of the desk. "Good morning, ladies and gentlemen. My name is Caroline Dickson. My Bachelor of Science in English is from Ohio State, and my MBA is from Duquesne University. I have a short questionnaire for you this morning. I want to know where you are in your business knowledge and needs. My goal is to tailor this seminar so that you get the most knowledge that you can."

She opened a folder on the desk and removed a stack of papers. "Please come take a paper and bring your belongings with you. We'll be filling up the class from the front row towards the back. I like to be able to see your eyeballs, or your eyelids, while we are learning. Questions?" No answer. "Okay. Simon says move your seats."

I landed in the middle of the fourth row. There were thirty of us in the class.

"Now, I will give you the next five minutes to answer any of the relevant questions. If a question doesn't apply to you, skip it. If you don't finish, that's okay, too." She set a timer and sat down in a swivel chair behind the desk. Her hand grabbed the edge of the desk, and she pushed off into a spin. The chair whirled around twice before she gave it another push. This time she lifted both of her arms in the air and closed her eyes.

I couldn't take my eyes off her. Who was this mysterious creature who appeared so mature and serious one moment and acted like a little kid on the playground in the next? Was she an expert in business or was this an elaborate shrek?[2] She stopped spinning, and I scrambled back to answering questions. When the timer beeped, she shut it off and collected our papers.

I thought six hours in class would be a drag, but the time flew by. My wrist begged me to stop taking notes, and my brain hit tilt from information overload.

I took my time packing up my old college backpack and made my way down the steps towards the door while Caroline stared at me. I turned away to check and make sure my fly wasn't open. No.

"I'm sorry," she said. "I know I've been staring, but I feel like I know you from somewhere. Have we met?"

I smiled. "Trust me when I say I would remember if we'd met before. You would be hard to forget."

She blushed but recovered quickly. "I can't put my finger on it." She picked up my paper. "Austin Mitchell. Austin Mitchell. It will come to me." Then she snapped her fingers. "I've got it! I read about you in Rolling Stone. You wrote that love song for that blockbuster movie last year. What are you doing here? Did you lose your fortune already?" She stood and unhooked her laptop from the projector before moving in front of me.

I hooked my thumbs in my belt loops. "No, nothing like that. I'm looking to take some of my money and invest in a restaurant. My business knowledge is limited to cashing my own paycheck. I had no idea there were so many moving parts to make a business successful."

She raked her eyes up and down my body as she spoke, pausing just below my belt buckle. "It can seem overwhelming. Would you like to take me to dinner and discuss your plan further?"

"We could do that, but I have a feeling you might be hungry for something else."

"Is it that obvious?" She barely breathed the words, but the power behind them was undeniable. I reached for her waist, but she slapped my hand away. "Tell me what you want to do to me."

"I want to put my head in between your legs and see what you're not wearing under that skirt. Then I want to please you with my tongue until you scream my name."

She crooked her finger at me and I lowered my face in front of hers. "I don't think you know what you're getting into. You will listen and obey my every command. Are we clear?"

"Crystal." I gazed at her without breaking eye contact. Her brazenness intrigued me. Even though I had no idea what she had in mind, I wanted to play. "I'm ready when you are."

She perched on top of the desk and spread her legs. The hem of her skirt rose up around her hips, revealing a glimpse of her trimmed bush. *I knew she wasn't wearing any panties.* "On your knees. Now."

I lowered myself, not taking my eyes off hers. I waited for her next command.

Her legs wrapped around my ribs on both sides. "You may look under my skirt, but you are not to touch me until I say so."

I leaned in and grabbed the hem of her skirt. I pulled on the stretchy fabric and covered my head with it. I had my face so close to her juicy lips that she could feel my warm breath on them.

"You may lick my lips, my clitoris, my sweet vagina, and around my anus. You will only use your tongue. No fingers. I want to come, but not too fast. Show me how good you are." She placed her hands on my head, encouraging me to begin.

I snaked my arms around her hips and pulled her into me. I licked and sucked at her lips, teasing her clitoris with short bursts of attention. She arched backward, laying her head and shoulders on the desk. This brought her tight little hole into view, and I moved to rim her in one direction and then the other. Her moans got louder and her pleasure spurred me on. I longed to kiss her silky inner thighs, but I stuck to the script.

I returned to her clitoris and focused my attention there. My tongue swirled around it, and I sucked the nub until it was swollen. Her breathing became rapid and the salty juices from her arousal clung to my taste buds as I licked them.

"Don't. Stop." She gasped between breaths. "Take me all the way home, stud." I increased the tempo of my licks. Her body started to shiver and I swear the whole building heard her screams of ecstasy. "Yes! Yes! Fuck me! Oh my God! Yes!" She bucked and squirmed, and I held onto her ass to ground myself. Then, in an instant, she became still and silent. I started to pull my head away but remembered her words.

She pushed my head away with her hands. "On your feet." I wiped my mouth with my hand and stood up. My rock-hard cock pressed against my jeans. She focused her attention on it for a moment. Then she looked up at me and hopped down from the desk, smoothing her skirt down around her thighs. "You can see your way out." She turned her back to me as she packed up her tote bag.

This was not the scenario I had pictured. It took me a moment to realize she was serious. I picked up my backpack off the floor and left feeling bamboozled, like Grandpa Joe and Charlie when Willy Wonka turned them away.[3] Looks like someone turned the tables on me, and I didn't like it. Not one little bit.

Seven
Sydney - Alpaca Farmers

The next evening, I plugged Micky's address into my phone. Their farm wasn't that far from the motel where I was staying, but it still seemed like its own rustic universe. The traditional two-story farmhouse with wraparound porch sat on the flattest part of the property. It still had an original slate roof. New beige aluminum siding trimmed with navy blue shutters provided the perfect pop of color. Micky had planted shrubs and flowering bushes in front of the porch and down the outline of the sidewalk leading to the driveway.

A humongous oak tree stood guard in the front yard, complete with tire swing. Behind the house, an enormous red barn peeked out from the right side, while up on the hills, groups of alpacas in a variety of colors and patterns grazed the grounds. A few free-roaming chickens pecked around the side of the house as I came to a stop. I heard a couple of low barks then watched the slowest moving golden retriever amble off the porch in my direction.

Micky appeared by the side door. "Come on in this way! Don't worry about Duke. He's an ol' slobbery teddy bear."

I felt relieved that I had left Samson at the motel. He wasn't friendly with other dogs, but I didn't train him to be, so that's not his fault. I grabbed my purse and gift bag and went inside.

Micky stirred something in a huge pot on the stove, steam wafting from the top. My stomach growled in anticipation.

"What smells so wonderful?"

"I'm cooking down this tomato sauce to can it. We love homemade sauce over store-bought any day."

"I remember my mom doing that when I was little. We would sit at the kitchen table and listen for all the seals to pop. She canned green beans, corn, beets, tomato sauce, and different jams. Those homemade jams were the best! Smucker's cannot beat that."

Micky nodded as she stirred. "Elderberry jam is my favorite, and I can't find that at Kroger's. The local Amish ladies make the best jam by far."

I couldn't help myself. My curiosity got the better of me. "I hope I'm not being rude, but I'm going to ask because you should never assume. Are you pregnant?"

She laughed. "No silly. I swallowed a watermelon whole about a minute before you arrived." She rubbed her belly. "Yes, I'm about 40 months pregnant. This little turkey better come on time, too. She's quiet all day long, and then, about the time I'm ready to sleep, she starts her gymnastics routine. For hours. Tumbles and kicks all night long. It's gotten a little tight in there and it's not quite as bad as it was, but I'd still like to be able to sleep more than an hour or two at a time."

"Yikes! That sounds awful!"

"It's the exact opposite of what I want her to do, but I haven't figured out a way to send a message through to her. Am I allowed to use subliminal messaging on my own kid?"

"Second question. You keep using feminine pronouns. Is she a girl?"

"Yes, we're having another girl. Poor Tony wanted a boy this time since we already have Ainsley. His sperm are to blame for that one. Oops! We kept it a surprise the first time because we didn't have a preference. But this time I yearned to start buying some blue clothes if needed. Ainsley is excited to be getting a sister, but I don't think she understands that they won't be playing together for a while."

"I don't mean to pry, so tell me to shut up if I ask something inappropriate. This is my first time on the rodeo circuit." I waited for her to connect the dots.

She prattled on without stopping. "I always said I longed for four kids, but this one may be the end of my uterus hotel. She's been cranky this whole time and—wait..."

There it was.

"...did you say you're pregnant?"

I nodded.

She shrieked. "Ohmigod! Ohmigod! You're kidding?"

I shook my head.

"You're serious! How far along? I can't even tell. Maybe your boobs, now that you said something. That's amazing! Can I hug you?" She came around the island and grabbed me. "This was meant to be. I'm so happy for you, Sydney! Tell me everything."

I took a deep breath. "It wasn't planned. I forgot to change my birth control ring and then this happened. I don't know who the father is. It's exhilarating and scary at the same time. To realize I have this life growing inside me that's causing me to outgrow my pants. That I will be responsible for someone else is a heavy load. You're the only person I've told besides my sister and my PCP."

Micky interrupted. "Have you been getting prenatal care?"

I shook my head. "I spoke to my PCP and she gave me prenatal vitamins. Other than that, no."

Micky clucked at me. "I'm going to give you my Ob/Gyn's number. He's fantastic. He's six foot five and, I will warn you now, has humongous hands. It goes to show you how elastic the vagina is. Call and schedule an appointment. That's so important, Sydney. Reality shows tell stories all the time about women who didn't know they were pregnant still having healthy babies, but that's so rare. Please take care of yourself. Your body is going through so many changes right now."

"Noted. I wasn't purposely neglecting medical care. I wasn't stationary long enough to establish a relationship with a doctor. I will take your doc's info. Thank you."

A loud slam sounded at the back of the house. "They're back!" Micky turned around and bent down, waiting. Fast footsteps came down the hallway and a black streak ran right into Micky's arms as she scooped up a little sprite. "How's my princess? Did you help Daddy with all the chores?"

Her ice blue eyes twinkled, and her little face bobbed up and down as she grinned. "Yes, Momma. I got to pet the baby, too." She turned to me. "Are you momma's friend from school?" Her cheek had a smudge of dirt on it, and her long ebony tresses needed a brush.

"Yes, I am. My name is Sydney. It's nice to meet you." She didn't look at all like Micky, but when her husband came through the door, I understood. Tony Allegro leaned against the doorway and lifted one leg to pull his boot off, and then the other. He looked close to six feet. His navy t-shirt struggled to keep his biceps and taut abs under wraps. His black hair and pale blue eyes matched his daughter's.

"Darling, dinner smells delicious." He came up behind Micky and kissed her on the neck.

"Sweetie, it's not dinner. I'm canning tomato sauce. You're on grill duty tonight. I marinated the steaks and was about to boil the water for corn. Meet my BFF from elementary school, Sydney Campbell."

He took my hand and kissed it on the top. "The pleasure is mine." He turned back to Micky. "Dinner with three beautiful women. I'm such a lucky man. I'm going to clean up and then I'll fire up the grill." He disappeared down the hall.

When I thought he was out of earshot, I exclaimed, "Micky! How did you convince your parents to agree to you marrying an Italian man? Did they die?"

She raised her eyebrows at me. "When we first started dating in high school, it was like in *My Big Fat Greek Wedding*. 'Is he good boy? I don't know. Is he from good family? I don't know.[4] Why can't you find yourself a nice Irish boy?' It took three years to wear them down. And then when we eloped, it started all over again. But Tony never allowed it to bother him, and they finally calmed down after Ainsley was born."

"About that. Ainsley is a beautiful name, but it's not a traditional Irish choice."

She nodded. "We didn't want traditional names from either one of our heritages. Another excuse for a family feud. We both love the show *The West Wing*, and we wanted strong names. We chose Joshua for a boy or Ainsley for a girl. This little turkey here is Zoey." She rubbed up and down her belly.

"I love them both. I haven't even thought about baby names yet. I'm still processing my swollen boobs and expanding waistline. I was already a solid size 22. Now I don't even know. I'm going to have to start wearing maxi dresses to keep my ass covered because I'm growing out of my shorts too fast."

Micky beamed. "That's a familiar feeling."

I looked around. "Where did your little munchkin go? I brought her something. Is she allowed to have Barbies? Some feminists have opinions about that, but I remember you and I used to play with them all the time. Remember that time my grandma bought us the gigantic Barbie condo with the elevator and swimming pool? Boy, my mom was livid. It took up so much of our bedroom." I smirked, remembering my mother's pinched face when she found out what was in the gigantic box.

"Yes, of course you can give her a Barbie doll. She has a few of them, but nowhere near the collection you and your sisters had." She went to the stairwell and shouted. "Ainsley, come downstairs please!"

Little feet two-footed the stairs and arrived in a blur. "Yes, Momma?"

"Miss Sydney brought you something. Would you like to open it?"

Ainsley squealed and clapped her hands together. "Is it my birthday?"

Micky shook her head. "No, love bug. Sometimes people bring presents without a specific reason. It's rare when it happens."

I held out a gift bag with unicorns and rainbows all over it. Ainsley took it and sat down on the floor to inspect it. She pulled the pieces of bright pink tissue paper out one by one, tossing them behind her. She came to a rectangular box that was wrapped in unicorn paper. Her little fingers worked around and found a corner to lift. Once she noticed the hot pink cardboard, she knew what was inside.

"Momma! It's a Barbie!" She ripped the rest of the paper off and ran over to show Micky.

"That's wonderful. What do you tell Miss Sydney?"

Ainsley hugged the box to her chest. "Thank you, Miss Sydney!"

"You're welcome. There's more in the bag."

I tried to remain in the moment, but Micky's term of endearment had triggered me. "Love Bug" was something I overheard Wendy calling Austin. I didn't think about him every minute or even every day now, but right now his face filled my head like a demented comic strip bubble. In moments of feeling alone, I almost called him several times, or started to text him, but then I remembered that he'd never tried to contact me. And that would stop me in the moment.

Ainsley opened all the new clothes for her Barbies, and there was one more present at the bottom. "Momma, this one is heavy. Can you help me?" She dragged the bag over to her. Micky sat down on a chair and Ainsley perched on what was left of her lap.

Micky picked up the wrapped package. "Sydney!" She looked at me and her eyes got misty. "Now this makes me think of your mother. She always included a book with our birthday presents." She slid her fingernail under the seam on the back, pulling the wrapping around each side, revealing two of my favorite books: *Knuffle Bunny* and *Knuffle Bunny, Too*.

"Bunnies! Stories about bunnies! Thank you, Miss Sydney!" She hopped off Micky's lap and ran over to give me a hug.

"I hear you like stories, and these are two of my favorites. I hope you'll love them as much as I do."

Tony chose that moment to reappear. "What happened here?" he bellowed. "Where did all this pink glittery garbage come from? Ainsley! What happens now?" He lifted arms above his head and growled. "The Garbage Monster is going to eat all the garbage. Don't let him gobble up you, too!"

She shrieked with delight and ran around, picking up pieces of wrapping and tissue paper as fast as she could. He started grabbing pieces off the floor. "Delicious! Like cotton candy! Grrr! I want more!"

He tapped her bottom. "I missed! She's so fast." He tapped her again as she giggled and fell on her knees. He scooped her up and hung her over his back by her ankles. "I can still smell her. Where did she go?" He twirled to the left and right, and she continued to laugh.

Micky rolled her eyes. "Hey. Garbage Monster! I think the grill is calling you!"

Tony came back to earth and laid Ainsley down on the carpet, still laughing. "Sorry, sweetie. Daddy has to make sure your pregnant mother gets fed. Thanks for helping clean up." He headed to the back deck.

Ainsley carried the pile of scraps to the trash can in the kitchen.

Micky looked at me. "I'd like to tell you he's putting on a show for you. But he's not. He's like that with us all the time. It's endearing and infuriating."

"He can't take his eyes off of you. Or Ainsley. He's totally smitten. I wish I had someone look at me like that. That's everything, right there. You have hit the jackpot, my friend."

Dinner went by in a blur. Micky and I took turns telling stories from back in the day. When the Campbell sisters and the Patterson kids got together, there was no shortage of hijinks. We lived four houses apart and we played together all the time. We never got into any real trouble, but Abby and Shauna, Micky's older sister, did their best to keep our noses clean. Brooke didn't participate with us much. She read her fashion magazines in her room while listening to alternative music or laid out in her bikini on one of the chaises by the pool, lathering herself with coconut oil.

Tony lit a fire in the stone fire pit in the backyard after dinner and we lounged in the Adirondack chairs surrounding it. Micky opened one of the benches and pulled out metal sticks with wooden handles.

"S'mores!" Ainsley exclaimed.

"Will you please go in the kitchen and bring out the basket with the fixings for your momma? *Don't run,*" Tony instructed.

She scooted off at a little less than a full-out bolt. I chuckled under my breath because it's exactly what I would have done. While we were roasting marshmallows, a figure came out on the deck. Boots clomped on the brick patio in our direction and we all turned to look. I could tell he was male, but he was backlit by the lights on the deck and I couldn't make out his face.

"Hey, brother! I cleaned out the truck bed and ran her through the car wash. Full tank of gas, too. I left the keys on the counter." He came to a stop in front of the fire ring.

Tony looked up from his marshmallow stick. "Thanks. Glad I could help. When do you want us to spread the mulch? I think I have some time tomorrow afternoon, if the last two mommas don't decide to give birth."

"Tomorrow could work. I'll text you in the morning." He turned to go, but Ainsley stopped him.

"Uncle Vinnie, do you want to make s'mores with us?" She held out a stick towards the shadowy figure. "This one is for you."

He took the metal rod and perched on the empty chair next to Ainsley. "How could I resist making s'mores with my favorite niece?" He took two marshmallows and slid them on the prongs. She held out her empty stick and he speared a marshmallow for her, then he helped her twist the handle to turn the outside golden brown. His own marshmallows caught fire.

I laughed out loud as he waved the thin pole around to put out the flames. "Let me guess, they taste better burnt to a crisp!" My third marshmallow turned a lovely shade of gold.

He looked at me, then my work of culinary mastery, then back at me. "Tony, do we have a ringer here? I haven't had the pleasure."

Tony chuckled. "Excuse my poor manners. This is Sydney, Micky's friend from elementary school. They bumped into each other at the thrift store yesterday."

He reached out his hand to me. "I'm Vincent, Tony's older brother." His dark hair and light eyes mirrored Tony's. "Do we need to have a marshmallow duel to determine who's the best?"

"Sure, why not? I can't remember the last time I made a boy cry." I smiled like the Cheshire Cat.

"That sounds like a direct challenge to your manhood, Brother." Tony punched him in the arm. "Are you going to take that kind of smack talk from a girl?"

Vinnie locked eyes with me and rubbed his hands together. "You're going down, little missy."

Micky gave us each a fresh marshmallow. "Should we time this? I think we should time this. Tony, give me one minute on that fancy watch of yours. Contestants: On your mark, get set, burn!"

We both leaned close to the fire, attempting to create the perfect crust. I was doing well until Ainsley came over to assist me.

"Miss Sydney, I want to help you." She grabbed onto my stick and wouldn't let go. It was too close to the flame and started to char on one side.

Tony gave the countdown. "Ten...nine...eight...seven..."

I pulled my ruined puff of sugar from the fire. Micky waddled over to inspect the entries.

"The judges have determined that there is a clear winner." She took Vincent's free hand and raised it. He jumped up and down like a little kid then scooped Ainsley up on his shoulders and marched around the fire. She squealed with delight. He took a victory lap and then came to shake my hand.

"Better luck next time." His smile was adorable.

"Agreed. Congratulations." I turned towards Micky. "Thank you for a lovely evening. I'm getting tired." I hugged the three of them goodbye and walked myself through the kitchen to collect my purse. Samson would take a brief bedtime walk tonight.

Journal Entry

Being neighbors with the Patterson family holds such fond memories for me. It tickled my heart to see Micky as a grown woman with such a wonderful partner in Tony. And their little Ainsley is adorable. They make me feel at ease with their warm and welcoming nature. As a kid, I loved being at their house more than my own. My mom had all these rules and my parents kept busy all the time. They never played with us and I hardly ever saw them relax.

Having dinner and roasting marshmallows was so enjoyable. Especially competing with Tony's brother Vincent for the golden marshmallow championship, even though Ainsley aided me in losing spectacularly. If I see him again, I'm totally asking for a rematch. All in good fun, of course

Being with their family makes me realize how much time I spend alone. Samson has been my only constant over the past few months. Tonight reinforced the concept that there is merit in having human companionship.

I haven't thought about where I want to park myself, but this small college town in Indiana looks attractive to me. I don't want to go back home and wind up under my mother's scrutiny. Having a friend nearby would mean the world to me.

Abby said she would help me with the baby if I came to NYC. But I left the swarming metropolis of L.A. for a reason, and I do not intend to run towards another overcrowded petri dish. I like seeing grass and trees, and not just the ones poking out of the holes in the sidewalks.

I still have some time to decide...

Eight
Vinnie - Fireside Chat

After Sydney left, we stuck around the fire, laughing and talking. Ainsley ran around all hopped up on sugar and attention. Duke lay at Micky's feet, watching Ainsley. These were the moments I cherished, when everyone was together and enjoying the moment. Micky rubbed her belly and called out.

"Ainsley, come here. Your sister is saying hello."

She scurried over to Micky and put her hand on her bump. "Hi baby!" She leaned in close. "I'm Ainsley. We're going to be best friends. I've got lots of stuffed animals and Barbies to play with. Are you coming soon? I love you." She patted her and went back to running around the fire pit.

Tony reached his hand out to hold Micky's "You are so gorgeous."

She pursed her lips. "You are so full of it. Every woman looks beautiful when you turn out the lights."

I chuckled. "I think you should quit while you're behind, Brother. She's right. There are two things guaranteed to make any woman look better: darkness and alcohol."

Tony shook his head. "I'm still going to tap this before bed. So maybe you could disappear."

Micky rolled her eyes in my direction. "He's such a romantic. How did I get so lucky?" She turned back to Tony. "If you want to tap anything, you will take care of putting Ainsley to bed."

"Done and done." He stood up and called Ainsley. "Love bug, it's time to go to bed. Give Momma and Uncle Vinnie hugs. Then I'll race you to the bathtub."

Once they were gone, we sat in comfortable silence, staring at the dwindling flames. The crickets volleyed their songs back and forth and an occasional lightning bug blinked through the air.

"I take it you have been friends with Sydney for a long time."

"We were in elementary school together. But after that, my dad's job moved him here. I haven't seen her in years. It's wonderful to reconnect. We always enjoyed each other's company. Her mother was always hard on her, and she kept trying to make her mom proud of her. It always made me sad, because I never had to prove anything to my parents."

"That sounds rough. I think Tony and Tommy and I spent so much time competing, it didn't occur to us to try to get our parents' approval. Sofia and Bianca were daddy's girls and got most of his attention. They still do. But the relationship between a father and son is different. He did his best to teach us how to be decent men. That responsibility sets up an extra barrier to being friends. I'm closer to Dad now than when I was living at home." I gazed up at the stars.

"Exactly. Momma and I are closer now. And when I became a mom, it changed everything again. Sydney hasn't spoken to her parents since she left California."

"What was she doing in California?"

"She was working as a songwriter for a record label. I can't remember which one. She had a huge Billboard hit and won a Grammy and an Oscar. You know that song from the summer blockbuster? *Our Dance*? She wrote it with a friend from college."

I nodded. "That's impressive."

"For sure. But from what she told me, it wasn't the lifestyle for her. She lived in L.A. for three years. She's looking for a house to rent or buy. I set her up with Callie."

"Oh, okay. I have a few friends who have rentals. I'll ask around. But you know it's a difficult game to find a place to live in a college town. They get swooped up by landlords looking to charge students top dollar not to live in a dorm room."

Tony sat back down next to Micky. "Why don't you have her stay with us?" "She can stay in Nanna's room. No one's using it."

She sat up in her seat. "That fact had escaped my pregnant brain. Honey! That's brilliant! I could kiss you!"

Tony grinned. "I'd rather cash in my chips for your earlier offer." He wiggled his eyebrows at me.

She held out her arms. "If you can pull me out of this chair, I will take those odds." She glanced in my direction. "I made an appointment with this studly man. Stay as long as you like. It's such a beautiful night."

Tony hoisted her to her feet and threw her over his shoulder. He carried her up the stairs into the house as she giggled. I shook my head as I watched them. It made me happy to see my brother so in love with his wife. Tony was the kindest person I knew by far and he deserved that kind of devotion.

At the same time, I couldn't help but wonder if I would ever find someone who made me feel that way. I'd had a couple of longer relationships that hadn't made it to that level of happiness. As the oldest son, I'd always thought I'd get married first, but Tony and Tommy beat me to it by a long shot. Mom never directly pressured me, but I knew she would feel better if I settled down with someone.

The fire dwindled and I used a marshmallow stick to cover the embers with ashes. A shooting star caught my eye and I made a wish. Couldn't hurt to put it out in the universe...

Nine
Sydney - Hearing a Heartbeat

A week later, Zoey still had not arrived. I accompanied Micky to her doctor's appointment to scope out the place and make an appointment for myself. She knew everyone in the office by name and chatted up the receptionist about the latest town gossip. I sat with an old People magazine. This was my guilty pleasure at the salon, too. Reading celebrity magazines. I never bought them for myself.

Micky sat next to me. "I hope you don't mind, but I got you an appointment."

"Did she give you a card? I'll put it in my phone."

Micky waved her hand at me dismissively. "It's right after mine. There was a cancellation. Isn't that the best luck?"

"As in an appointment *today?*"

She squeezed my knee. "In mere minutes, we'll see your little peanut! How exciting!"

"No. *No.* I'm not prepared for this. I haven't shaved my legs in…it doesn't matter. Micky, why didn't you ask me? I was going to make an appointment before we left."

"As if Dr. Aaron hasn't seen hairy legs before. I think I stopped shaving six months ago. So, no big deal."

I sighed. "Okay. I suppose I need to do this sooner than later."

I didn't have time to think about it because the nurse called for Micky. In the exam room, Micky stepped on the scale and covered her eyes. "Don't tell me. This bowling ball weighs a hundred pounds already." She shooed the nurse out, saying, "Yes, I can handle donning these fancy garments."

I sat in the corner and averted my eyes, looking at a poster of babies at various stages of growth in the womb.

Micky laughed at me. "Honey, I have no shame at this point. My lady bits have been seen by all kinds of nurses and aides in the hospital, and I pooped right in front of my husband on the table while I was in labor with Ainsley. Trust me, your modesty will not exist by the time you take your baby home."

"That makes me feel so much better. Thanks."

Dr. Aaron knocked and entered. "Hi, Micky. How are you feeling? Is this gremlin still keeping you awake at night?"

"Yes. I'm guessing she won't give me a moment's peace when she arrives, either." She lay back on the table. "This is my friend Sydney. We went to elementary school together. She's your next appointment."

He shook my hand. Micky wasn't kidding—he stood at least six foot five. Dark hair, stubble beard, brown eyes, and absolutely the largest hands I'd ever seen. A bulletin board hung in the hallway, full of pictures of him with tiny burritos he could hold in one hand. I had this flash image of Dwayne Johnson in scrubs as an Ob/Gyn. I could handle that.

"So, Micky is pimping patients for me. Excellent! Now, let's find out what's going on with this little pixie." He measured her bump and checked her cervix. "You're two centimeters dilated. Which is the same as last week."

Micky groaned in disappointment. "Doc, I am done cooking this turkey. Please give me some good news."

"If you're still pregnant this time next week, we can schedule an induction. I prefer the baby to come on her own time. Now, any questions or complaints?"

"Not that pertains to you, Doc."

Dr. Aaron turned towards me. "We're going to have your appointment in the room across the hall. Take your time and ring the bell by the door when you're ready."

Mickey and I switched roles, with me donning the glamourous paper gown in the new room. Dr. Aaron came in with a nurse right behind him.

"Julie is my new ultrasound tech. Would you mind if she takes a look at your baby?"

"Of course not."

Julie parted the middle of my gown and squirted gel on my stomach. She moved the wand back and forth, and we focused on the black and white monitor. What was I even looking for?

"There he is." She pointed to this tiny dot on the screen. "The sac is intact and everything looks good. I'm going to take some measurements to give us a better idea of how far along you are." She pushed a white ball around and lines appeared on the monitor. "The whooshing sound is the baby's heartbeat. He sounds strong."

"Am I having a boy? You said 'he'."

"It's a little early to tell the gender of your baby. Do you want to know? We will mark your chart if you want to keep it a surprise for a gender reveal party."

My head started to spin. *Gender reveal party?* I'd barely wrapped my head around being pregnant. "I want to keep it a surprise for now."

She finished her measurements, but her furrowed eyebrows alerted me.

I started to worry. "Is something wrong? Something is wrong." I started to hyperventilate. *Breathe, Sydney, Breathe...*

Micky took my hand. "It's going to be fine. Let Julie do her job. Doctor Aaron is right here." She held on and didn't let go.

Julie locked eyes with Doctor Aaron for reassurance. "Do you hear it? It's so faint. I'm going to check around." She resumed the exploration with her wand. She moved down my ribcage to the left and around my kidney. That's when the rhythm of the heartbeat changed. My musical ears picked up on that kind of anomaly.

I tried to sit up. "Why is it different now? What happened? Is something wrong with your equipment?" The more I spoke, the higher my voice rose in panic.

Doctor Aaron smiled. "Good catch, Julie. We could have gone at least another month without hearing it." He put his hand on my bent knee in the stirrups. "Sydney, your babies are thriving. We often have one twin who likes to hide."

I was dumbfounded. "What? I don't understand."

Micky squeezed my hand. "Sweetie, you're having twins."

I heard her words, but it sounded like a foreign language in slow playback.

Doctor Aaron nodded in confirmation. "Julie, let's try to obtain some measurements on baby number two. We may have to wait until your next appointment if he or she doesn't want to cooperate. But we have two strong heartbeats."

I lay on the table, numb, as Julie tried to find my second peanut. This was not what I expected at all. I was just getting used to the idea of having one small person to take care of, but two? Frightening. If I hadn't been laying down, I might have fainted.

We stopped at a coffee shop on the way home. Micky found a table and I carried our iced coffees. My life was not going according to plan. I'd mapped out a route to head over and explore the New England states and then work my way down the Atlantic coast all the way to the Florida Keys. I put my elbows on the table and my head in my hands. I needed some time to process all this new information. *Pregnant. Twins!* It overwhelmed me.

Micky sipped her frothy concoction. "You're not in this alone, Sydney. You have our support. I know you won't get that from your mom, that's for sure. But family isn't always blood. I'm so glad we've reconnected and our children will grow up together."

"Me too. And you're right. I haven't had the courage to tell her that I'm pregnant. What does that say about the kind of relationship we have? I can hear it now. *'Who's the father? Why isn't he marrying you? How could you let this happen? No one's going to want to marry you now. No man wants to raise someone else's kid.'* She's so cold and judgmental. And my dad plays along with her. I'm fortunate to have Abby, but it was hard to be left alone with my mom when she went to New York."

Micky took my hand in hers. "I want you to come stay with us. Tony's grandma lived with us for five years. She passed three months ago. We built a small suite on the side of the house when she moved in with us. You would have your own bedroom, sitting room and bathroom. Plus, you can get out of the motel and won't have to worry about housing right away. You stay as long as you like."

"Micky, that is way too generous. I couldn't impose on you and Tony. You're about to have another little one to take care of yourself."

"Hush. I checked with Tony while you were changing and it's settled. Bring your bags over from the motel tomorrow."

I mulled it over. "Samson is the only variable. If he gets along with Duke, I'll take you up on your offer. On one condition: I am not a guest. I will earn my keep."

She grinned and jumped up to hug me. "Let's go tell everyone!"

Journal Entry

Twins! Crap on a cracker! Now I'm in for it. I was just wrapping my head around having one baby. I better get serious about finding a place for the four of us to live. An extra person with a dog in Micky's house is one thing, but three? I can't impose on her, especially with her having a new baby too. She knows a local real estate agent who can help me find a suitable rental or home purchase. Samson may hamper my rental options since he's considered part of the bully breed group.

Micky was not kidding about Dr. Aaron. His hands are massive, along with the rest of him. I wonder what made him decide during medical school that being an OB/GYN was the way to go. I think I've watched way too many episodes of Grey's Anatomy.

I have to tell my parents about my pregnancy at some point. Maybe I can put off that news until the twins are in college. Works for me. It's not fair to Abby to ask her to stay quiet, though. At least I have 500 miles between here and my mother's withering look of disappointment. More to come...

Ten
Austin - Food for Thought

"What can I make for you this fine Saturday afternoon?"

I leaned forward towards the window of my food truck to take the next order. I realized we're at the beach but damn, that last woman's bikini barely qualified as clothing. When I was in this truck, I was all business, or at least I tried to be. Some of these women made it extremely difficult with their skimpy suits. This was the second weekend I'd brought the food truck out to the beach. It reminded me of when someone spotted a celebrity in public and leaked it to their followers on social media. Except my face wasn't famous; my tasty food was the celebrity.

We had a never-ending line of people waiting for these pulled pork sandwiches, which totally thrilled me. I sweated through my t-shirt before the end of the first hour and we didn't stop until we ran out of food.

I realized early in my planning that I needed two people in the truck—one to take orders and one to make them. I figured I'd make the food and let my assistant take the money. So, I put an ad in the newspaper at the college three weeks ago, and one online. Zero promising results. David suggested I try culinary schools, and that's where I found Zach Hutchence. He informed me, no surprise, that barbeque cuisine was not an area of concentration in culinary school. But he had some interest in it. Studying under demanding chefs meant he worked under immense pressure and didn't rattle. He gave off a relaxed and friendly vibe the ladies would like, and his sun-kissed California surfer dude appearance didn't hurt. I hired him.

I still worked with Jack, Marcus, and Crissy during the week. The genuine comradery of our group sustained us through the loss of Sydney. Venus wanted us to replace her, but we collectively vetoed that. Sometimes I thought I'd see her as I turned the corner into our studio, like she never left. Her absence was palpable for me. I never brought her up, and between myself and Marcus licking our wounds, Jack and Crissy steered clear of mentioning her name.

On occasion, Venus would bring us some lyrics without a melody. She told us the music that came with it wasn't a good fit and they wanted a fresh take. When I read them, I easily identified Sydney's writing style, but I never confronted Venus. Instead, I pushed my feelings down into the depths and added more bricks to my wall.

When I left rehab, I intended to stay sober and do better for myself. But then Sydney left, and my world crumbled around me. The flight attendant in first class kept the cocktails coming on my flight to Nashville, and I came down from my buzz in the limo on the way to Tim McGraw's ranch. Alcohol is called "medicine" for a reason. There wasn't a big enough dose to cure the emptiness in my heart. When I got home, my sponsor met me at the airport and took me straight to a meeting. He probably saved my life by doing that.

I compensated for my pain by amping up my sexcapades. Karaoke nights drew the bunnies into my lair. My silky-smooth voice was my weapon. It wove a spell around many a horny woman as I sang Garth Brooks and Chris Young songs to them in the crowd. From the stage I assessed my prospects and selected someone to buy a drink for after my performance. My game was on point and I never went home empty-handed. Or with the same woman twice. I learned my lesson on that count the hard way.

One night as I sang, I noticed a woman in the crowd that I knew I'd slept with previously. Heather. She had a particular set of skills in the bedroom that I appreciated, and I decided to find out if we could play those games again. And we did. And again the following week.

But then she started texting me incessantly. Getting clingy and possessive. I stopped answering her. Most of the time, when I stopped communicating, women got the hint and quit trying. Not Heather. But I stuck with my no-reply strategy.

Our third weekend slinging BBQ went by as fast as the last two. My favorite Chiefs ballcap kept my sweat at bay as Zach and I hustled to fill orders as fast as possible. My mind was on the grill and keeping things moving when he tapped me on the shoulder.

"A majorly hot woman outside the truck says she is not leaving until she speaks with you. I tried to help her, but she will only talk to you."

I sighed. Could only be one person. "Have her come around to the back door." I put my spatula down, pulled off my sanitary gloves, and swung the door open. There she stood. Heather.

She lowered her hot pink sunglasses and peered at me over them. "Well, how you doing, Austin? Since your phone won't let you text me back, I thought I'd go old school on your ass and show up where you work." She wore a white low-cut sundress and clearly wasn't wearing a bra. The hem of her dress flirted with revealing her assets, and the pink ribbons of her white platform sandals crisscrossed all the way up to her knees.

I stepped down to the pavement to meet her. "What do you want?" I snapped, crossing my arms across my chest.

"When someone you've been sleeping with says they would like to speak with you, the least you could do is fake it. The silent treatment is for five-year-olds."

"You've been blowing up my phone for days with ridiculous texts. If I wanted to respond to you, I would." I locked my jaw shut.

"Would you mind giving me an explanation. I thought we were having fun." She pushed her hip to the side and placed one hand on her waist.

"We were. At first. But not anymore. You want a boyfriend. Someone to boss around and keep tabs on constantly. That's not me, sweetheart. Never has been. Never will be. I've been completely transparent about my intentions the whole time. Sex. Fun. Period."

She slapped me in the face. "Asshole. I can't even believe you right now."

I glared at her. There were so many things I wanted to say, but my rage prevented me from coming up with a coherent thought. Mostly I wanted to pull up her excuse for a skirt and tame her wet vagina with my cock, but that would have only exacerbated the problem.

She waited for a minute, giving me an opportunity to respond. The sounds of the boardwalk drowned out the silence that overwhelmed us. She raised her eyes and looked at me one last time. "What a disappointment. Goodbye, Austin." She slid her sunglasses back in place as she turned her back.

My eyes trailed after her as she sashayed away. Then I remembered I left Zach alone with a hungry crowd and I hustled back into the truck.

Zach pounced the moment I returned. "Who was that slice of heaven? I don't think I've ever seen a skirt that short in broad daylight." He wiped his forehead with the hem of his t-shirt.

I shook my head. "That ... was Heather. Sometime when we're not slammed, I'll tell you about her. Now put your eyes back in their sockets and go flirt with the ladies waiting in line." I picked up my spatula and started the next order.

Eleven
Sydney - Twins Checkup

A month went by in a blur and I found myself back at Doctor Aaron's for another checkup. The twins were now fluttering in my stomach, which was a surreal sensation. I gave up on wearing anything with a zipper. I bought some roomy maxi dresses at the thrift store and used Micky's sewing machine to hem them so I wouldn't trip. Short people problems.

Doctor Aaron and Julie came into the room with the ultrasound machine on wheels. He took my hand. "Nice to see you again, Sydney. Let's find out how these peanuts are doing."

Julie got everything prepared while Doctor Aaron looked at my chart. "There's not a father's name here. You're on your own?"

"Yes. Is that a problem?"

"Not at all. I want you to have as pleasant an experience as possible. Having a support system is always a good idea, especially when you have two babies."

"I like it here and I'm considering staying for a while. Micky wants me to stay here so our kids can grow up together. My heart wasn't done traveling yet. I haven't decided what to do."

"I've been living here for about five years now. My wife and I like it. Being in a college town like Perdue is a unique experience, although I still can't put my finger on why." He changed the subject: "Were you using birth control?"

"I used the birth control ring and I swapped it out once a month. I forgot to change it, and now, here I am. Knocked up and all alone."

He listened. "Not to intrude, but perhaps telling the father is a viable option. He might surprise you with his support."

I laughed. "Doc, I'm in my own personal hell version of *Mamma Mia!* without a soundtrack. I don't know who the father is because I slept with two different guys in the same week. It's embarrassing. I'm usually a responsible human being."

"I'm not here to judge you. I'm here to give you the best prenatal care possible. One last question: are you planning on keeping the babies? Adoption options are available if you're leaning in that direction. Termination is another choice. Only information, not persuasion."

"I hadn't thought about anything besides keeping them."

He turned to Julie. "Are you ready?"

"Let's take a look." She put the gel and wand on my stomach. The whooshing began and the outline of a jellybean appeared on the screen.

"I see him now! Or her!" *I'm so proud of myself.* "Where's the second one? Come out, little peanut!"

Julie giggled. "I wish that technique worked. That would make my job so much easier." Her petite frame made me think she still shopped in the junior's section in the mall. She looked too young to be a tech. The braces did it. Or maybe the scrub top covered with kittens. She tied her long blonde hair into a ponytail at the base of her neck. Her bright blue eyes focused on the monitor as she collected data on my little peanuts.

"Dr. Aaron, how do you want me to distinguish them? Baby A and B?"

"That's fine for now. Sydney, they will change positions, and we can't give them name tags with any amount of certainty. We will be as accurate as we can."

Julie pushed the wand over to the left where she'd found my second peanut the last time. The whooshing changed, and the wand picked up the heartbeat of my second peanut. Now I observed it on the monitor.

"There he is! Or she! This makes it so real!" I couldn't stop staring at the monitor. "Can I have a few pictures? I want to show my sister."

"Of course! Let me take a few snaps now since I have Baby B in my sight. Do you want me to find out the sex?" Julie looked up from the monitor and waited for my reply.

Micky had planned to come with me today, but Ainsley woke up with a bad earache. Tony took her to the pediatrician and Micky stayed home with Zoey. Without my sounding board, I made a split-second decision. "I didn't think about that after my last checkup. I'm going to say no for now."

"I think it's fantastic when you let it be a surprise, but I understand why some people want that information in advance."

Dr. Aaron concurred. "I like the surprise, too. Your babies are in separate sacs, which means they're fraternal, not identical. You may end up with one boy and one girl, or a same-sex pair."

I took all this information in—so many things to think about, so many decisions to make. The most important one being whether I wanted to keep my babies.

I wasn't a teen mom still in school. I was a grown woman making a life altering decision. I crossed off abortion immediately as an option, which left me with two choices. Did I want to tackle life as a single mother? Perhaps a married couple could give them a better life. If I gave them up, what would I tell them later on, if they came looking for me? It's so difficult to know what path to choose. This "whatif" road is long and winding with no clearcut path to an answer.

On the way home, I took a detour through the Starbucks drive-thru. Instead of going for an iced coffee, I chose a fruity pink iced tea concoction. I paid for my drink and for the car behind me, then parked in the lot. I needed to make a phone call.

"Hello? Sydney?"

"Yes, Mom. It's me."

She sniffed. "Do you need money?"

What? Unbelievable. I've never asked them for money. "No, Mom. I didn't call you to ask for money. I'm doing fine. I bumped into an old friend from elementary school. Do you remember Michelle Patterson?"

"Yes. They're a lovely family. It's a shame they moved away. You and Abby spent a lot of time at their house."

"Michelle and her husband Tony live outside of town here near Purdue. They raise alpacas. And they have an adorable little girl with another one on the way."

"That's wonderful." She shifted gears to twist the screw. "I haven't heard from you since you left on your road trip."

"Didn't you receive my postcards? I sent them from all the national parks I visited." The guilt trip in her voice beckoned me to take a ride, but I wasn't buying a ticket.

"It's hard to tell if you're still alive with a postcard. You could have called."

"Yes, I agree. The phone works both ways, Mom."

"Don't you sass me. I was concerned."

I sighed. "Mom, I didn't call you to argue. I want to tell you something important. Can you round up Dad and put me on speaker?"

"Hold on." She put down the phone. "ROBERT! Sydney is calling with some news. She has requested your presence." It took a minute.

"Sydney! How are you, sweetheart?" my dad asked.

"I'm doing well, Dad. I have something to tell you and Mom. Are you both in range?"

"Yes, we are."

"Please listen to me. I'm not asking for your help. I want you to be aware of what's going on with me." I paused. God, this was hard. "I'm pregnant. With twins. I'm due in November. I haven't told anyone else. I'm telling you first. The babies are healthy. I think that's about all I wanted to say."

There. It was out.

My mother sucked in a breath. "Who is the father?"

Of course. "That's not important."

"Sydney, it most certainly is important. He has an obligation." My mom behaved in her typical fashion, the queen sitting on her throne of judgment.

"Gretchen, Sydney is an adult. She should handle this how she decides is best."

"How is this going to look? That I have two bastard grandchildren!"

"Gretchen! That's enough!"

For once, my mother shut up. I felt relieved to have him stand up for me.

"Thanks, Dad. I'm gonna go now. Love you."

I did it. I ripped off the Band-Aid. Now Abby didn't have to be careful when she called them. I gave in to my overloaded emotions and let some tears run down my face. My mother had this incredible superpower to make me small and insignificant. No way I'd do that to my children. I vowed to love them without setting impossible standards for them. And that's when I decided being a single mom wouldn't be so bad. I survived for twenty-two years with my mother; I could do anything.

Journal Entry

I can only imagine the filibuster my mom went on after I hung up with my parents. My dad is probably still pretending to listen to her go on and on about it. Her reputation, and the scandal when the ladies in the neighborhood and at church find out about it, blah blah blah. I feel bad for my dad on one level, having to live with her being appalled and ashamed of her own daughter. But he married her and knows what she's like.

It kills me that she was more concerned about which man to blame than she was about my well-being. She is right about one thing: What about the father? Would he want to take part in raising our babies? I don't even know who that is right now.

If it's Austin, he's likely to run in the opposite direction. Based on what Danny told me a long time ago, I don't see him embracing fatherhood. Ever. And that makes me sad. I miss him. I think about him every day. But I'm afraid of what he'd say if I attempted to contact him after all this time.

Marcus would step up to the plate. His strong bond with his family impressed me and how much he respected his mother. It might not be the way he wants to become a father, but he would embrace these little people and love them unconditionally. That's what every child deserves.

So yeah, I'll be able to provide for my babies. I don't need to involve the father. That may be a consideration down the road, but for now, I must keep moving forward. It's just me, kiddos. I hope I don't screw it up too much.

Twelve
Austin - Stroke of Luck

Sunday produced a rare thunderstorm, and I ended up with more leftovers than I cared to eat. I gave a container of pork and a package of hoagie buns to Zack for him to share with his roommates. My roommates got two hoagies each, and I saved the rest to bring to work. Everyone loved it when I brought it in, so I figured why not try to sell them? I couldn't freeze the meat for next week, and I didn't want it to go to waste.

When they saw me pulling a sizable picnic basket out of my car, Jack and Crissy slowed down to investigate.

"Are you on the way to grandma's house? Inquiring minds want to know." Jack wagged his eyebrows in the direction of my basket and stuck his tongue out.

"Mighty fancy next to my sad, brown bag lunch," Crissy echoed.

I laughed. "You vultures are an embarrassment. Yes, I brought leftovers. The thunderstorm yesterday killed my profits. From now on, I'll check the weather before I start smoking meat. So, for the price of a Lincoln, you can have one delicious day-old sandwich. Can't give them away for free this time."

"No worries. I've got a Hamilton to trade for two of them. One for now and one for later." Jack pulled out his wallet.

"Just don't leave anything in the fridge unattended or it may walk away from you." I warned. "No refunds, and no replacements. Sydney used to have her coffee creamer go missing almost weekly." I said the words without thinking. The energy changed in our conversation and goosebumps formed on my arms. She was a taboo topic around me, and Jack and Crissy remained silent, waiting for my cue.

I changed the subject in a heartbeat. "Who wants odds on how long it will take me to unload these thirty sandwiches?"

"That's not a fair wager. They'll be gone in an hour," Crissy said. "I'm going to take four of them. My boyfriend will be thanking me for not attempting to cook."

"You can't be that bad. What do you cook?"

"Kraft Mac and Cheese™. SpaghettiOs™ are hard to screw up. Oh, and ramen noodles!"

I shook my head. "Crissy, Crissy, Crissy. I can give you a few pointers to make your boyfriend stick around, if you would like."

"Super! I'm going to hold you to that."

We traded sandwiches and cash. Crissy and Jack went left down to the hive, and I made a right towards the elevators.

I tapped on the door frame and poked my head into view. "Knock, knock! It's the Candyman!" I held out my basket.

Venus waved me in and gestured towards a seat while still on the phone. I sat and waited. When she was finished, she grinned at me. "Were your Spidey senses tingling?"

"I relate more to Batman, so no."

"Brooding, emotionally scarred, handsome man. The resemblance is uncanny. Can I be Catwoman?"

Was she hitting on me? "I don't need anything. I'm peddling yesterday's sandwiches the thunderstorm didn't let me sell. Don't tell anyone, but yours is on the house." I put my index finger to my lips and then slid an aluminum foil packet across her desk. She surreptitiously slipped it into a desk drawer.

She put her elbows on the desk and gestured for me to sit. Her pen twirled in between her fingers. "You must live under a charmed star, kid. I can't even believe what I'm about to tell you."

Curiosity overwhelmed me. "I'm not sure I understand. What do you mean?"

"I mean you have hit the jackpot yet again. As if it isn't enough to win an Oscar, now you've been hand-selected to participate in the next viral reality show." She paused for dramatic effect. "A barbeque competition."

I leaned forward in my chair. "What? Are you serious? When? How?" I was dumbfounded. This was incredible!

"Your food truck culinary delights reached the lips of one of the producers. His girlfriend brought him one home from the beach and he has been looking for you like Cinderella's other slipper. Luckily you have a brilliant agent who caught this on the internal gossip line and introduced herself. You have a screen test on Wednesday, and if they like you, you will be on the show."

My jaw hung open. A thousand thoughts raced through my brain and I finally settled on one. "What's going to happen to my food truck? I was just getting started."

"Filming won't start for a month or so, so continue with your regular plans. I'll receive more specific details once you're chosen. What did I tell you? A charmed star!"

This was fantastic news because it would give me TV time to showcase my business and build a following. I could already imagine the light fixtures and place settings for my restaurant. Maybe my career lived under a charmed star, but my love life didn't. I decided to ask.

"Have you heard from Sydney? I hate to ask, but I still think about her. I recognize her lyrics when you give them to us. I worked with her too long not to decode the voice."

Venus leaned back in her chair. "Yes, I do keep in touch with her. I can tell you she currently lives near Purdue University and is doing well. She reconnected with a friend of hers from elementary school. Her freelance agreement gives her more freedom and works for both of us. She asks about you but never asks me to pass along a message. I'm in a difficult spot with both of you." She traced around the block numbers on her desk calendar with her pen.

"I appreciate you telling me that much. I screwed things up with her. It's difficult to make it right when I don't understand what I did wrong."

She kept her eyes on her desk. "I truly don't think it was about you. She needed to put herself first and live on her own terms. There might be a chance for you two down the road, but it would be a mistake to pursue her now." She glanced up at me. "That's my gut feeling. Take it for what it's worth."

I felt relieved Sydney was doing well and thriving. It still punched me in the gut that she hadn't communicated with me all these months. But I couldn't focus on that. I laid more bricks on my wall and kept my eyes on the present.

"Can you text me the details for the screen test? Then I won't lose them."

"Consider it done. What else can I help you with today?" And with that, she switched back to being all business.

"I'm good for now. Thanks for everything, Venus." I stood. "Now I'm off to unload the rest of these sandwiches."

She turned back to her computer. "I can't wait to put your meat in my mouth later. The sandwich, I mean."

I didn't imagine it this time. She wanted me.

Run from the maneater, Austin. Run fast.

Thirteen
Sydney - Labor Day

Once I received confirmation from Tony about Micky's offer, I moved in the next day. We put my tent and household goods in the corner of the garage, and I rolled my luggage into the house. Nanna's suite was gorgeous. Cream-colored walls from ceiling to the chair rail, with pale blue bead boarding below. Navy blue carpet covered the floor, and photos of the beach hung on the wall above the sofa in rustic wooden frames. The bedroom and bathroom were in the same color scheme. The whole vibe was soothing and peaceful.

"Micky, did you decorate this? It's so beautiful! It's akin to a decadent B&B."

"No, that would be Tony's sister Sofia. She helped me decorate some parts of the house, and when we wanted Nanna to have a comfortable place while she lived here, Sofia stepped up. The woman is gifted."

"I may have to hire her. I could use some help with a double nursery."

"Can I help you unpack?" Micky sunk into the rocking chair next to the bed.

"You are right where I want you. I can handle hanging up my clothes. You have done so much for me already. Most of my clothes don't fit right now, and I didn't take much with me when I left. My bedroom furniture and some other minor things like my awards dresses are in storage. Since we purchased the rest of the furniture together, I left that for Austin."

A picture frame fell out onto the floor as I unzipped my overstuffed suitcase. The frame held a strip of three snapshots of me and Austin from the photo booth on the Santa Monica boardwalk. When we came to Los Angeles to record our demo, I insisted we take the pictures as a souvenir. In the first picture we're smiling at the camera. We're sticking our tongues out at each other in the second. In the last picture, Austin is kissing me on the cheek, and I have a surprised expression on my face.

I sat down on the bed, holding the frame in my hand. What happened to these two crazy kids, full of life and optimism? Lefty started his kickboxing class in my uterus, and I rubbed my belly to calm him. I was determined not to tell Austin and Marcus about my pregnancy. That was the best option, I was sure of it.

But ... what if it wasn't?

Maybe I was hormonal and not thinking straight. That's what I kept telling myself when I did things that were out of character for me. Micky called it Pregnant Brain and insisted it is indeed a real symptom of some pregnancies. Not that I needed any encouragement.

Micky interrupted my thoughts. "I don't like to pry...oh that's a lie. Have you spoken with Austin at all? It sounds like the two of you were close."

I turned and gazed out the window so I didn't have to face her. "I thought we were close. I'm sure he's upset with me and hurt by how I left. But he doesn't deal with things the way most of us do. If he wants to call me, I haven't blocked his number. It's been difficult not to have him in my life, but I can't focus on that. My babies are my priority."

Micky rocked as she thought. "One other question, and then I won't bring him up again. Is he the father? Because if he is, I think you should tell him, Sydney."

"As I told Doctor Aaron, I don't know who the father is. I was in a relationship with a wonderful man, Marcus. He treated me like a queen, and I've never felt so seen in my life. But he saw Austin and I sing together, and he figured out we had feelings for each other. He made a choice to step away from our relationship. I would never have acted on my feelings for Austin. I love Marcus. His decision was non-negotiable and I chose to respect him. I found myself in Austin's bed just days later, which makes it difficult to determine who knocked me up."

Micky didn't speak for a few moments. "Sydney, that's a lot to unpack. I understand why you've been stressed out."

"I'll be fine no matter who the father is. I'm not sure that's going to be the case on the other end. That lingering question mark is what worries me. I don't want to upend anyone else's life."

"That's fine for now, but what are you going to do when these babies start asking about their daddy? Because they will once they go to school and other kids ask them."

I groaned. "I didn't think about that." But she was right. Kids asked each other about their parents as a natural course of conversation. What would my kids say? "I've got a little time to figure this out, don't I?"

"You'll have to at some point."

She sat in the rocker, rubbing her swollen belly. Tendrils of her hair escaped from her braid and the bags under her eyes magnified her tired appearance. I sat down on the carpet in front of her, legs crossed, and held out my hand. "Give me your foot." She raised her eyebrows.

"It's a little late for the Cinderella routine. My Fred Flintstone feet can't fit into flip-flops, let alone a glass slipper."

I picked up her foot and started rubbing it with my fingers, starting at the balls, moving from side to side. She leaned back in the rocking chair and closed her eyes. "Oh, Sydney. Don't stop. That feels so good."

Tony came around the corner while Micky was moaning. "Cheating on me already. A guy can't catch a break," he teased. "How are you settling in, Syd? What do you need?"

"I can't think of anything. Your sister Sofia really is super talented. This is way better digs than the little Sunset Motel I've been staying at. Samson agrees." Samson was camped out on his new dog bed next to the sofa with his eyes closed.

"Sweetie, I put lasagna in the oven about twenty minutes ago. We'll have dinner at six. Okay?" Micky asked.

"Perfect. I came to tell you I'm taking Ainsley out to feed the herd with me. Be back at six." Then he vanished.

I finished rubbing one foot and switched to the other. Micky relaxed and dozed off. I covered her with a throw blanket and walked out to the kitchen to put together a salad for dinner. Vinnie's sleek black BMW sedan sat in the driveway, and I guessed he might stay for dinner.

When I pulled the lasagna out of the oven, little steps rushed down the hallway. I turned to Ainsley and whispered, "Shh! Momma's sleeping. She's so tired."

Ainsley's eyes grew wide and she placed her finger up to her mouth. "I'll be quiet."

"Go wash your hands, sweetie. Dinner's almost ready."

She skipped to the bathroom. Tony and Vinnie came in the side door.

"I would accomplish a lot more if I ran everywhere like Ainsley does," Tony joked. "Sydney, are you on dinner duty too? Micky is already overworking you." He scanned around the room. "Where is my lovely bride?"

"I left her taking a nap. She looked exhausted. Do you think I should wake her?"

"Nah, let her sleep. Our naughty little turkey Zoey kept her up all night. I would trade places with her if I could."

"Okay. You two go wash your hands and I'll bring dinner to the table."

The four of us ate our meal in silence. Micky came out as we were collecting plates. "Why didn't you wake me for dinner?"

Vinnie spoke up. "When a queen is sleeping, you let her sleep. You already got true love's kiss, right?"

Micky wrinkled her nose at him and grabbed her swollen belly. "Sure, smarty pants. Did the lasagna turn out better this time?"

"Nothing tastes as good as Mom makes it, right Tony?" Vinnie mopped up the remaining sauce on his plate with a piece of buttered bread.

"I can't put my finger on what's missing. Doesn't matter, though—as you can see, there's not much left." Tony pointed to the casserole dish with two decent-sized pieces remaining. "Hungry men don't complain about a delicious, hot meal put in front of their face."

Micky turned to me. "Tony's mom gave me her recipe for lasagna, and I keep trying to make it like she does. I think she left something out of the recipe, but I can't prove it. It's maddening."

"Let me warm up some lasagna for you. Here's a salad while you wait." I scooped a piece onto her plate and took it to the microwave. Ainsley carried our water glasses and the empty breadbasket back into the kitchen. Vinnie opened the dishwasher.

"Let me take care of that," I scolded him.

He cocked his head. "We all help each other. I'm not a guest, and neither are you. Now go bring in the rest of the dishes so I can finish my job." He waved his hand to dismiss me. Back in the dining room, I handed Ainsley dishes, wiped the table, and put the placemats back for the next meal. I sat down next to Micky, who tackled her lasagna.

"I'm still so tired. This fork is heavy." Micky slumped in her seat.

"Change into your jammies and crawl under the covers. There's no prize for staying up the latest."

She shuffled to the stairs and inched up them. I could feel my little jumping beans dancing on the ceiling and rubbed my belly to settle them down.

Vinnie finished loading the dishwasher and came out to sit with me.

I spoke first. "I'm sorry if I overstepped in the kitchen. I'm still getting used to the routine."

He made a dismissive sound at me. "Pssh. I'm not offended. I don't want you to think kitchen work is women's work around here. My parents didn't raise us that way. We all took turns at dish duty, garbage night, mowing the lawn, and folding laundry. I think that's the way it should be."

"I didn't have any brothers, just two sisters. I'm the baby, my sister Abby is in the middle, and Brooke is the oldest. My parents had a similar philosophy. My dad made me learn how to change the oil in my truck and change a tire."

We sat in the dining room chatting for a little while. Tony came downstairs after putting Princess Ainsley to bed. She'd worn a crown and a fluffy tulle ballgown all day long. He carried the soiled dress under his arm.

"I think her Royal Highness is asleep. She cracks me up with her imagination." He paused. "I've been reading *Knuffle Bunny* every night."

"She loves listening to funny stories. It warms my heart when kids ask for someone to read to them."

"Do you read a lot?" Vinnie asked.

"Yes, it's almost criminal. I haven't read much since I got here, but I have a huge litany of books on my TBR list."

"TBR?"

"To Be Read. I had them all in order once, but I came across more I wanted to read. I like stories about animals, biographies, and memoirs. Some of my favorite authors are John Grisham, Lisa Scottoline, Jennifer Weiner and Jodi Picoult. I can't remember them all."

"That's cool. I read when I'm on planes and in airports. At home, I have so many projects to tackle that I end up watching Netflix from behind my eyelids at bedtime." He chuckled. "They should be paying me for the things I don't finish from falling asleep."

"Speaking of bedtime, I've been chasing a princess around all day. I'm going to follow her and her mother. Excuse me, gentlemen." I padded to my room and closed the door.

A knock on my door woke me from my slumber. Samson let out a low woof in a warning. A tenor voice came from behind the door.

"Sydney? It's Tony. Zoey is about to announce her arrival. Micky is already in the truck waiting for me…"

I hopped out of bed and hurried through the sitting room to the door. Rubbing my eyes, I confirmed with Tony. "Okay. I'll take care of Ainsley."

"Vinnie will feed the herd this morning. I'll keep you updated about when you can bring Ainsley to the hospital."

"Sounds good. Take care of our girl." I hugged him and he hustled toward the side door and to Micky. I couldn't remember what time Ainsley got up in the morning, so I left my door open. And promptly fell back asleep.

Noises in the kitchen woke me. I checked my phone. 7:30AM. I pushed the covers off and went to find out who was making such a racket. Vinnie's back was towards me as he pulled dishes from the dishwasher and stacked them back in the cupboard. It impressed me how they all worked together, even though this wasn't Vinnie's home. He had his own job and responsibilities, but here he was, helping his brother and his family.

Samson snuck by me and butted his head against Vinnie's leg. "Hey, boy. Is it breakfast time for you yet? Or do you need to go out?" He turned around and caught me standing there.

I held my hand up and waved. "Morning. I'm going to have to let my bodyguard go. Do you know anyone who wants a lazy bull mastiff?" I laughed. "Samson, let's go out." He padded towards me and I opened the door for him.

I turned back towards Vinnie. "Tony told me you were feeding the herd this morning. I got Princess Ainsley duty. What time does she wake up?"

Vinnie thought. "I want to say 8AM, but I'm not sure. That may be bedtime instead. I'm no help."

"That's okay. I'll go ahead and make the pancake batter. Are you staying for breakfast?" I opened the pantry and found Bisquick and Mrs. Butterworth.

"I planned to go home and eat some cereal, but you said the magic word. Pancakes. Twist my arm a little and I'll stay." He held out his arm and I slapped it out of my way.

"Okay. Breakfast for four, coming up."

"Four?"

"Samson likes pancakes, too." He barked at the door and I let him back inside.

Cooking wasn't my favorite thing by far, but I managed not to starve. It wasn't fun to cook for one person. I preferred cooking for dinner parties or celebrations. The griddle warmed up as I slid a tray of bacon into the oven. That way, the top of the stove wasn't overloaded.

Vinnie took plates from the cupboard and silverware from the drawer. "I take it Samson doesn't need a plate."

I blushed. "No. He's too spoiled."

A little voice piped down the stairs. "Momma? Daddy? Where are you?"

Vinnie stuck his head in the stairwell. "Ainsley, we're in the kitchen. Come down to breakfast, please."

Her bed head was out of control, and her pink nightgown with tiny white stars hung off one shoulder. She yawned and rubbed her eyes. "Where's Momma and Daddy?"

Vinnie answered. "They went to the hospital because Zoey is coming."

Ainsley clapped her hands and hopped up and down. "Is she here? Can I see her now?"

"Daddy will call when we can come to the hospital and meet her. It might be a few hours or more." He switched topics. "Are you hungry? Miss Sydney is making us pancakes and bacon. Doesn't that sound yummy?"

She sat down next to him. "Can I have some milk, Sydney?"

"Of course." I poured a small glass and brought it over to the table. I set it down, along with a plate full of fluffy pancakes. "I'll be right back with the…oh shoot! I forgot to make coffee. I'm so sorry. I don't drink it much and it didn't occur to me you might want some." I smacked my hand against my forehead.

He stacked pancakes on his plate. "Don't worry about it. If I want caffeine, I'll find some. Ainsley, let me cut up your pancakes." He leaned over her plate with his fork and knife.

We dug into our plates of sweet deliciousness. The only sounds were the clanking of silverware on plates. My mother always said that the food is good if everyone stops talking. If only she could see me now. I was proud of me, and that's what counted.

We cleaned up the kitchen together. Vinnie leaned against the counter. "I'm heading home to work for a while. I'll go to the hospital when Tony calls. Do you and Ainsley want to ride with me? I'll pass by here on my way."

"I take it you don't live far from here. Of course we'll ride with you."

"I live just a couple miles over. Most of us chose to stay close to home. Our brother Thomas, or Tommy, is the only one who defected. He lives with his wife and pack of shelter dogs in the Florida Keys and sells expensive real estate. They'll come up for Zoey's christening celebration."

I finished wiping the counters and around the stovetop. "We'll await the good news."

As I watched him walk down the sidewalk, I couldn't help but think how lucky Tony was to have a brother like Vinnie. I put on one of my maxi dresses, brushed my hair and teeth, and went to help Ainsley do the same. We couldn't wait to meet Zoey.

Journal Entry

Ainsley spent the morning asking me every five minutes if Zoey was here yet. Barbies and games of Memory only distracted her for so long.

I never did get a phone call. Vinnie showed up a little after lunch and took us to the hospital. We stopped in the gift shop in the hospital lobby and let Ainsley pick out a balloon to take them. She picked a gigantic one in the shape of a birthday cake with a single candle on top. It announced "Happy Birthday!" in colorful letters across the cake. It was perfect.

So was little baby Zoey. So tiny and so pink. Micky looked exhausted but invigorated by the attention. It gave me a glimpse of what I might experience myself in a short amount of time. I got to meet Tony's parents and reconnect with Micky's parents briefly before Ainsley got antsy and Vinnie and I took her to the playground.

The more time I spend with Vinnie, the more I like him. He's not difficult to look at, either. Tall, with a muscular build from manual labor. I can't stop staring at him. It's probably my hormones on tilt. It's definitely not my heart. I'm not on the market, or in the market for anything resembling romance right now.

I have more important things to think about.

So why can't I get him out of my head?

Fourteen

VINNIE - ZOEY ARRIVES

Tony called me with the good news after lunch. I closed my laptop and grabbed my keys off the hook by the front door. My excitement took over and I remembered about halfway to the house that I neglected to let Sydney know I was on my way. I smacked my forehead as I parked in the driveway. Oh well. I'm here now.

Ainsley streaked towards me when I opened the door and I caught her as she jumped into my arms. "Uncle Vinnie! Is Zoey here now?"

I squeezed her. "Yes, you little monkey. Are you ready to go meet her?"

She wiggled in my arms. "Yes! Let's go."

Sydney came through the kitchen archway. "I thought you were going to call first."

She didn't sound upset but I apologized anyway. "I'm sorry. I got excited and forgot. I can wait for you two to get ready."

"We just need our shoes. Ainsley, what did you do with your other sneaker? Go look under your bed, please."

I put Ainsley down and she scampered towards her room.

"I'm going to put Samson out on his run and make sure he has fresh water. That should give Ainsley enough time to find her shoe."

"I'll go help her look. We just need to find two shoes that match, correct?"

"Yes. Doesn't matter. You know Micky isn't fussy about her wardrobe." She turned and went out the back door with Samson.

Ainsley came back wearing both of her sneakers, laces dragging on the floor. "Can you help me tie them?"

I kneeled down. "Of course, monkey." She held out each foot as I made the bunny loops and crossed them together. "Let's go meet your sister."

Ainsley picked out a gigantic balloon in the hospital gift shop to bring to Zoey. "Happy Birthday Zoey! I brought you a balloon!" She ran over and climbed up on the bed with Micky. "Hi, Momma and Daddy! I came to play with Zoey."

Micky held Zoey in one arm. She took Ainsley's hand and whispered, "Zoey's sleeping right now. She just ate and she's a tired little baby. Would you like to meet her?"

"Yes, Momma." She bounced on her knees on the bed.

She pulled back a corner of the blanket and held Zoey at an angle for Ainsley.

"Momma, she's all red."

We all laughed. Micky explained. "That's normal, love bug. She was growing inside me, so she hasn't had her skin exposed to the air. Your skin was red, too."

Tony scooped Ainsley in his arms. "Come over here and sit with me, little monkey."

Micky looked up at me. "Do you want to hold her?"

"I was waiting for you to ask. Of course!" She held out Zoey, swaddled in the requisite blue and pink striped hospital blanket. I took her and sat down in a chair next to the bed. Sydney looked over my shoulder.

"She's perfect, Micky," Sydney murmured.

"Another beautiful princess," I concurred. I stared at little Zoey, so fragile and strong at the same time. I knew I wanted this. Being a fun uncle warmed my heart and I loved Ainsley unconditionally. But I wanted my own children, too.

Micky's parents' arrival interrupted my thoughts. They carried gift bags and a bouquet of daisies.

"Where is the new princess?" her dad bellowed. His hearing wasn't as sharp as it used to be. "I'm taking her to Disney World right now."

"Okay, Dad. We can arrange that." He came over and hugged her. "I hope I didn't pull you away from something important."

"Hush. What could be more important than family?" He shook Tony's hand and hugged him, too. "Family hugs, remember?"

"Yes, Sir. So glad you both came." He looked over at Micky's mom. "Grace, what is all this fuss?" He pointed at the gift bags. "We already had a baby shower."

She waved her tanned hands at him. "You should know by now that I can't come to festive occasions without bringing presents. Besides, these aren't for you. They're for your girls." She sat in the chair on the other side of the bed.

Ainsley perked up. "Presents? For me?" She turned to Micky. "Momma, is it my birthday, too?"

"Remember what I told you the other day? Sometimes people bring presents for fun, like your Barbie from Miss Sydney. Grandmas do that sometimes, too."

Grandma Grace picked up one of the bags. "Ainsley, this one is for you." She held it out and Ainsley grabbed it eagerly.

She pulled out the tissue paper and found a pink t-shirt that said *I'm the Big Sister!* She held it up. "Daddy, what does it say?"

"I'm the big sister," Tony replied.

"Yay! Thanks Gramma and Pop Pop!"

Grace picked up the other bag. "Tony, why don't you open this one for Zoey?"

Her t-shirt onesie said *I'm the Little Sister.* Tony laughed. "Of course!"

"I was with your aunts a couple of weeks ago in Myrtle Beach. While we were shopping, I came across these in a store window and couldn't resist. I don't think you got anything like this at the shower."

"It's perfect, Mom. Thanks," Tony replied.

"Mom. Dad. You remember Sydney Campbell?" Micky said.

Sydney stood up and hugged them both. "Mr. and Mrs. Patterson. You haven't changed a bit."

"You need an eye exam, or I need to fire my bathroom mirror," he joked. "Your momma isn't here, so please call us Brian and Grace." As a child, my mother always insisted I call people Mr. and Mrs., no matter what they said. Sydney's must've done the same. Old habits die hard.

"I'll do my best. How wonderful to reconnect with all of you." She sat back down as more visitors—my parents, Tom and Leona—came into the room. They fussed over Zoey.

"Micky, she's got a full head of hair! Remember how Ainsley was bald for so long? In her first birthday pictures, that gigantic pink dress with all the ruffles was the only way anyone knew for sure she was a girl," Leona mused. "I have a few frozen casseroles I made for you. Tom, you will remember to take them over tomorrow."

"Yes, my darling," Tom replied.

The few chairs in the room all held occupants. I rose from my chair. "Momma, come sit here."

Everyone talked back and forth. Ainsley squirmed on Tony's lap. He spoke up. "Sydney and Vinnie, I think Princess Ainsley is ready to go to the playground. Can you give Momma and Zoey a kiss before you go?"

Tony swooped Ainsley down in front of Micky. She kissed her and Zoey. "Bye, Momma." He put her down and she ran over to Sydney. She took her hand and skipped out the door.

I followed them. "Guess that's my cue. Let me know what I can do to help with the herd, brother."

Fifteen
Sydney - At the Park

I couldn't unbuckle Ainsley fast enough when we got to the playground. Her little legs kicked up and down in anticipation. When I freed her from the booster seat, she scrambled out and ran full-speed to the swings.

She hopped on and shouted, "Uncle Vinnie, come push me!"

Vinnie jogged over and obliged.

"Higher! Higher!" She shrieked with laughter and pumped her legs up and down to reach the sky.

I strolled over and stood next to Vinnie. "Does she jump?"

He turned his head towards me. "No, not yet. Do you realize how many kids break their arm or leg on the playground every year? I don't intend to bring this little princess home to my brother with a cast. Not on my watch." He didn't crack a smile.

I nodded. "Kids have accidents all the time. I don't think anyone would blame you for a playground injury."

"They won't have to if it doesn't happen in the first place."

I wasn't sure how to continue the conversation and remained quiet as I watched them. After she had her fill of giggles on the swings, Ainsley headed over to the climber that resembled an upside-down metal soccer ball. Vinnie and I found a bench nearby and sat down.

"Uncle Vinnie! Come play with me!" She waved from the top of the bowl.

He laughed. "That contraption is not made for gorillas like me. Only little monkeys like you."

She responded by bending her hands up to her armpits and cheeping like a monkey. We all laughed, and she went back to exploring.

"How are you adjusting to life in the slow lane?" Vinnie asked as he leaned back onto the bench.

"Fine. I didn't expect to reconnect with Micky, but I'm so glad I did. Getting to connect with your family has been the most normal thing I've done in a while. I spent most of my time alone while I was traveling cross country. Well, I had Samson, but you know what I mean."

"I spend a lot of time alone on my trips, too. I take care of business and eat takeout in my hotel room. They all look the same to me now. It gets old after a while. But it pays the bills."

Ainsley came hobbling over to us. "Can you fix my sandal, Sydney?" She held it up and I noticed her ankle was caught in the back strap.

"That's an easy fix. Hop up here on the bench."

I unbuckled the offensive strap and repositioned it properly. "Do you want to play some more, or are you ready to go home?"

"Play some more," she chose.

"Great. I notice a few more kids coming, so now you'll have someone to play with you." A minivan had just pulled up, and two girls about Ainsley's age streaked towards us. Ainsley got excited and ran off to greet them like they were old friends.

A woman pushing a stroller followed behind them. Her streaked blonde-brunette hair sat cockeyed in a messy bun on top of her head, and she wore an oversize sweatshirt and colorful leggings. She settled next to us, standing but not sitting. Her confused expression unnerved me. Then she spoke. "I don't mean to be rude, but are you with this little girl?" Her confrontational tone set me on edge.

"We are." I bristled a little. "What's the problem?"

"I recognize her, and I know you're not her mother." She narrowed her eyes. "I'm trying to decide whether I should call the police."

I held up my hands and Vinnie stood up in response. I stumbled over my words, trying to decide if I was offended by her busy-bodiness or impressed. "I'm a friend of her mother's, and this is her uncle. We brought her here to play while her parents are at the hospital."

She relaxed and held her hand to her chest. "I'm so relieved! It appeared suspicious from my end. I hope you can understand I was only trying to protect Ainsley. Did Micky have Zoey? I wondered about that."

I settled on impressed. "Yes, Zoey arrived late this morning." I held out my hand. "I'm Sydney. This is Uncle Vinnie."

She shook my hand. "I'm Danielle. Micky and I meet up here after preschool sometimes to let the kids run wild and chat over our Starbucks drinks. My girls go to preschool with Ainsley."

"I wondered why she was so excited. Now it makes sense."

"Micky told me she'd reconnected with an old school friend. I'm guessing that's you."

"Guilty. We were best friends until junior high. Back then we didn't have Facebook, or the internet. We just lost touch. We found each other in the thrift store. Can you believe it?"

We chatted for a while, and Vinnie kept track of Ainsley until finally she came over, her braids slightly askew. "Sydney, I'm hungry."

"I didn't bring any snacks when we left the house. I guess we need to go home. Go say goodbye to your friends."

"Wait a minute." Danielle reached over and grabbed her giant diaper bag. She unzipped a compartment and handed Ainsley a juice box. Another compartment held goldfish crackers and granola bars. She called her girls over and distributed snacks all around. They sat on the grass and devoured their snacks.

"How generous of you! Thank you." I remarked. Another reason to be impressed—what else was in that magic bag?

She smiled. "Can you tell I've been doing this for a while? My husband wanted a boy in the worst way." She pointed towards the stroller with the blue blanket covering it. "Third time's a charm. I'm done pushing out watermelons. Next stop is to 'snip-snip' town to prevent any happy accidents."

"That sounds like a smart idea. An unexpected pregnancy can be overwhelming." *I should know, right?*

Vinnie interjected. "I think however children come to you is a blessing. So many couples out there can't have kids. I would love to have a few of my own, but I haven't found my partner."

Then he said the thing I didn't want him to say.

"I have to give single mothers credit. I can't fathom how they do it. But then they keep going back to these useless men who knock them up again and leave. We have all these kids growing up without fathers, and it's not right."

I couldn't help myself. "I'd rather be a single mom than be in the wrong relationship. You can do everything right, play-by-play out of the book, and still end up in a less than desirable situation. Let's not play the blame game here, shall we?"

Vinnie held up his hands, his eyes wide. "I'm sorry. I didn't mean to offend you. I'm sure it doesn't apply in every scenario."

Offend, you did. My rage started to boil. "Oh no, that's fine. Tell me how you really feel. These women end up bamboozled by worthless men who want a free ride. Many of these losers find ways to avoid paying child support by working under the table for cash. Then she can't have his wages garnished by the court. He still manages to obtain visitation because *he has rights*. When he doesn't show up, she's left to console sad little people because they still love him, regardless of what a douche canoe he is. There are few impactful consequences for men when they behave like assholes and don't take responsibility for their actions. Could you imagine what people would say if Micky just took off one day and didn't come back? The backlash would be akin to *The Scarlet Letter*."

I stared at him the whole time, my face hot and my heart pounding in my ears. *Seriously?* No one even asked him to expound on the subject of single moms. My hands shook and I clasped them together, hoping he couldn't tell.

Danielle broke the tension by getting up from the bench. "It's getting to be nap time. I better take these hooligans home before they run out of juice. Please tell Micky I'll stop by once she's home and settled. I'm glad we met." She grabbed the handle on her stroller and I swear she sprinted away from us.

Vinnie was the first to speak. "I never thought about it that way."

"I apologize. I'm rarely confrontational." I only meant it halfway.

He chuckled and ran his hand through his short black hair. A few gray strands peeked through at his temples. "That's okay. I like women who aren't afraid to speak their minds."

"I had a friend out in L.A. who got a raw deal from a worthless guy. It just rubs me the wrong way. I'm not a big fan of Taylor Swift, but every word in her song *The Man* is true. Our world is not an equal playing field for men and women[5]. The double standard is alive and well. I wish I'd written that song."

Over his shoulder, Ainsley trudged toward us.

"We have a very tired little princess coming this way," I said.

Vinnie turned. He jogged over to Ainsley and swooped her up in his arms. "Did you have fun with your friends?"

She clung to his chest. "Yes, Uncle Vinnie." She yawned. "Can we go home now?" Her eyes closed.

"Of course." He loaded her into the booster seat with a content expression on his face and she fell asleep before Vinnie started the car.

Journal Entry

I take back what I said about Vinnie. What a neanderthal! He's got some 1960s ideas about women. No thank you. Hard pass.

Seriously, how can men keep thinking like this? Women can do whatever men can do and run circles around them while doing it. I admit I got a little carried away lambasting him, but he deserved it.

I have an uphill battle on my hands if I'm under the delusion that a man is ever going to want me with so much baggage – and the stigma of being a single mother. At least I saved myself, and don't need a prince to do it for me. **I'm my own hero.** *If I have a girl(s), I hope I can instill the idea she can do anything a man can do and be anything she wants to be. If I have a boy(s), I'm going to raise him to understand women are powerful. And EQUAL to men. We haven't come as far as I thought we had as a society. Geez. Guess we still have a way to go.*

Sixteen
Vinnie - Planting the Seeds

Tony texted me and asked if I could pick Micky and Zoey up from the hospital. Their Houdini alpaca Larry escaped again and he was out in the woods chasing him.

I peeked around the doorway to Micky's room. "Is it safe to approach?"

She waved me in and I made my way to the bassinette. "Zoey, I'm going to spoil you as much as your sister. I promise." I leaned over and kissed her forehead, then turned to Micky. "How are you doing this morning?"

"The nurses took Zoey last night, so I got to sleep. I'd almost forgotten what that's like. I'm still sore, but I feel fantastic otherwise. How was the park yesterday?"

"Ainsley had a splendid time. We met a couple of her preschool friends and their mom, Danielle. She got hyper when she noticed us with Ainsley instead of you. I swear she thought we were kidnapping Ainsley. No joke."

"That must have been uncomfortable. I didn't think about it when I told you to take her to her favorite park. I'm sorry."

"Why are you sorry? We talked Danielle down from the ledge and then had a regular conversation. It was fine. Except for the part where I got schooled by Sydney for my remarks about single mothers. That was a real treat."

"What did you say?"

"I don't remember exactly. But Sydney got fired up and put me in my Neanderthal place."

She sucked in a breath. "I take it no one told you Sydney's pregnant. And facing the difficult reality of becoming a single mother."

"That information might have been helpful before I stuck my face in it."

"I think we all say things we shouldn't from time to time. But you know now." She waved her hand casually, like she'd absolved me.

"What do you think of Sydney? I'm so glad we've been able to reconnect and be close."

Subtlety was not Micky's strong suit. "I'm glad you two are friends. However, I'm certain she's not my biggest fan."

Micky winced. "She's got a lot to digest."

"Why's she by herself? Where's the father?"

"Unsolved mystery. All I know is she's here now, and I'm going to help her. I think it'll do her a world of good to have stable friends in her life who won't abandon her."

I leaned back on my heels. "Whatever you want to do is fine with me. I should apologize to her for being such an insensitive ass."

"She's probably forgotten about it already. They're going to grant me early parole this afternoon."

"Tony told me. I'm your Uber."

"Wonderful. The car seat is in the closet. It'll be a bit though. They have to do all my discharge stuff."

"I need to make a few calls anyway. Text me when you're ready to split."

I made a left out of Micky's room and found an empty family lounge. Now Sydney's disgust with my comments made sense. If the roles were reversed, I would have responded the same way. *She must think I'm a misogynistic asshat.* I need to apologize.

After I made my phone calls, I returned to assist Micky. I placed the carrier on the bed and Micky expertly buckled Zoey into it. A nurse came in with a wheelchair and Micky didn't protest. When I picked up the carrier, its heaviness surprised me. "Holy moly! Is this thing made of bricks? It didn't seem heavy without the baby in it. I'll need bigger biceps than The Rock to carry this. How do you do it, Micky? Geez."

"Motherhood is my superpower."

I had no doubt.

Seventeen
Sydney - Pregnant in NYC

Being pregnant as a plus-size woman is challenging, to say the least. People take one glance and just think I'm fat. Or fatter than I used to be. I should be joyful about the lives growing inside me, but instead I have to deal with that nonsense.

At five months, which already seemed like ten or eleven, I flew to visit Abby for a long weekend. She sprang for my business class ticket, but I still needed a seatbelt extender. People gave me side eye as I waddled my way through the airport and onto the plane. *No one wants to be seated next to the fat chick.* I wanted to wear a T-shirt that said *Fat AND Pregnant* on it, but I wasn't quite brave enough. It wreaked havoc on my psyche to wear so much emotional armor in public all the time. When I was with Abby, I didn't pay attention to negativity. I was always too busy soaking up every moment I spent with her. Knowing I'd get to be with her for a few days improved my mood tenfold as I flew through the clouds.

Samson perked up when he saw me put my suitcase on the bed. He pouted and turned his back to me when I told him he wasn't coming. As if I told him I was abandoning him permanently. "Micky and Ainsley will spoil you rotten after I leave," I told him. Honestly, the guilt trip.

New York City was one of my favorite places in the world. The electric energy in this city was unmatched. I could see fabulous Broadway plays and musicals until my heart burst from happiness. Abby scored complimentary tickets to something she said I'd love but wouldn't tell me anything else. I hoped it would be *Waitress* because I loved Sarah Bareilles.

I only had one request for this trip: I wanted to see Her Copper Majesty, Lady Liberty, up close and personal. The day after I arrived, Abby and I got up early to ride the subway to the ferry. Abby knew this city so well, we never needed a map. All I did was follow her lead.

My excitement grew, watching Lady Liberty inch closer and closer. No photograph compared to seeing her in all her glory with my own eyes, but I took tons of pictures anyway. Abby and I explored the exhibits inside the pedestal on Liberty Island, learning about the architect and process for construction, as well as the restoration in the 1980s. The original torch sits in the middle of the first floor, and the full-size replicas of her face and her foot put her sizable presence in perspective.

The view of the Manhattan skyline from Liberty Island was magnificent during the day, and from the postcards I'd seen, it was even more amazing at night. We didn't go up the 300+ stairs to the crown because I wasn't sure I had the stamina for it.

The museum at Ellis Island was impressive. All these people who left their homelands to come here, hoping for a better life. I didn't know much about my own genealogy, and now my curiosity was piqued.

On the way back to the subway, we splurged for a ride on the Sea Glass Carousel they built in Battery Park next to the ferry. What a genius marketing money pit for families to open their wallets and bribe their kids to behave at the same time. My anxiety kicked into high gear as I wondered if I would be able to fit in the fish pods with the size of my stomach. Once we got up close and saw how roomy they were, I relaxed. Abby and I each chose a car that looked like a fancy fish. We spun around in a random pattern, laughing and enjoying ourselves.

"I'm bringing your peanuts here when they come to visit Fun Aunt Abby."

"I figured as much." It's a blessing to have a sister to be silly with.

Afterwards, we stopped for a hot dog and pretzel from a nearby cart and gazed across the harbor from a picnic bench. By this point, my pregnant feet ached, and we agreed to head back to Abby's apartment. The evening commuting hour began, and the subway car got more crowded the further we went. I observed people standing and using the poles and hand grips to maintain their balance as the car rocked back and forth along the track.

An attractive businessman in an expensive-looking suit got in the car and stood at a grab bar a few feet from me, focused on his phone. I wouldn't have paid him any attention, except that his cologne triggered me, and not in a good way.

It was the same cologne Jason wore when he attacked me.

My breath got short and my head started to pound. I tried to ignore it but I couldn't. I grabbed Abby's hand and squeezed it a little too tightly.

She leaned in and whispered, "Sissy, what's wrong?"

I couldn't find my voice.

She took in my expression. "My god, you look like you're terrified. Are you in labor? Tell me what's wrong."

Still nothing.

"You're making me nervous. Do we need to get off the train? There's a stop coming up in two minutes."

I nodded, tears rolling down my cheeks.

"Excuse me!" She sounded shrill as she stood and pulled me up with her. I let her propel me through the throng to the doors as the car came to a stop. Once outside, she drug me over to a pillar and leaned me against its cool tiles. She pressed her open palm against my forehead and cheeks.

"Sissy, are you okay?" she asked, fear tinging her words.

I swallowed. "His cologne." That's all I managed to utter.

"Whose cologne? The suit? It was kind of strong. I read somewhere that pregnant women can have extreme sensitivity to aromas."

I shook my head. "That's not it. It was the same cologne Jason was wearing." I started to sob.

Abby took me in her arms. "Oh my god, Sissy. You've never talked about what happened. I understand why." She tightened her grip around my shoulders and didn't let go. After a few minutes, I managed to calm myself.

I wiped my tears with the back of my hand. "I think I'm okay now. I'm sorry. That's never happened to me before."

She put her hands on my shoulders and looked me in the eye. "Never apologize for that." A small smile curled on her lips. "We have a few more subway stops to go. Let's pick up takeout from this great little Korean place. I think we earned some relaxation in our jammies." She patted my stomach. "I don't want my future nieces or nephews to get hungry."

"We could eat." I returned her grin, and it actually felt genuine. My sister was the best. "Lead the way."

We slept in the next morning and had a leisurely breakfast at a diner in the neighborhood before heading into the city. Today we would spend some time at the Museum of Broadway, have dinner in the theater district, and then hit the show after dinner. I put on the one dress that still fit over my growing baby belly and Abby helped me tie my sneakers. As we strolled to the subway, she told me she arranged for a car to pick us up after the show, which made me less cranky.

While we poked around the museum, Abby probed about my, eh hem, growing situation.

"Have you decided what you plan to do about the babies? I mean, are you going to tell the father soon?"

"I would if I knew who that was without a shadow of a doubt."

"Have you spoken to Marcus or Austin since you left?"

"No. I've thought about it, Abby. But what should I say? Silence feels like my best option now. My whole life is consumed with these swirling thoughts about what will be best for these little people once they arrive."

Abby sighed. "I will support you no matter what."

"Yes. I appreciate you. Mom helps pile on the criticism. She's more concerned about what her precious church members think than my feelings. What else did I expect?"

I stared at the famous sequin-covered dress from *Hello Dolly!* Two scenarios kept playing in my head regarding telling Austin/Marcus. My birth control mistake was just that, a mistake. Did this mean his life should be upended along with mine? Would he think I lied? That I trapped him into parenthood? He could have chosen to wear a condom to protect himself from this situation. Why should I be the only one who pays for joint adult consent?

When we sat down to dinner at Skirt Steak, my little peanuts started a dance contest in my uterus. I took Abby's hand and placed it on my beach ball. She squeaked and removed her hand when she experienced a kick.

"Oh my! He's a strong one! Does it hurt, Sissy?" She gingerly placed her hand down again and received another impact.

"No, it doesn't hurt. They do get rambunctious when I lay down, which makes sleep challenging."

"That's bizarre." Abby wrinkled her nose.

"You would think so. But I spend all day moving around and rocking them to sleep. When the ride stops, they wake up."

She tapped her finger against her forehead. "Now you're making sense."

I took a sip of my Shirley Temple. "The strangest part was when I first started sensing them move. It felt like I had butterflies flitting around in my abdomen. They've grown too much now. Occasionally, one of them presses their foot up against the wall and I can view the whole outline against my skin. It's the craziest thing."

"You haven't found out what you're having, have you?"

"Nope. I think it's one of the last great surprises in life. I don't care if it makes it more difficult to shop for the baby shower. What did we do before gender reveal parties?"

"I think I would have to know. Are you excited about being a mom? I'm nowhere near ready myself."

"Truthfully, I'm a little bit terrified. I don't want to do to my children what was done to me. To us. I don't want them to feel inadequate, or that their achievements are not quite good enough. They need to believe I'm proud of them and love them without expectation or reservation. I never even entertained the thought of being a mom much. And now it's staring me down. It's intimidating to say the least."

Abby reached over and took my hand. "Sissy. You're not going to end up like Mom. That's what you're afraid of, right? That you will repeat with them what was done to you and me. And Brooke. It's not going to happen, because you experienced the unhealthy hurt firsthand. You're going to be an amazing mom. And I intend to be the best auntie ever." She pointed at her heart.

Our steak dinner arrived and our conversation faded. Knowing what you don't want to do as a parent was only half the battle. I'd still make mistakes all the time, I knew that. It's inevitable. But I hoped Abby was right about most of it.

We walked from the restaurant to the theater. As it turns out, Abby did score tickets to *Waitress* and I was beyond thrilled. Box seats, no less. Sarah Bareilles had completed her stint in the lead role, but the new actress did a phenomenal job bringing her character to life. I sat enraptured through the whole show. Abby called it right, getting a car to take us home. I fell asleep from having too much fun all day.

Journal Entry

My feet are so swollen from three days of walking. I bought a pair of compression socks to wear on this plane ride home. But spending time with Abby has always been one of my very favorite things, so I wouldn't change a thing. This weekend was amazing.

I can now check the Statue of Liberty off my bucket list. I'm inspired to look into our family tree once I'm home. I want to learn when my ancestors came over from Europe to start their new lives here.

The only low point of my visit was when I got triggered on the subway. I didn't realize how much the scent of his cologne was tied to that memory. I don't want one creep to affect me in such a negative way. The part that bothers me the most is that I never know when my brain will get triggered and short circuit into fight or flight mode.

I've been thinking about Marcus and Austin. I wonder if I'm cheating them out of the experience of anticipating the arrival of their babies. But mostly I obsess over what kind of mom I'm going to be. Abby's right—I don't want to end up like Mom. I'm going to do everything in my power to prevent that.

Eighteen
Austin - Show Business Blues

I had no clue what I was getting into when I signed the contract for this competition. Sitting in a chair letting someone put makeup on my face was not part of how I pictured it. But here I am, letting Lori, the HMUA (Hair and Makeup Artist) make me look less ugly. *Okay, I'm exaggerating.* I'm not going to stop traffic in horror, but I held no grand delusions of being swoon worthy like Brad Pitt.

After makeup, I traipsed down to wardrobe and they handed me something to wear. My regular clothes are not suitable. They have to gussy me up for the cameras. It's all unnecessary in my opinion, but I wouldn't want to tell them how to do their jobs. I let them shuffle me around until they were satisfied, and waited until they were ready for all twelve of us.

It was all a game of "hurry up and wait." Every morning they acted like we were behind schedule, but then we'd wait for them sometimes until after lunch. *Infuriating.* I brought my guitar most days and worked on songs for the hive. Other times, I perfected my video game prowess on Grand Theft Auto and Rocket League. Sometimes a group of us gathered for a friendly (no betting) card game. Anything to pass the time.

One of the other contestants got my attention from the first introduction: Cheyenne. Her warmth and bubbly personality enraptured me, and she had sass for miles, like a compact powder keg. I'd never met someone so petite. I could probably pick her up in one hand. Her grandpa taught her about smoking and grilling. He owned a restaurant for many years in Houston, and he won plenty of competitions back in his day. They found her in much the same way they discovered me. The right person tasted her secret recipe while she sold pulled pork sandwiches at the county fair.

For every challenge, three core judges and one guest judge ranked our dishes. This week Guy Fieri sat in the guest seat. I'd met many celebrities in my line of work and wasn't fazed by them. Normally. I'd been a fan of Guy's for a long time, and cooking for him totally excited me. He seemed like someone who'd be cool to hang out with in real life. I wouldn't mind his job either, driving around and trying out food at all those interesting places.

Someone knocked on my door. "Everyone to the set!"

I checked my hair in the mirror and headed out to the set. Cheyenne was a few feet in front of me, so I picked up my pace to catch up with her.

"Hey, pretty lady! Ready for the next challenge?" I bumped her with my shoulder as I pulled up alongside her.

She glanced in my direction but kept walking. "As ready as I'm going to be." She tucked her chestnut hair behind her right ear. "It's counterintuitive to improvise when you're making food, but who am I to judge? I only wish they'd stop putting me in dresses that make me a reject from the Strawberry Shortcake gang." She waved her hands up and down her outfit. The pale pink dress had miniature white polka dots all over it. The short sleeves capped off with ruffles on the ends, along with the hem of the skirt. "All I need is pigtails and a pet turtle for a sidekick."

"Oh man! I remember those little dolls! My cousin owned the whole set, and I sniffed all of them like glue. Awfully embarrassing to think about it now. Makes me sound like a pervert." I laughed at myself. "Have you asked Angela to give you something else to wear?"

She nodded. "She doesn't even pick out the clothes. Someone who's not even on set does. It gets approved by the producers and becomes my outfit whether I want to or not. My friends will be laughing their butts off when they see this getup. At least you wear pants."

"Next time we can trade. I'll wear the dress." I curtsied, holding out my imaginary dress, and she cracked up.

"Thanks for making me laugh about it."

"I aim to please." I tried to figure out how to ask her out, but my usual pickup lines in the bars weren't going to work this time. It needed to be sincere, and not like a horny toad trying to feel up her skirt.

She beat me to it. "Would you be interested in going out sometime?" She glanced up at me. Good lord, did she grasp how sexy she was?

I gulped before I answered. "Actually, I planned on asking you out. You beat me to it. I would love to go out with you. Let's talk after this.

Cheyenne and I didn't talk after today's shoot. I shot my mouth off during the instructions for a challenge and got in a tangle with the producers. They sat down with me in a meeting, explaining who's in charge. It reminded me of a teacher trying to explain to politicians what schools need. The politicians nod their heads like they understand but do the exact opposite of what they recommended. Completely unproductive.

It was all so stupid. We stood on our marks as the cameras rolled and the hosts explained the challenge of the day. The longer they talked, the more certain I became that a monkey determined this series of events by pulling them out of a hat. Mentally, I struggled to calculate the logical progression for this challenge. They told us we only had five hours to accomplish our task.

I opened my mouth and words spilled out like vomit. "Wait a minute. There is no way any of us can perform all those steps in five hours and have anything but a subpar, half-cooked mess. It would take me at least eight to ten hours using my smoker at home. And if I turned up the heat to meet the time deadline, it would be closer to the consistency of a hockey puck."

The hosts turned towards each other, speechless. All the other contestants looked at their shoes. I'm sure they thought I'd be canned immediately and didn't want to pack their suitcases next.

I kept going. "This is supposed to be competition to find the best barbeque chef, correct? We should be given an appropriate amount of time to complete this challenge. Five hours is not going to cut it. Who decided this? They have little to no knowledge of the nuances of this craft. *And it is a craft*. The average Joe with an apron and a spatula in front of his gas grill on the holiday weekend can't do this. There are ways to make this show interesting without placing impossible demands on us."

"CUT!" the director hollered. He hopped from his chair and came out in front of the camera to speak to me.

"Austin, is it? Listen. These challenges were curated to give all the contestants a fair chance at winning."

"I doubt that. This is the third week, and none of the challenges so far have been appropriate. Have you ever been to a rib cook-off? They start smoking their meat before the rooster wakes, and baby it all day to achieve its unique flavor and tenderness. Cooking any kind of food is a science, and you aren't following the rules."

"Maybe this competition is not the right place for you," he seethed. He looked past me to the remaining contestants. "Go back to your trailers. I'll call you again when we're ready to start shooting." He turned on his heel and started marching in the opposite direction. He stopped and turned towards me. "I would pack your suitcase now, Mr. Mitchell."

I made my way back to our alley of trailers. I passed the first three trailers and heard a voice behind me.

"Psst! Austin! This way."

I turned my head and saw the rest of the contestants huddled on the side of a trailer where they couldn't be seen. I changed direction to join them.

"What's going on? You guys planning on kicking my ass?" I joked. "He told me to pack my suitcase."

Bubba, one of the more seasoned contestants, took the lead. "Not at all. We agree with you. If they try to can you, the rest of us are leaving too. You're right about all of it. And I doubt the director has ever deigned to lower himself to eating pork, period."

I chuckled. "He strikes me as someone who eats a lot of vegetables. I appreciate the backup, but it's not necessary. I meant every word. This contest is ridiculous and pointless. No legitimate barbeque cook-off works like this. I bet they don't have one person on their creative team who could find a rack of ribs in the dark."

I followed Mr. Fancy Pants Director to the emergency meeting called on account of my big mouth. Without raising my voice, I explained my reasons for being less than cooperative. And I clued them in that the rest of the contestants intended to walk out with me. The producers listened to me, and we got the show back on schedule. I gave them suggestions on challenges that made more sense for the competition.

I accepted the outcome of the meeting and agreed to stay. Mr. Fancy Pants and I shook hands as a show of faith, and I took the news back with me to the trailer pod. Everyone thanked me, and I got a few hugs, too. I was proud of myself for taking a stand.

I caught up with Cheyenne after dinner. She sat outside her trailer on a lawn chair, eyes closed, with her head tilted up to the sky. Her face caught the last rays of the sun as it dipped between the trailers for the night. I stopped and observed her for a moment. She had a faint scar on her left cheek that I hadn't noticed until now. She intrigued me. I wanted to get to know her better, but without jeopardizing the spirit of competition. I hadn't felt this way about anyone in quite a while.

I approached her from the side and whispered in her ear. "Greetings and salutations."

She jumped a little at the sound of my voice. "Oh, hi. I needed my daily dose of vitamin D. Artificial lighting on a sound stage doesn't count in my book."

"I'm living out in L.A. right now, so it's not something I think about much. It's always sunny."

"Must be nice. Although I don't think I want to live in a place where it never snows. A blanket of frozen water makes the whole world magical. Don't mistake my meaning. I am a Texas gal through and through. But those Rocky Mountains have been my home for a few years now. Those rich, hungry snow bunnies are my bread and butter, so to speak. Food trucks do well at the slopes."

"Things got out of hand today. I've never stood up to anyone like that before. I usually keep my mouth shut and grumble about it under my breath later."

"I'm glad you did. It all worked out the way it was supposed to. I would have been sad if they dismissed you. And I'm glad they listened to your input. They didn't do very much research before throwing this competition together."

"I hope things progress smoothly moving forward." I hooked my thumbs through my belt loops and leaned back on my heels.

She gasped. "Where are my manners? Would you like to come in and talk? I don't want the rumors to start flying." She stood up and folded her lawn chair, resting it against the side of her steps.

"Thank you. I wouldn't mind some time to chat." I followed her up the four steps and into her trailer, pulling the door closed.

She opened her small fridge on the countertop. "I have Coke, fresh-brewed sweet tea, and a few Coronas. What's your poison?"

In the past, after the day I'd just experienced, I would have knocked out a six pack without any effort. I reached into my pocket and grasped my one-year sobriety chip. It reminded me daily of how far I'd come in my recovery. "I'd love some tea, thank you."

She poured tea into two blue Solo cups and came over to sit with me on the couch. My hands were grateful to have something to hold onto so I wouldn't fidget. Cheyenne made me nervous, which wasn't typical of me. My usual confident demeanor with women vaporized.

"I recall they gave a little bit of information about each of us at the first taping," she said, "but you'll have to refresh my memory. How did you become interested in mastering the barbeque world?"

I took a sip of my tea. "I'd like to say something profound about a relative who taught me like you did. My Consumer Economics teacher in middle school, Miss Hollis, turned me on to cooking. My mom didn't much care for cooking, and we ate takeout food at least twice a week, if not more. Miss Hollis helped me build a foundation to competently cook whatever I wanted.

"*Diners, Drive Ins and Dives* got me interested in barbeque. How they would let meat marinade for days, then take eight to ten hours to cure properly. I used the oven for my first experiments, but when my mom surprised me with a used smoker for Christmas, I was hooked. Now I use different combinations of spices and types of wood to create unique flavors. When I didn't have to work on Saturday or Sunday, I selected a roast or rack from the freezer and spent all weekend creating a masterpiece. As a bonus, we ended up with leftovers for two or three days. I made sides to complement the masterpiece: loaded baked potatoes, grilled corn on the cob, dill potato salad, or my favorite, pulled pork with mac and cheese."

"The mac and cheese combo sounds delish. I'll have to try that."

"Trust me, it's like crack. You'll be addicted and I won't be held responsible."

She tilted her head and looked at me. "What would you be willing to be responsible for?" Her tone shifted. A little bit softer and a whole lot more inviting.

I didn't want to blow my chance with her. I moved my cup to the side table then leaned in close and inhaled her floral perfume. "Would it be okay if I kiss you?"

She gazed up at me and nodded.

I placed my hand on the side of her cheek. "I need you to answer me. Consent is sexy."

"Yes," she breathed.

I closed my eyes and found her lips. I touched mine against them. She responded, kissing me back. My toes tingled, and a warmness rippled through my body. Kissing meant feelings, and I hadn't felt this way in a long time.

Her lips parted, encouraging me to continue my discovery of her. I slid my tongue into her waiting mouth. We continued kissing, neither one of us wanting it to end. I pulled back, giving her one last soft kiss.

We opened our eyes and I removed my hand from her cheek. "Wow! That was something!"

She blushed. "You've done this before."

"I'm not the only one. Who taught you those moves?" *I'm impressed.*

She waved me off with her hand. "When you have the right partner, they make you look good."

I counted myself completely sprung on her, but I didn't want to show my hand yet. Instead, I pulled myself off the couch. "I better be going. I've already gotten in enough trouble today."

Cheyenne started to stand up but I stopped her. "You stay there. I would like to do this again soon." I took her hand in mine, brought it up to my lips, and kissed it. Turning around, I strode to the door and made my exit.

When I got back to my trailer, I pulled off my boots and socks, and flopped down on the couch. Thinking about Cheyenne warmed me in places I almost forgot existed. I spent so much time mourning the loss of Sydney, and I didn't want to risk that kind of hurt again. But the heart wants what the heart wants, and I couldn't stop thinking about Cheyenne. I wanted to take her out at least once before one of us got sent home. To do that, we'd have to sneak past our chaperones and security.

Game on.

Nineteen
Sydney - Nesting Assistance

I kept getting up later and later. Ainsley came in for a hug every morning, but then I rolled over and went back to sleep. The contractions, along with the twins fighting for the most room in my uterus, made it difficult to sleep well at night. Around dawn, the babies settled and I could get some rest.

Staying with Micky and her family was a blessing and a challenge at the same time. The rhythm of the farm differed greatly from the environment in L.A. Farming of any kind is a lifestyle, not just a business. It's not a nine-to-five job or a bricks and mortar store where you can lock the door and walk away. Animals require constant care, feeding and maintaining their living quarters round the clock.

In addition to the alpacas, Tony and Micky planted an extensive garden and tended a variety of fruit trees. They devoted a section of their acres to a large grove of blueberry bushes and a strawberry patch where people could come and pick their own baskets. Micky canned beans, tomato sauce, beets, cabbage, sauerkraut, carrots, and zucchini from the garden. Tony made amazing pickles from their cucumber harvest.

I did my best to fit in and assist wherever I could. That meant entertaining Ainsley, helping with meal prep and laundry, and changing Zoey's diapers. When I was in school, I didn't babysit very often; that was Brooke and Abby's territory. Hanging out with Zoey made me feel better prepared for my upcoming role as a mom.

As my due date approached, I purchased basic necessities for the twins. Two matching cribs and a changing table replaced the sofa in the sitting room. Micky told me not to purchase a stroller, then she instructed me to practice my surprised face. *Happy baby shower to me!*

Micky put Tony and Vinnie on furniture assembly duty. They bickered back-and-forth the entire time they were putting the cribs together. It was comical and I found myself trying not to laugh out loud multiple times.

"I told you panel A gets screwed into panel B. How dumb can you be and still breathe?"

"You're still breathing, so pretty dumb, Vinnie."

"Keep it up, buster. You're cruising for an ass whooping."

"You'd have to catch me first, which will never happen, you clumsy ape."

I texted Micky, who had taken Ainsley to gymnastics.

> Are they this way all the time when they work together?

> Oh, dear God. I asked them to behave.

> I already peed my pants. I can't stop laughing.

> I have toddlers. Not men. Toddlers.

After about an hour, I ventured into the sitting room to check on their progress. They had one crib assembled and the second almost completed.

"Would you like some refreshments?"

"Yes, please," they replied in unison.

I brought them their drinks and went back to cutting vegetables for crocodile stew.

After a while, I heard Tony call my name.

"Sydney, we're finished."

I waddled into the room. They stood on either side, waving their arms up and down like models showing off the prizes on *The Price Is Right*. I clapped for them. "Oh, my! They're perfect. Now Samson won't have to give up his bed."

Samson perked up his head at the mention of his name. I hugged them both around my humongous belly, thankful to have help. Vinnie was starting to grow on me. I couldn't forget his negative comments about single moms, but he came across like a decent guy otherwise.

"Do you two argue back and forth like this all the time? I'm just curious."

Tony and Vinnie looked at each other. Then at me. Then back at each other.

Tony explained, "It's just brothers busting each other's chops. We don't mean what we're saying. You should be here when Tommy gets involved. Come to think of it, Sophia and Bianca can throw some zingers if we rile them up enough. But when it comes down to it, we have each other's backs. You better not mess with one of us, or you'll be dealing with all of us."

"All I'm going to say is I peed a little a couple of times while I was laughing, and that's not a nice thing to do to a pregnant woman," I joked.

"We are bottom-feeding scoundrels, Tony. There's no redemption for us."

"I think putting those cribs together is your redemption. Thanks again."

"Okay, Vinnie. Back to the barn." And they disappeared outside.

I sat in my rocking chair and dialed Venus.

"Hiiiiiiiiiiiiiiiiiii!! So glad you called!"

"I've been thinking about you. I go to bed so early most nights and you're still working. I might be up past my bedtime tonight."

"How are you? How are my babies doing? You're taking care of yourself, right?"

"I take so many cat naps, it's ridiculous. Lefty has kickboxing classes every night as I'm trying to go to sleep. Righty marches to his own drummer, but not quite as exuberantly as his uterine roommate." I rubbed my belly.

"Did you find out if you're having boys or girls? You're using 'he' pronouns...."

"Nope. I think it's one of the few remaining surprises in life and I will find out when they arrive."

"You don't make it easy to select shower gifts."

I got excited. "Does that mean you're coming to the shower?"

"Do you want me at the shower, or do you want me to come for a week once you're home and settled? I can do one or the other. They dog me whenever I decide I need a vacation and act like the whole company will vaporize if I'm not there to hold it on my shoulders. Why give me vacation days if I'm not allowed to use them? It's madness."

I nodded. Lefty started kicking. "V, I wish you should check out the kickboxing Lefty is doing right now. It appears I'm about to give birth to an alien through my belly button. It's hilarious."

"I can imagine. You are one brave woman, Sydney. I'm certain I couldn't do what you're doing. Now, back to my question."

I thought about it for a moment. "I would rather you come for a week afterwards. Abby and Micky have blown off the rails on this shower. If you came, I would ignore everyone but you and Abby, and that wouldn't be fair."

"You got it. I will have my new assistant attempt to book a flight for me without screwing it up. I hate training new people. It makes me channel Miranda Priestly more than it should."

Venus didn't have any patience for incompetence, and she went through assistants frequently. Her demanding job required someone who kept up with her and complemented her efficiency. The temp agencies did their best, but it was a steep learning curve. Sink or swim. Few survived the first week.

"Speaking of little people, I need to check on Ainsley. It's too quiet upstairs. I love you and can't wait for you to visit."

"Ditto." And she was gone.

Journal Entry

What did I do to deserve such amazing friends? Tony and Vinnie took care of the crib assembly and disposed of the packing remnants. I couldn't resist laughing at them while they were working. They reminded me of the brothers in Ocean's Eleven who can't stop hurling insults at each other. Right now, I pee a little every time I sneeze or cough, so it's unfair to have that happen when I can't stop laughing. Their banter back and forth was too hilarious!

I'm glad I got to chat with Venus even for a few moments. I miss having her nearby. We developed a tight bond while I was in L.A. and the time difference makes it difficult to connect. Her upcoming visit will be something for me to look forward to, besides the arrival of my babies.

Samson lays by my side in bed most nights and jumps a little when he senses a kick nearby. He's been around Ainsley and Zoey and seems comfortable with them. I wonder how he'll behave when he has two more humans to protect. It's been the two of us for so long. We both have some big adjustments to make.

I'm still mulling over baby names. I have so many dog-eared pages and highlighter marks in my books. How will I ever decide? I hope by the time they arrive my choice will become clear.

Dr. Aaron told me to assemble a hospital bag, and my pregnancy books have helpful lists of recommended items. I found a few yellow and green infant outfits and bought two in each color. If I have a boy and a girl, it will be easy to tell them apart. But if I have two boys or two girls, I'll need a way to distinguish who is who. I don't want to dress them alike. That's just asking for confusion.

I'm getting excited about meeting my babies, but I'm scared, too. Labor isn't for sissies. Even this Sissy. Micky said she won't leave my side the whole time. I'm so lucky to have her friendship. I don't know what I'd do without her.

Twenty
Austin - Secret Date

As it turns out, it wasn't difficult to sneak by our chaperones. I "borrowed" a golf cart from the stadium and picked Cheyenne up at her front door. She wore a simple sundress with skinny straps and her flip flops had rhinestones. I had some surprises stowed behind our seats for us. Then I drove right through the gate and waved at our chaperones as we passed them in their booth. They were both watching TV and didn't even notice us.

I steered the cart all the way around the stadium, up to the top level. I parked by a railing and turned off the cart. Cheyenne stood and leaned against the top bar of the railing, peering out at the city. I went around beside her and observed the picturesque view. We stood in silence, absorbing the ambiance as the city lit up in the twilight.

I caught a glimpse of her profile, obscured by the tendrils of hair blowing across her face. God, she was a vision! I reached over and turned her face towards me. I gazed into her hazel orbs and leaned in to kiss her. We melded together, taking our time to acquaint our bodies with each other. It was tender and sweet—a perfect moment.

When we finished, I put my finger to her lips. "Stay here. I need to set up a few things."

She nodded and I dropped her hand as I scampered back to the cart. I drove a little way down the open-air walkway so I was away from her sight line. The blanket from my couch served as the base for our picnic, and I laid it in an open spot with a panoramic view. I arranged grapes, crackers, cheese and meats on a wooden tray. Two red Solo cups™ served as our fancy glasses, and a bottle of sparkling white grape juice rounded out our feast. I left the chocolate-covered strawberries in the bag for a surprise later.

When I brought her back with me, we sat down on the blanket facing each other. We chatted as we nibbled on our treats.

"How many brothers and sisters do you have?" I asked her.

"I'm an only child. My mom and dad both grew up in big families and I have lots of cousins around my age. Too many."

"I'm an only child, too. My home is with my mom in Kansas City. I miss her and her optimistic outlook on life. She always put me first and I don't call her often enough. I took her to Disneyland when she came out to visit me in L.A. She's such a kid at heart and I loved watching her have fun."

"She sounds delightful. I'd like to meet her sometime. Let me think … what can I ask you? Do you have any pets?"

"We have a bunch of barn cats we feed and shelter in exchange for rodent removal. I've lost count because they come and go as they please. We have one fat housecat, Oliver. He's aloof and sassy most of the time. How about you?"

"We have hound dogs for hunting, and they stay outside. I've never had a pet to call my own. Growing up on a farm gives you a different philosophy when it comes to animals and what purpose they serve. Your turn."

"I understand. My grandparents farmed for a long time and we had various farm animals like chickens, pigs, and goats." I changed the subject. "Do you have a boyfriend? Are you married?" I held my breath waiting for the answer.

She locked eyes with me. "No boyfriend. No husband. How about you? You're a handsome guy. Who do you go home to?"

I answered her without blinking. "No one. Not in a long time."

"Follow-up question: Who was she and how long ago was it?"

Is it that obvious? "My writing partner, Sydney. We spent every day working together for three years. It took her leaving for me to realize how much I loved her. It was difficult to recover. But I'm ready to invest in a relationship again." I hoped she heard the sincerity in my voice. I didn't want to blow it with her.

"I appreciate your honesty. It sounds like she meant a lot to you."

"Yes, she did." I swallowed. "There's something I need to tell you before we go any further." I shared the short version of my childhood trauma and how it affects my life and the way I dealt with things.

We got so busy talking that I almost forgot. "The strawberries!" I blurted out.

Cheyenne looked confused. "What strawberries?"

I pulled them out of my reusable grocery bag. "I got them for dessert, and as a joke. Since you mentioned Strawberry Shortcake the other day."

Her face lit up. "That's terrific! You put a lot of thought into this date. I'm impressed."

My chest puffed out a little and I attempted to remain cool. "Thank you. I like you a lot, and I wanted to make this memorable."

She blushed. "I will definitely remember this evening. I like you a lot, too. It's too bad I'm going to wipe the floor with you in the next challenge."

"Oh, ouch!" I clutched my chest in fake horror. "I'm not worthy!" Then I burst out laughing. "Bring it on, sweetheart." I leaned in and kissed her. Her floral perfume and the strawberry flavor of her lips flooded my senses. I could have stayed like this with her, but we got interrupted.

"Excuse me. You're not allowed to be here." A security guard pulled up to us on his golf cart.

I scrambled to my feet. "Pardon me, officer. We were just having a picnic. We're not causing any trouble, are we?"

"I can't let you stay here. You need to vacate the stadium. I don't want to call the authorities."

He didn't appear armed, but I wasn't taking any chances. I held up my hands. "We'll go. Not a problem." I helped Cheyenne to her feet and we collected our picnic. The security guard followed our cart all the way down the serpentine ramp. We didn't talk. When we got to the bottom of the ramp, I stopped and motioned him to come up next to us.

"We're going to go that way," I pointed to my right, "back to our trailers. Thank you, officer."

His mouth gaped open. "Are you contestants for the reality show? Gosh! I'm sorry. I thought you were trespassing."

"Yes, we are. We're going to mosey back to our camp now. Have a good evening." I waved and turned our golf cart to the right.

Cheyenne grabbed my right hand. "You handled that so well! I was afraid we'd end up arrested."

"Not on my watch, sweetheart." I squeezed her hand.

We pulled up to her trailer, and I kissed her goodnight. "I had fun on our picnic. We should do this again. Not the security guard part, maybe."

She smiled. "I agree. Do you want to come in?"

I wanted to. Badly. But I didn't want her to think I only wanted sex. "I think I should take this coach back and call it a night. I want you to think I'm a gentleman."

She gave me a kiss on the cheek. "Thanks again. See you tomorrow."

I made sure she entered her trailer, then took the cart back. As I walked back to my trailer, I replayed the evening in my head. The more time I spent with Cheyenne, the more I wanted to be with her. I'd never had this kind of desire, but I liked it. Winning this competition was important to me, but not if I couldn't have Cheyenne. I'd already lost one woman I loved, and I was not about to lose another. *Cowboy up.*

Twenty-One
Cheyenne - Catching Feelings

I thought I was too old for magic like this. I leaned back into my trailer couch and closed my eyes, thinking back to our first kiss. Austin gave me all the feels, and I couldn't wait to spend more time with him. It's disappointing that he declined my invitation to come inside, but I also felt relieved. In this age of online dating and easy hookups, how refreshing to find a man who wanted to take his time and not rush to sex.

Our picnic was fun, even when security got involved. Austin executed a thoughtful date, even though we didn't go anywhere. The views of the city from the stadium were spectacular. I wouldn't have ventured up there on my own.

One part of our conversation replayed in my mind. I asked Austin whether he wanted children.

He took his time responding. "I never thought about my life with children in it. I'm not opposed to kids, but I don't think I'd make a good dad."

"What makes you say that? I think you would be an amazing dad, from what I've witnessed. Standing up to the director impressed everyone. I'm not just saying that."

"I know." He looked off into the distance.

I sensed he wanted to say more, so I waited for him to elaborate while sipping my sparkling juice.

"I'm going to tell you something about me. I don't grasp how you will react, so I'm hesitant to do so."

"You can tell me anything. No judgement here."

He took a deep breath. "I was molested and abused when I was very young. Some of it I don't remember, and some of it comes in flashbacks. I've been in therapy most of my life, dealing with my past. People don't realize how screwed up you can be when these things happen.

"I want you to comprehend what you're signing up for if we continue to have a relationship. Most days I function like a normal human being. But sometimes I have a flashback or a trigger and I become a different person. I am moody and withdrawn from everyone. Especially the people I love the most. My mom has seen more of it than anyone else."

Knowing no details of what he'd been through, it was difficult to wrap my brain around it. He spoke with no emotion and his eyes lost their sparkle as he revealed his monsters. I grew up in a loving home with doting parents and supportive grandparents nearby. The mere thought that someone else could have a different childhood experience made me so sad for him.

"I don't want this to have control over my whole life. My defense mechanisms are well honed. I keep my distance and have built up emotional walls no one will ever break through. I have to, to keep myself safe and keep the monsters at bay."

He finished by saying, "I like you, and I can envision you becoming an important part of my life. Give me a chance to prove it to you." He held out his hand and I clasped it with mine.

"That's a lot to unpack," I'd remarked. "I've been through a lot, but nothing like that. It makes me angry that some people think it's okay to do horrible things to other people. Don't let the monsters have power over your life and your happiness. Life is too short. I will keep your secret safe."

We sat in silence for a spell. I wasn't sure what to say. No words were adequate to heal from trauma like this. The only thing I could compare it to is when someone you love dies. Grief wasn't something you recovered from; you simply figured out a way to carry on with that hurt in your heart.

While we rode back to our trailers, I thought about what he said. He told me about his past because it was important, but also because it gave him a way out. I had a suspicion that if things got too intense for him, he would bolt.

We pulled up in front of my steps. I turned to face him. "Thanks for trusting me with your story. It took a lot of courage to tell me." We leaned into each other and spent a few more moments kissing. His cologne made me dizzy, and when our lips parted, I asked. "What cologne are you wearing?"

He responded, "Hugo Boss," and went back to kissing me.

"It makes you smell amazing." I inhaled his scent. "Would you like to come in?"

He stopped and looked at me. "I think I should take this coach back and call it a night. I want you to think I'm a gentleman."

I gave him a kiss on the cheek. "Thanks again. See you tomorrow on the battlefield."

Twenty-Two
Sydney - Baby Shower

As promised, Abby and Micky pulled out all the stops and held the most outrageous baby shower. They rented out the V.F.W. and transformed it into a pink and blue wonderland that would have made Willy Wonka jealous. The tables were covered with linens and flower arrangements spaced at intervals down the rows. A chocolate fountain with fruits, marshmallows and graham crackers sat next to a table full of a variety of cookies in an elaborate pyramid pattern. Along the back wall they hung a cream-colored backdrop and put an elaborate balloon sculpture in front of it for photo ops. Right in the center of the room was a cake made to resemble a stack of building blocks.

I couldn't take it in all at once. It took a lot of time to make this happen and I became overwhelmed with emotion. I started to sob.

Micky grabbed me by the shoulders. "What's wrong? Are you okay? You're not having contractions, are you?"

I shook my head but continued crying.

"Come over here and sit down." Abby steered me to the rocking chair at the front of the room. She knelt in front of me with her hands on my knees. "Sydney, I don't want to have to give you tough love, but we have guests coming in about twenty minutes, and we don't want a sad pregnant lady. Tell me how we can help."

Micky handed me a box of Kleenex and I took three. I blew my nose and attempted to collect myself. They regarded me anxiously.

"I think you're so amazing for throwing me this..." I waved my arm and gestured around the room, "...party. How are you going to fill all these tables? I only know like ten people here. This is too much." I shook my head and blew my nose again.

"You remember Danielle, right? I invited her and a bunch of my gal pals. I've lived here a long time and know lots of lovely women. They all want to shower you with love and support. You're going to love them. Trust me."

Abby nodded and rubbed my arm. "You deserve this, Sissy. Sit here and relax. This is your special day. We even bought you this gorgeous yellow dress that doesn't appear as if you're wearing a tent."

I didn't want to wear a dress in the first place but pants had become an impossibility. Abby selected a body-hugging canary dress with cap sleeves, and asymmetrical rouching. The plunging neckline showed off my swollen décolleté. It would be the only time I could wear something this bold without people commenting behind my back on how fat I was.

"I'll be fine. I need a minute." I smiled at Abby and tried to reassure her I wasn't going to ruin this. "I will sit here and behave while you do whatever you need to do right now. I'm fine. Really." I closed my eyes and rocked back and forth. I must have fallen asleep because someone tapped my shoulder and called my name. It was Micky.

"Sydney, your guests have begun to arrive. Would you like me to move your chair closer to the door so you can greet everyone?"

I nodded and followed Micky. The first people I greeted were Tony's mom Leona, and his sisters, Sofia and Bianca. Grace and Shauna Patterson arrived after them. I knew some of the others, but not many. I turned around to grab a Kleenex from the table when I heard a voice behind me.

"Oh. My. God. I can't believe it! I had to view this with my own eyes."

I would recognize that voice anywhere. "Brookie!" I grabbed onto her and embraced her around my huge belly. "What? How? I can't believe you're here!" I started to cry. Again.

She whispered in my ear. "I don't always follow through, but I had to be here for you today. You are my sister, after all."

"I'm so glad you're here! They didn't tell me you were coming."

"I didn't know for sure until two days ago. It was easy to keep a secret." Micky brought over a chair for Brooke and she sat next to me while I greeted more people. At the very end of the line, I got another surprise. I glanced up and Tori stood there.

My mouth fell open and I held out my hands to her. "Help me out of this chair so I can give you a proper hug. Oh my God! This is the best day ever!" We hugged for a long time. "Please tell me you are staying for a few days. I can't believe it!"

"I absolutely am!" She met my gaze with wet eyes and nodded. "One of Daisy's mommas just had a new litter of puppies, or she would have been here, too."

I was the luckiest woman alive. Beloved old friends, kind new friends, my sisters... There was only one face missing from the room.

My mom.

Brooke and Tori stayed after everyone had left. Tori didn't have her requisite notebook and marker with her, but I didn't ask her about it. Micky called Tony to load up the truck and take all the gifts over to the house.

Micky, Grace, and Shauna bought me a fancy double stroller that did everything but change diapers. Leona, Sofia, and Bianca bought me what appeared to be a whole pallet of diapers. The twins got some matching outfits, two different mobiles for their cribs, and some toys for tub time and tummy time. A few of the gifts were for me. Venus sent a couple of massage gift certificates along with two onesies that said "I'm Mom's favorite" on them. Abby and Brooke got me gift cards for Door Dash when I didn't want to cook.

My entire being was exhausted and overwhelmed with happiness. Lefty started his kickboxing, and Brooke stared in amazement as he made my belly jump.

"He's a live one," Tori remarked. "Does it hurt?"

"Not at all. I can feel it, but it's not painful. Lefty is a lot more exuberant than Righty. I can't wait to meet them. They already have their own personalities." I took Tori's hand. "I have to ask: where's your notebook?"

She winked at me. "Some people don't need translations."

Tony came over to us. "We've got your loot in the truck. Where would you like us to put it?"

I thought for a moment. "How about the dining room? That sounds like the perfect place for now."

"Your wish is my command." He whistled as he made his way to the door.

Brooke took notice. "You have some wonderful friends here, Sydney."

"I'm blessed. I don't know what I would do without Micky and her family."

Brooke and Tori followed us back to Micky's house. We spent the evening in the living room, laughing and talking. Tony started a fire in the fireplace, and Micky brought out the wine – and grape juice for Ainsley and me. When it was time for bed, Tony wrangled Ainsley and hung her from the back of his shoulders to carry her. She giggled and hung onto the doorway as they passed it.

"Daddy, no! I have to kiss the babies!" He set her down and she scrambled over to me. She hugged my belly and kissed it twice. "Good night, babies!"

After Ainsley made her exit, Brooke stood up. "I hate to be a party pooper, but my plane leaves in a few hours. I'm so glad I got to be here for you today, Sissy." Abby helped me out of my chair and the three of us hugged. How long would it be before we were in the same room again?

Tori stood up after her. "You're not going to get rid of me. I will be back tomorrow around ten." She kissed me on the cheek. "I'm glad we could surprise you like this. Venus is going to be so jealous when I tell her about that chocolate fountain."

Journal Entry

Today was memorable on several levels.

First, I couldn't believe Brooke came to the shower! With all the times she's flaked on me, I didn't expect her to come today. Such a fantastic surprise!

Then Tori showed up! I miss her and think of her often. Her fierce friendship, along with Venus and Daisy, kept me going in L.A. when I didn't want to. I'm so glad she will be here for a few days! And Micky's friends were so generous to come and support me. I'm still overwhelmed and grateful thinking about it.

It disappointed me when I learned my mom opted to stay home instead of coming to my shower. These are her first grandbabies, and it shouldn't matter how they come into our lives. Her religious zealousness is too much for me to handle sometimes. She's disappointed in me (yet again), but for some foolish reason, I still want her with me for important moments like this.

With all these people surrounding us, my babies will be loved and cared for, not just by me. That's a feeling more precious than gold.

Twenty-Three
Austin - Final Round

Reality shows have many secrets that contestants aren't allowed to talk about, even after the show has wrapped. When a competition involves eliminations, they don't send home the ejected contestants. They ship them to another house and they are required to stay until filming is completed. This amounts to being under house arrest. It would ruin the drama of the competition otherwise.

Cheyenne and I made it all the way to the finals. I sighed with relief after every elimination round. During the fifth round, I blew it by overcooking the ribs, but the guest judge saved me. If you get too cocky—and I did—the tables can turn against you.

After the picnic with Cheyenne, I decided to behave like a gentleman during the competition. I didn't want to lose my focus by daydreaming about Cheyenne when it should be all about the barbecue. In the immortal words of Alex Hitchins, *Daydreams are for private time. When you're in the room, be in the room. Concentrate. Focus. Women respond when you respond to them*[6]. In other words, keep your head in the game.

They taped the final competition in front of a live audience. They brought in two guest judges, which cranked up the intensity. I've performed for audiences many times as a singer, and I'm used to getting nervous just before I go on stage. But this was different. The stakes were much higher and it had my stomach churning, not in a good way. Cheyenne and I stood behind the curtain, waiting for our names to be called. The eliminated contestants sat in the front row to record their reactions on camera and to cheer us on.

Me and her. Finalists.

Damn.

We didn't speak and we didn't look at each other. I had hoped it wouldn't come down to the two of us, but that ship sailed. Cheyenne won one less challenge, but she didn't receive a mulligan like me. They called her name and she hustled out through the curtain, wearing another unfortunate dress from the wardrobe department. She looked like she'd stepped out of line at a square-dancing competition.

I couldn't tell what happened in front of the curtain, but I grew impatient waiting my turn. An intern with a clipboard waved me back to reality. I jogged through the part in the curtain and waved at everyone. The artificial lighting blinded me, but I could hear the clapping and whistling. I hit my mark and turned to chat with the hosts.

"Austin, how are you doing this evening?" the hostess in sequins and too much makeup asked.

I glanced over towards Cheyenne. "I have some tough competition to beat, but I'm ready."

"Do you have a specific strategy you plan to use during this challenge?"

"I'm not revealing my secret ingredients, if that's what you're asking." All of us had mic packs clipped onto our clothes and I didn't understand why she pointed a microphone in my direction.

She swiveled towards the camera. "We have a surprise for you tonight. Your mom is here, all the way from Kansas City."

I had the sensation of being underwater, trying to understand what she said. But then I saw Mom. Sitting in the front row, clapping. I forgot myself and ran over to her. I lifted her up off the floor in a gigantic hug.

"I can't believe you're here!" I whispered in her ear, forgetting my hot microphone amplifying my voice for everyone. My eyes got misty, but I caught myself and resumed my composure faster than Danny Zuko. I set her down and ran back to my mark next to Cheyenne.

The host read the challenge requirements and set the timer. We hustled over to the pantry to gather our ingredients before taking our positions at our cooking stations. I planned in my head as we stood there, but my gut feeling told me Cheyenne would take that route as well. Our styles overlapped and the final verdict would come down to the palates of the judges.

With a live taping, we did not have the time to smoke ribs or a brisket. This final challenge involved steaks, and that suited me. As I began, I thought back to a phone conversation with Zach a few weeks ago. We discussed how to diversify the menu to attract more customers. Our idea was to blend spices in a marinade with a tropical vibe to it – not too tangy and not too sweet. Right now, a captive audience of five well-versed palates would experience something new and different.

I decided to go for it. I dropped my knife and ran back to the kitchen. The judges deconstructed the possibilities of my selections the moment I put them in my basket. Guy Fieri and Bobby Flay sat in the audience, and they traded remarks as well. At least I had their attention.

As the clock counted out the last few minutes, I plated my dish and garnished it. Cheyenne and I stepped back from our workstations and stood in front of the counter to await feedback from the judges. They talked to Cheyenne first, complementing her on the aroma of her dish, the balance of spices in the sauce, and the tenderness of the beef. She credited her grandpa, and he smiled at her from the audience and gave her a thumbs up.

They turned towards me. It became difficult to concentrate, but I heard them mentioning the unique combination of ingredients I used. Judge #1, Alton Brown, commented, "I can't say I have ever seen anyone use these ingredients for this type of challenge. What made you take a left?"

I licked my lips. "I have a food truck out in L.A. A few weeks ago, my assistant and I discussed how to diversify our menu. This is what we came up with, and you are my first taste-testers."

Judge #2, Rachel Ray, chimed in, "That's a big gamble. Do you think it will pay off for you?"

I replied, "If it didn't, at least I got your attention. Every single one of you were intrigued." I tried for confident and hoped it didn't land on cocky.

The host pulled the microphone back. "Okay judges, let's have your decision."

Alton Brown handed him an envelope and he turned it over to open it. "In a three to two decision, the winner of The American Barbeque Challenge is...Austin Mitchell!"

I couldn't believe my ears! Confetti and balloons rained down over me. I shook Cheyenne's hand and ran over to my mom. Her tears caused a lump in my throat. This turned into the best day ever! I won $50,000 and a bunch of shiny new restaurant equipment to invest in my business. I called Zach and told him we were moving up in the culinary world.

Long after the audience dispersed, and my mom went back to her hotel, I walked over to clear out my trailer. As I approached, I spotted Cheyenne coming down the steps from her trailer. She wore a pink t-shirt and cutoff denim shorts. I jogged over to talk to her.

"Hey, Cheyenne! Are you leaving now?"

She held a rolling suitcase in one hand and her phone in the other. "It's about that time. I'm flying home to Houston tomorrow. My grandpa got an extra room at the hotel for me. In all the competition craziness, I didn't even think about it. Congratulations again."

It caught me off guard because I hadn't thought about what would happen once the competition ended. "My mom did the same thing. I didn't think past this day."

We stood in awkward silence. Then we both started to speak at the same time. We laughed and I gestured for her to go first.

"I'm glad I got to meet you and compete against you. You were a worthy opponent." She fiddled with her phone. "I'm sorry. My extended family is blowing up my phone with texts." She shoved it in her back pocket. "If you happen to be in Houston some time, look me up."

My eyes grew wide. "Is this the *Dear John* brushoff? I want to keep seeing you. I like you, and I think you're a talented chef. What I want to do is offer you a place in my restaurant. That's what I'm doing with my prize money, opening my own restaurant."

"I don't know what to say. It's clear we would go our separate ways, and I didn't want to make it awkward for either one of us."

I took her free hand and laced it with mine. "I didn't want to come on too strong while we were competing for the same thing. And I don't want to assume that you would leave your family to open a restaurant with me. It's just a guess, but there might be enough barbeque joints in Texas."

She nodded. "It's a pretty good one."

I tipped up my Stetson a bit and leaned in to kiss her. I grazed her lips and whispered in her ear. "You are the sexiest woman I've ever met, and I am not going to let you get away." Then I kissed her again, hard, leaving no doubt as to my feelings.

She pulled back and looked at me. "Can we take this back to my trailer, handsome?" I grabbed her hand and raced up the steps to her trailer. I led her down the short hall and tossed her onto the bed. I had no intention of being a gentleman.

Twenty-Four
Cheyenne - Naked Fun

(explicit chapter)

"Can we take this back to my trailer, handsome?"

He grabbed my hand and we hustled up the steps and down the hall to my bedroom. He tossed me onto the bed and stood there, gazing at me. Then he pulled his shirt over his head and onto the floor in one fluid motion. I licked my lips in anticipation as he lay down beside me.

He hooked one arm and one leg over me and pulled me in close. Our lips met and my body tingled in all the right places. His body pressed against mine as he laid his full weight on top of me. He took his time touching me, firm but gentle at the same time. I inhaled the bold, masculine scent of his cologne.

He straddled himself over my hips and leaned back on his knees. "What would you like me to do?"

I didn't speak. Instead, I shimmied my t-shirt over my head, revealing my red bra with pink lipstick prints all over it. He reached out and took one breast in each hand, teasing my nipples through the thin silky fabric. I gasped and squirmed underneath him. He smirked and lowered his head towards them.

I wrapped my arms around his neck and let him explore. He pinched my nipples, making them hard and sensitive. Then he pulled me up to unclasp my bra, freeing my breasts for more attention. He took one in his mouth and flicked his tongue back and forth against my erect nipple. I moaned, spurring him on to his mission.

He peered at me. "You are so sexy. You sure you want to take a chance on a broken cowboy like me?"

I looked at him through my lashes. "Do you think I invite all my competitors to see me naked, Silly? Of course, I want to be with you. Why don't you take off our pants and prove you're worth it?"

Without hesitation, he hopped up and pulled on his belt buckle. He hurried at first, but changed his pace, pulling his belt out of the loops in slow motion. He unbuttoned his jeans and turned away from me. Bending over, he pulled his pants down inch by inch, revealing his navy-blue boxer briefs over his well-rounded cheeks. But he pulled them back up.

"What's wrong? I was enjoying the view." I pouted.

"I forgot I need to take my boots off first. Then I can finish the show." He pulled off his boots while standing and resumed his strip tease. When he turned to face me, his rigid cock strained against the fabric of his briefs. My pelvic muscles clenched in anticipation. I crooked my finger at him and he crawled on his hands and knees towards me on the bed. He leaned in to devour my lips again.

"You forgot my pants, stud." I breathed between kisses.

He shook his head. "No, I didn't. That's next on my agenda."

He reached in between us and unzipped my pants. Grabbing the fabric, he tugged my jeans over my hips and down my legs, revealing my cheap white cotton panties. Once he removed them, he kneeled in between my legs and lowered his face towards my wet lips. He kissed along the insides of my thighs, stopping just short of my sweetness.

My pleasure rose with every touch. I had been thinking about Austin nonstop since our picnic and all I wanted him to do was flip me over and pound me until I came. But he had other ideas.

He teased my wet lips with his fingers, searching for my sweet spot. Once he found it, he dove in and licked around my clitoris until it became a swollen ball of nerves. Every time he touched it, I shivered with excitement.

"Put your ankles on my shoulders," he commanded.

I obliged. He continued to tease my sensitive spot, my moans growing louder and more frequent. My climax built up with every sensation. "I want your dick. Now." I hissed above his head.

His shocked face popped into view. "Yes, ma'am. One minute." He pulled down his briefs and ripped open a condom that he had placed on the bed. Sliding it on his shaft, he half-closed his eyes from his own touch. His dilated pupils matched the arousal of his penis.

"Take me now, stud." I reached for him.

He took my hand and flipped me over. "I have a feeling you like this position better." He grabbed my waist and pulled me back towards him on my hands and knees. The tip of his rock-hard dick poked at my entrance. I wiggled my ass in anticipation.

"Are you ready?"

I nodded.

He put one hand on my ass and guided his cock into me. Filling me with every inch of him. Moaning with pleasure, I pushed my ass towards him, encouraging him to continue. He pulled back out and waited a few beats before doing it again. And again. And again. About the time I thought I would lose my mind from his dick teasing me, he began to stroke me without stopping. My clit dangled on the brink of exploding.

"Come with me, babe," I demanded. "I'm ready for you."

He increased the pace and intensity of his strokes. I moaned and gasped with immense pleasure. His moans made me clench my muscles around his rod, and I gave in to my aching body. It shook, releasing all my tension and more of my salty juices as he pumped me. He grasped my hips on both sides and cried out with his own orgasm before pulling out and flopping onto the bed next to me. Breathing heavily, I crumbled onto my stomach next to him.

We turned our heads towards each other and lay there, coming down from the high, our breathing fading back to normal.

He propped himself up on one elbow and leaned in to kiss me. He shared the flavor he captured in his mouth, a mixture of soft and salty. I wanted the moment to last forever. He gazed at me, and I wondered what he was thinking.

I touched a jagged scar on his lower abdomen. "What happened here?" I wondered aloud.

He put his hand over mine. "Stupid boys. We were playing chicken on our bikes. Danny and I collided and I ended up with his bike gears in my side. I needed some stitches but it missed my major organs. We didn't have plastic surgeons on call back then to sew me up. They put me back together and no one made a fuss if it didn't look perfect." He touched the scar on my cheek. "Tell me about yours."

I blushed. "I can't hide this one under my clothes. When I was in elementary school, I ended up with a terrible case of chicken pox. My mouth and throat had so many pox that it made it difficult to breathe. I spent several days in the hospital being monitored and on oxygen. It's from the little oxygen tube. No one noticed it rubbing and it created a blister. I scratched it and it didn't heal properly. They did a fantastic job covering it in the makeup chair for the show."

He kissed it. "It gives you a badass edge. I like it."

"I don't think any of us escape this life without some scars, visible or not. I've seen some cool tattoos where a scar has been incorporated into the tattoo. It probably wouldn't look as cool on my face though."

He sat up and changed the subject. "I better skedaddle. I don't want your grandpa to wonder where you went."

"Oh my!" I looked at my cell phone. "It's later than I thought." I rolled off the bed and grabbed my clothes off the floor. When I turned around, he was already dressed.

He came around to me and wrapped me in his arms. "I meant what I said before. I want you to come to L.A. and be with me. Help me open the restaurant. I want you with me."

I leaned against his chest. "That's a lot to ask. I need some time to think about it. In the meantime, I want to keep in touch." We exchanged numbers and shared one last passionate kiss before going our separate ways.

Twenty-Five
Sydney - Happy Birth Day

Tori pulled into the driveway the next morning as promised. I waddled to the front door to let her inside. We hugged and moved to the living room, where I sat in the giant recliner, and Tori sat across from me on the couch.

"I did boil some hot water for tea, and I always have a pitcher of iced tea in the fridge. Please help yourself to some of the dozens of cookies left over from yesterday. I'd forgotten how the Patterson women like to feed everyone and we'll have leftovers for weeks." I pulled on the lever of my chair and put my feet up. "My poor swollen feet do not appreciate being overworked yesterday. I don't have any shoes left that I can force my feet into. I'm the stepsister in Cinderella saying 'I knew it was my slipper. It's exactly my size.' while the other half of her foot is hanging out the back."[7]

Tori chuckled. "Other than your feet, you look fantastic. The amazing yellow dress you wore yesterday was killer. You should show off your assets more often."

I blushed. "This is the only time I can wear whatever I want without getting told I look fat. No one at the shower would have said that. Except for my mom. It's probably a good thing she didn't come."

Tori frowned. "I thought for sure I sat next to your mom. She was gushing over you and how she couldn't wait for the twins to arrive."

"You must have been sitting next to Grace. She's Micky's mom, but in a way, she has been mine, too. She's a special lady." A stabbing pain sat in the small of my back. It only lasted a couple of seconds. Ugh. *Thank you, Lefty or Righty, for sitting on my nerves.*

"By the way, I have to thank you for your shakedown of the patriarchy before you left."

I didn't understand what she meant. "Elaborate, please. Pregnancy brain here."

"I was informed you requested a settlement from the record company because of the incident with Jason. I had a meeting with HR and the in-house lawyers, and they deposed me as a witness. I told them what happened, and I thought that was the end of it. A few months later, I signed a nondisclosure agreement and the dictation of my testimony in a gigantic conference room. They handed me a generous check. Did you receive one?"

I snapped my fingers. "That's why Venus has left messages! I have been so tied up with everything going on here that I haven't returned her calls."

"I hope yours is bigger than mine, especially with little people to take care of. That slimeball Jason went across the street to work for one of our competitors. I don't think he ever had to answer for his actions. Which burns my toast, if you know what I mean."

I nodded as I lay back further in my recliner. The sharp pain turned into a knot of gigantic proportions. "Tori, will you do me a favor? There's a bottle of Tylenol in the medicine cabinet in the powder room. And I could use a Snapple from the fridge."

Tori got up and retrieved my requests. I opened the Tylenol and took three. I leaned back and closed my eyes.

"Are you sure you aren't in labor? You don't look so hot, Sydney."

I attempted to breathe evenly. "I've never been in labor. Those pregnancy books I read contradict each other."

"Humor me. Who's going to be with you in the hospital? Where is your hospital bag? Who do I call? I want you to answer me before you become hysterical, so I understand what to do." She kneeled by my chair and squeezed my hand.

"My bag is in my room but I haven't finished packing. Micky is supposed to take me to the hospital and stay with me."

She pulled out her phone and typed something and scanned her screen. "I'm not an expert, but Google says low, intense back pain is one of the symptoms of labor. I think it's time to meet your little ones." She stood. "I'm going to put some comfy clothes in your bag, along with your hairbrush, toothbrush, toothpaste and slippers."

"No slippers!" I protested.

"Suit yourself. They will make you wear those ugly socks with grippers on the bottom."

I rolled my eyes. "Ok. Slippers."

She disappeared down the hall, and I reclined with my feet up, counting my breathing. The knot wasn't going away, and my gut told me Tori was correct. I picked up my phone.

"Hello, Sydney."

"Micky, where are you?"

"Dropping Ainsley off with my mom for a day with grandma. Then stopping at Agway for alpaca feed. Do you need something while I'm out? Ainsley, don't run with a lollipop in your mouth."

I exhaled. "I think I need my birth coach."

"Oh! Really? Okay! How far apart are your contractions? Do I have time to get the alpaca food before I pick you up?"

"Tori's here. You can meet us at the hospital. She's grabbing my overnight bag. I think we're going to wait a little bit to make sure it isn't false labor. Dr. Aaron said the babies could come any day now."

"Why don't you call me back when you're sure. Tony is out fixing a hole in one of the fences. Larry, our Houdini alpaca, got out again while we were celebrating yesterday. I'm going to keep my phone in my pocket for you."

Tori came back with my purple, patterned Vera Bradley overnight bag. "Fancy bag! I love the color."

"Purple is my go-to color. It always makes my mood better."

"Now we wait. Maybe you should try to rest."

"I don't want to be rude and take a nap right in front of you."

She waved her hand at me. "Poppycock! I have books on my phone I can read." She grabbed a blanket from the back of the couch and laid it on top of my huge belly. Sleep sounded like an excellent idea.

Once my feet were up in the stirrups, it was go time. Micky held one hand and Tori held the other. I was using muscles I didn't realize existed before this moment. I had never felt so in tune with my body. It squeezed me in a vice and split open at the same time. Noises came from me that sounded primal and not human at all.

Doctor Aaron came in with his mask on and gloves in the air. "Sydney, are you ready to meet your babies?" He sat down on a stool in between my legs. "You're doing amazing. I can see the top of the head. Let's make some big pushes. Are you ready?"

I nodded. Micky and Tori each took one of my thighs to give me more leverage. I lost count of my pushing and counting. Noises from machines and people shouting encouragement came all around me, but I was in a fog and couldn't focus on them. All I wanted was to meet Lefty and Righty.

Doctor Aaron's voice made it through. "We've got the head and shoulders. Stop pushing, Sydney." He pulled out the first baby and cut the umbilical cord. "It's a boy! Time of birth is 11:55PM. We'll clean him up and you can meet him." He lowered the baby into a blanket held by a waiting nurse, and then my precious baby began wailing. That was the most beautiful noise!

"A couple more pushes and his sibling will be here. You can do it, Sydney!"

I was exhausted. I didn't have the strength left. "No. I'm done. I think I'm going to keep this one."

"I know you're tired, but you got this. Home stretch."

I reached down deep inside and found the strength I needed. Three more pushes and I was finished. Doctor Aaron exclaimed, "It's another boy! Congratulations! Time of birth is 12:02AM. One of the nurses will bring Baby #1 over to meet you while we clean up Baby #2. You did a phenomenal job, Sydney!"

Two little, magnified voices cried and fussed. The nurses were aflutter, getting them clean and dry. Micky wiped my forehead with a cold washcloth and Tori offered me some water. It meant so much to me that they were here with me. A nurse brought over my first baby. He was all red, just like Zoey had been when she was born.

A different nurse brought over Baby #2. She gave me a tight-lipped smile. I didn't understand, and my heart sank, thinking something was wrong. I pulled down the blanket to see his face, and it became clear why the nurse had acted strangely: Baby #2 had light brown skin, brown eyes, and a full head of black tiny curls.

"Is this my baby?" I looked over at Tori and Micky for confirmation. "What happened?" I began to hyperventilate. "Where's Doctor Aaron? Something's wrong! Why are my babies two different colors?"

A nurse picked up the intercom and paged Doctor Aaron. He breezed in wearing clean scrubs and stood at the side of my bed.

"What happened? My babies are two different colors!" My worried face must have caught him off guard, because he took a couple steps back from me.

"Sydney. Calm down. Nothing is wrong. Both of your babies are healthy."

"Why aren't they the same color? I don't understand."

He rubbed his bald head. "I'm the one who delivered them, so I know that these children belong to you. We put ID bands on their ankles with your name as soon as we cut the umbilical cord and took them over to the warmer. That's procedure. I have a few ideas, but I want to do some research before I speculate. I'm going to discuss this with a few colleagues. Let me get back to you on this." He patted my shoulder. "Your babies are healthy and beautiful. Enjoy them."

They wheeled me back to my room and I attempted to feed both boys before drifting off to sleep. Micky and Tori went back to Micky's to sleep and made phone calls while I was snoozing.

When I woke up, I thought perhaps I had dreamed the whole thing. Then reality hit me. I had one vanilla baby and one chocolate baby. How was I going to explain this to them later? Or to other people we met. I didn't even want to guess how my mother was going to react when I sent her a picture of the twins.

Abby was the first to arrive to meet the boys. She came in holding a big bundle of blue balloons with "Congratulations!" and "It's a Boy!" on them. She tied them to the foot of my bed and moved towards the bassinettes. "Hi, Sissy! I came to spoil my nephews."

I threw up my hands and shouted, "Wait!"

Abby stopped in surprise and shock.

"Sit down. I need to talk to you first." I pointed to the chair next to my bed. She eyed me cautiously but sat down. She waited as I tried to find the right words.

"I found out who the father is."

"I bet that's a relief."

I grimaced. "Not the slam dunk I had hoped for. Even if I dress them exactly alike, I will not have trouble telling them apart. I'm pretty sure one belongs to Marcus. And the other belongs to Austin."

Her eyes grew wide. "I'm confused. How is that possible?"

"I don't know. I'm guessing my uterus had an egg release party when I forgot to change my birth control ring. I'm lucky I didn't have octuplets. Doctor Aaron said he would investigate to give me an explanation. The only explanation I can come up with is that I'm a white trash ho bag."

Abby clucked at me in an attempt to stifle her laughter. "Sydney, you are not a white trash ho bag. Except for the one time…"

She attempted to lighten my mood, but I wasn't having it. "I have one vanilla baby and one chocolate one. I can't hide this. What am I going to do?"

"Snap out of it for starters." She leaned in and took my hand. "Are your babies healthy?"

I nodded.

"Do they have a home with a mother who loves them to pieces?"

I nodded again.

"Do they have family and friends who will love them and take care of them?"

I could have been a bobblehead.

"I don't think you have a problem. At least not one that's important."

My mouth fell open but no words came out.

"Now, I am going to hold my nephews and smother them with kisses." She picked them up, one in each arm, and sat down. "Sydney, they are beautiful!"

She leaned in to talk to Baby #1. "Hello, little angel. I'm your fun Auntie Abby. I cannot wait to take you places and teach you all kinds of ways to torture your momma." She turned to Baby #2. "Yes, of course, you are going to come with us, too. We are going to have grand adventures together."

I teared up as I watched Abby love on my babies. She meant every word and that meant the world to me.

Micky and Tori came in next. Micky handed me a small white paper bag. "They don't have any alcohol in this place, which is a crime. We brought you the next best thing."

"It better not be a puppy." I unfolded the flap and peeked inside. A hot fudge sundae! "Oh, my glob! You two are saints!" I pulled out the treat and cracked the protective plastic on the spoon. "I'm going to be rude and eat it right now."

Tori laughed. "Go ahead. You deserve it. After helping you in the delivery room, I don't think I'm ever going to sign up for that. Veto!" She took Baby #1 from Abby and sat in the rocking chair in the corner.

"By the way, what did you do with Samson?" In all the commotion, I'd forgotten about taking care of him.

"We chained him up in the basement."

My eyes popped wide in horror.

"*Kidding*. He's playing with Ainsley and Duke right now. Did you figure out names for these two perfect babies yet?" Micky asked.

"I pondered that while nursing in the middle of the night. I was thinking about naming Baby #1 Austin James after his father but calling him AJ." I waited for feedback.

Micky spoke up. "That's perfect, Sydney. And Baby #2?"

"I wanted to incorporate his father's name as well. I think Andre Marcus works. This way, they both have first names that start with the same letter, in twin tradition. What do you think?"

Everyone murmured in agreement.

"It's official. Now I can fill out the birth certificates."

Journal Entry

I thought being pregnant with twins was my biggest surprise. Wrong. Plot twist! I'm glad I didn't have sex with three different men in one week. Then I would have had an actual Mamma Mia scenario on my hands. Geez.

Even after my valiant attempts to run as far as I can in the opposite direction, I am still my mother's daughter. After the twins arrived, I had all these thoughts in my head about the shame of having two different baby daddies, and AT THE SAME TIME. That has to be a Jerry Springer episode if it isn't already.

Doctor Aaron came back to speak with me before I left the hospital. He told me that what happened is a phenomenon called heteropaternal superfecundation. *I had two eggs fertilized by two different sperm owners. That makes AJ and Andre half siblings. He said this happens in about one out of four hundred twin births. A lot of times it goes unnoticed because their hair and skin coloring is close in shade. In my case, it was extremely obvious. If Dr. Aaron read about it in a medical journal, at least I'm not the only one. I can't decide if that's a good thing or a bad thing.*

Abby brought me back to reality. My babies are healthy. They are already loved by our family and friends. Their different skin colors don't matter. That's where I'm going to leave it. I'm sure my mother will have some feelings about it, but I'm going to ignore her as best I can on this matter. I hope she can overcome her moral objections and love these two perfect little people like I do. They deserve that much.

<u>My Place</u>

    It's my turn
    To know the joy
    Of your smile,
    Warmth of your skin,
    Sound of your laugh.
    I never knew before
    How you would change me
    Completely.
    I am transformed by
    your presence;
    my heart is yours
    Unconditionally.
    Your devotion shows me
    No one else
    Can take my place
    In your world.
    For I am your mother
    and you are my child.
    Our souls are bound
    Together in the stars
    Forever.

Twenty-Six
Sydney – Motherhood

After two days, the hospital let me loose. Tori left for the airport this morning with tons of pictures on her phone and a goodie bag with cookies to share with Venus. I swore her to secrecy since I had not contacted their respective fathers. Although with Tori I didn't have to worry about her gossiping. That wasn't her style.

I had a brief conversation with my parents yesterday. I told them the babies were healthy and so was I. There was no way I could tell them the whole truth. My mother's "holier than thou" disappointment track already had free rent in my head. It was so difficult to absorb her verbal condemnation. She did it without thinking or acknowledging that perhaps it wasn't the best way to approach people.

I thought about Austin and Marcus a lot. At this point, I couldn't be away from the boys, and this was not the kind of thing to explain over the phone. The reveal to their fathers would have to wait. As far as I was concerned, it didn't need to be brought to light. As long as I could care for them by myself, I didn't need to involve them.

Micky drove us home in the minivan I purchased a couple weeks ago in preparation for their arrival. I wanted to buy a small SUV, but there wasn't enough cargo room for my double stroller. This minivan was so fancy. Remote sliding doors on both sides, along with a push button for the back hatch, and enough cup holders for a whole baseball team! It even had a small TV behind the driver's quarters for back seat entertainment.

My favorite part was the color; it was a bright cobalt blue. It drove so smoothly compared to my bumpy old pickup. I hung onto my truck because it was paid for and I couldn't bring myself to let it go. But it wasn't going to be driven much until the boys didn't need to be in safety seats.

We pulled into the driveway and both of us carried a heavy car seat into the house. I unbuckled them and laid them on a blanket in the living room, then totally collapsed in the rocking chair. Watching my babies was better than any TV show—they lay awake and wiggling, with Andre making short noises and AJ turning his head towards him. He mimicked whatever noise Andre made.

Micky brought in the bags of extra diapers and supplies from the hospital and took them to my room. The nurses said if I didn't take them, they would be thrown away because of sanitizing protocol. Micky sat cross-legged on the blanket with the boys. She stared at them, mesmerized.

"I need to go help Tony in the barn. Are you going to be okay?" She glanced up at me.

"Of course." *Nope, totally terrified.* Taking care of Ainsley and Zoey didn't compare to being one-hundred-percent responsible for my own babies. But this is what I signed up for, right?

Micky backed out of the room. "I know it seems like a lot. You'll get the hang of it, I promise."

I turned to my sons. "Well, boys, this is it. You and me."

The first few weeks were rough as I attempted to function on minimal sleep. It took over a month to adjust them to the same schedule—which, *oh my God*, made things a million times easier. Micky was a godsend, often holding one of them on her hip while cooking or changing a smelly diaper. I attempted to breast feed, but my milk never came in like it needed to for two hungry babies. Andre was good with the tit or the bottle, but AJ only wanted a bottle. The dishwasher ran nonstop with loads of bottles and pacifiers.

Ainsley loved the boys from Day One. She sat in the rocking chair, holding one at a time and talking to them. Sometimes I'd let her help me give the boys their bottles; her little face lit up whenever I asked. When we put the three babies in the playpen together, it was the cutest thing on the planet.

It took me so much time to prepare three people to leave the house. I used to be on time everywhere I went. Now, appointment times were guidelines. Flying by the seat of my pants went against my punctual nature.

As requested, with Micky's assistance I took the boys with me to my follow-up appointment with Doctor Aaron. The whole office staff gushed over them and took turns holding them. I brought in little bags with personalized blue M&M'S® with the boys' names on them and handed them out to everyone. Doctor Aaron told me to take it easy, and I out-right laughed when he told me to refrain from sex for at least six more weeks. That wasn't on my agenda. At all.

The only other time we ventured out was for the boys' checkups and shots. They had so many of them in this first year, and I felt awful every time they cried from the needles. They kept getting bigger and stronger, and hit their milestones on their own timetable.

Andre figured out how to roll over first, and AJ followed soon after him. They fascinated me and I couldn't wait to discover what came next.

Time flew. I barely blinked and they were six months old. Abby surprised me with a plane ticket to visit her for a long weekend. I wanted to spend time with her, but I couldn't leave the twins for long. At least that's how our phone call started.

"Abby! I can't believe you! A plane ticket? I think I'm only allowed one lap baby on the plane."

"I didn't invite the twins. They will have adventures with Fun Aunt Abby in due time."

"I suppose I can leave them a bowl of food and water…"

"Sydney, you're hilarious. My co-conspirator, aka Micky, will be taking care of them while you are away."

I stalled. "I can't leave them, Abby."

"Nonsense. You can and you will. I won't take no for an answer."

New York City never disappoints. My flight landed at three o'clock. I pulled my small suitcase from the overhead bin and headed for the AirTran. Abby worked in Manhattan but lived in Brooklyn. She had a hefty commute each way for work and spent her time on the subway listening to audiobooks. She used to read a printed book but kept getting approached by creeps. The headphones kept all but the most aggressive men at bay.

At home, I had been living most of my postpartum life in sweats and oversized t-shirts. That way, it didn't bother me when I got spit-up or pee on my shirt. When I packed, I had to try on my jeans instead of assuming they fit. Out of five pairs, I got one to zip with some effort, and one to zip up with ease. I packed a pair of black flowy dress pants with an elastic waist, and a sparkly top in case Abby planned to go out to dinner.

I could only cram one pair of shoes into the small pouch on the outside of my carryon suitcase. I wasn't willing to pay $25 to check my bag. Charging passengers for a suitcase is, in my mind, extortion. Take a page from Southwest or add a few bucks to the price of a ticket. Geez. The rest of my wardrobe and toiletries barely fit in my suitcase, but I managed to zip it on the third try. I flashed back to Austin zipping my suitcase with ease and my chest tightened. *Stop it, Sydney. That was a lifetime ago.*

I switched trains at Penn Station and rode out to Brooklyn. The brain games on my phone plus people-watching kept me entertained. I checked the directions in my phone notes multiple times to make sure I didn't miss my stop. Abby had upgraded to an apartment in a better part of town since I last came to visit her. I walked the five blocks to her building and hiked up the three flights of stairs. She hid a key for me behind the welcome sign on her door.

This apartment screamed Abby. Everything was pink. The couch, the drapes, the rug – everything. The tiny living space combined the living area and kitchen. Her bedroom and the bathroom sat on the left. I parked my bag by the front door and walked around it. The windows over her kitchen sink and table faced the building next door. She could pass a cup of sugar to her neighbor in the next building without a rope and pully. The stove and fridge stood against the wall with the bathroom on the other side. She kept some cold drinks in the fridge, and I helped myself to a Snapple iced tea.

My god—her bathroom was drowned in roses. I had to laugh. It was lovely, but also a lot. The curtain, the bathmat, the hand towels, the little decorative soaps – it was charming and overwhelming at the same time. I opened the door to her bedroom expecting more pink. Instead, everything was white. Not a pop of color anywhere. It belonged in another house. Or an insane asylum. I couldn't decide.

I lay down on the piles of pillows and looked out her window. She placed a bird feeder on her windowsill, and I observed as the menagerie flitted back and forth for seeds. They chirped at one another, and I wondered what they were saying. I closed my eyes, intending to relax for a few moments...

"Ha! Ha! I feel like the momma bear who found Goldilocks sleeping in her kid's bed." Abby doubled over with laughter, waking me from my nap.

"My god, have you heard of the gentle wakeup?" I tried to orient myself to where I was. *Abby's apartment. New York. A million miles from my babies.* "This is the only nap I've taken today, so that's an improvement." I peeked at her through the slits in my eyelids then closed them again. "By the way, what's with the sterile bedroom? I was afraid to touch anything."

"It's my own personal social experiment. I'm looking for a man who isn't freaked out the first time I bring him home. So far, I've tried it four times with no success."

"Why didn't you go with black? Hang a couple of questionable paintings up with black lights?"

"Then they assume I like kinky shit. I'm not saying I don't, but it's not the message I want to send."

I shook my head. "Whatever makes you happy and doesn't get you arrested." I sat up. "Are we going to chill this evening? Pajamas and pizza?"

"No can do, Sissy. My boss hooked me up with a table at an exclusive place. Lots of celebrities and New York royalty will be there. It's so exclusive it doesn't have a name. It's this unassuming door in an alley. But when you enter, it's like Willy Wonka opening his door to his candy fantasyland. It's extraordinary! We have reservations for nine o'clock."

"Jesus, Abby, that's past my bedtime in any time zone." Her face fell a little, and I caved. "Okay, okay. I'll go."

She squealed and wrapped me in a huge hug. "Let's put some makeup on and find something sexier to wear. Show off your assets." She took a handful of my hair in her hand. "And maybe go to the salon tomorrow."

I groaned. "Do I have to?"

She grabbed my face in her hands. "Sissy, please let me have my fun."

"Okay," I mumbled between smooshed lips. She steered me to the bathroom and got to work.

When Abby let me look in the mirror, I didn't recognize the glamazon who stared back at me. My sister missed her calling. She could have been an A-list hair and makeup artist. I saw the best possible version of me. She sent me to dress while she touched up her own perfection.

Abby outfitted me in a scarlet body-hugging wrap blouse that shimmered like an ice skater's leotard, with a V-neck highlighting my bosom. My breasts had not gotten smaller once I had the boys. Nothing had gotten smaller. I had to buy bigger shoes and bigger bras. I paired the blouse with my black pants and new black flats.

The exclusive restaurant was phenomenal. The food tasted scrumptious, the cocktails were top notch, and the celebrity sightings were mind-blowing. Over our four courses, we saw Justin Timberlake and Jessica Biel, Kevin Bacon and Kyra Sedgewick, and Jon Bon Jovi with his wife, Deborah. The only downside was I couldn't take pictures. While technically this is a public space, it's poor form to approach a celebrity while they dine. True New Yorkers ignore celebrities on the street and in public places like any other stranger. Which I imagine appeals to them, to have a few moments of normalcy on occasion. I fangirled under the radar and tried to remain calm.

"I can hardly sit still being in the same room with Jon Bon Jovi a couple of tables away from us. His smile is everything. How do you not go teenage girl cray-cray when you notice someone you really adore?" I asked Abby.

"It was a challenge when I first started moving in these circles, but I'm used to it now."

"Isn't there even one celebrity you would fall on your sword for? Risk your reputation for? There has to be at least one."

She bit her lip. "I can think of two. Josh Holloway from *LOST*, and Christian Slater. Gawd he was so hot in *Mr. Robot*. If he showed up at my door, I would ravish him. Josh, too. I watched *LOST* for Sawyer and his cute nicknames for everyone. He can call me 'Freckles' any time."

"Good choices. They would make my Top Ten. I think my top pick would have to be Keanu Reeves. He's got machismo from *The Matrix* and *John Wick*, but he's also sensitive and funny. I love watching his TikToks about how to be a good boyfriend."

We passed Sarah Jessica Parker and Matthew Broderick on our way out. I couldn't help myself. I stopped right in front of her. "Oh my God! I can't believe it! I have been your fan since I saw *Girls Just Wanna Have Fun*. And I want to be Carrie Bradshaw when I grow up. Except for the smoking."

To her credit, she acknowledged my hysterics with a smile. "It's always nice to meet a fan. Would you like a selfie with me and Matthew?"

Somehow, I managed to hand Abby my phone and she snapped a quick photo.

"Thank you so much!" I gushed as they hurried into the restaurant.

I turned towards Abby, who shook her head in disbelief. "Did you hear a word I said?" She looked mortified. "Sydney. I'm going to be telling this story about my country hick sister at parties for years to come, so you know."

I smiled sheepishly. "I couldn't help myself. I behaved the whole time we were in the restaurant."

"Yes, you did. Thank God. Now, let's call an Uber and go home before I have to commit you."

On top of the exclusive restaurant, Abby took us to an upscale salon for pampering the next day. She insisted I needed a haircut and a pedicure, at the very least. We shopped. I bought a couple of designer handbag knockoffs from a street vendor, and cute onesies for the boys that said "I Heart NYC" on them.

We had pajamas and pizza night. Abby took this opportunity to confront me.

"I want to talk to you about something, Sissy. It's important, so please listen to everything I have to say before responding. Okay?"

Did I have a choice? "Um, okay."

"I love you so much, and I always want what is best for you. This includes your precious boys as well. You are doing an amazing job being a single mom. I am so proud of you, and I admire you more than you will ever understand.

"So, here's the thing. I want you to consider telling Austin and Marcus they are fathers. They both love you and I'm sure they would hear you out. It might not go well, but I don't want you to look back in five, ten years and regret it.

"It's one thing to sleep with someone and then break up. It's quite a different tale when you create another life. If they don't want to be involved, their financial support can still pay for college, or whatever the boys need down the road. You make good money, but when you have kids, there never seems to be enough.

"You've had time to adjust to this new life as a mother, and you will give them time to process this change for them. I hope you understand I'm coming from a place of love and as someone who wants the best for you and the boys."

She went silent, and folded her hands in her lap in a waiting pose.

My turn. "I heard every word you said. I wrestle with this issue in my head about it. My fear is they will want shared custody or a difficult visitation arrangement. I'm going down the *What-If* road. What if that's what they ask for? I don't want to share."

"I'm glad you've thought about this. Whatever I can do to help, I will."

"I appreciate your candor. I need a little more time."

Abby nodded. "I'm here if you want to talk."

"Thanks, Abby." I hugged my sister long and hard. "I love you."

On my last day, we hit Broadway to try for half-price tickets to a show. While we waited in line, I showed Abby tons of photos of her adorable nephews. Micky was texting me new ones constantly. She was one helluva babysitter. It was hard being away from the boys, but this made it bearable enough that I could give myself over to the fun my sister was trying to show me.

Once we scored our tickets to *Phantom of the Opera*, we had a few hours to spare. Abby got excited. "I have the perfect idea!" She pulled out her phone. "I'm going to make reservations. Hang on."

"Where are we going?" I tapped my foot as she worked on her phone. "Abby?"

She held up her finger to shush me. "Sissy, I can't concentrate with you whining in my ear."

I rolled my eyes and waited. She pocketed her phone and glanced left, then right. "This way is quicker." She made a right and walked right across the street without waiting for the light. I had no choice but to risk my life and follow her. Despite all the times I've visited NYC, I've never learned how to find anything. Abby is my tour guide and she never gets lost.

Without warning, she stopped. "We're here."

I turned towards the building next to us: *Serendipity*. "No! You didn't!" I gaped at her with my mouth open.

"I know I'm fabulous. Yes, I did."

"We're going to have frozen hot chocolate!" I squeaked and clapped my hands. I don't lie: New York never disappoints.

After three fun-filled days with Abby, my heart needed to go home to my babies. No amount of photos and videos could replace holding them in my arms and smelling their precious baby heads.

I hugged Abby and held on for a few moments. It might be a while before we would be together again. "I had such a wonderful time, as always. Next time, you come visit your nephews, okay?"

"You've got a deal, Sissy. Are you sure you don't want me to take you to the airport?"

"That is the one place I can locate without an experienced tour guide. I love you and will text you the second I get home."

"Please think about what I said. Those babies deserve a father in whatever capacity they decide to participate."

"It's at the top of my list."

Journal entry

On the flight home, I thought about what Abby said. In theory, I want my boys to know their fathers. In reality, it might be a lot more complicated than I like. How would I share custody if it came down to that? I've made a new life here, and I'm so thankful to have support from Micky and her family. It wasn't something I would dismiss so I could move back to L.A. I want my boys to have outdoor space to be kids with Ainsley and Zoey, enjoy the farm, and play with Samson.

Next to Abby, Venus is my most level-headed friend. She never lets emotional attachments dictate her decisions. I have a bit of a plan, and I need help putting it in motion. I need to stop dreading the inevitable.

As Austin would say, Cowboy up, Sydney.

Twenty-Seven
Austin - Taking a Meeting

When I got home from the competition after being away for two months, my roommate Avery appeared happy to have me home. After Sydney left, I handled the rent by myself, but I didn't like the emptiness of the house. My ad on Facebook Marketplace had dozens of interested people within minutes. Avery came to his interview with Dale tagging along. We got along from the start, and they've been here almost a year.

"How did it go?" Avery asked from his seat on the couch. He held a script in his hand. "We waited to finish the finale episode with you. We've been rooting for you the whole time. That one week in the middle when you overcooked the brisket, we thought you were packing your bags. You had some stiff competition with Bubba and Cheyenne. If I was straight, she'd be on my radar. She's a sassy stick of dynamite, although her wardrobe needs an upgrade."

"It was exciting and exhausting all at the same time. Do you want me to give you the rundown now or save it until Dale gets home?" I sat on the opposite side of the couch and pulled my boots off. I gestured towards his script. "Audition or gig?"

"Audition. For once, Dale and I aren't competing for the same role. His manager passed on this one. It's a minor recurring role in an unnamed prime time soap. I'm guessing *Grey's Anatomy*, but it might be *Chicago Med*. I'm not going to pass that up. If your show goes into syndication, you receive royalty checks for years. I've been googling so many medical terms. I want to understand what I'm saying, what tests I'm ordering and such. It makes memorizing my lines easier. But WebMD probably thinks I'm a hypochondriac by now."

I nodded. "Makes sense. Is Dale working?"

Avery didn't look up from his script. "He has a new boyfriend and hasn't been home much. I hear the shower some mornings, but by the time I decide to go to the gym, he's already gone again. His boyfriend has his own place where they can have privacy."

I leaned back onto the couch and propped my feet up on the coffee table. My phone started playing "Maneater" and I pulled it out of my back pocket.

Avery chuckled. "I wonder who gets that honorific."

"My boss."

He laughed harder.

I answered. "Hello, Venus. I literally just came through the door. Your radar is spot on."

"Perhaps. Is it possible for you to come in to the office tomorrow? I have a client I'd like you to meet with."

I scratched my head. "Sounds okay. What time?"

"Ten works for me. Come to my office. How did it go with the show? I don't have the patience for reality competitions."

"How about I give you the lowdown tomorrow?" I didn't want to spoil things for Avery.

"Sounds good. See you then."

I hung up and turned towards Avery. "We've never caught her with a man. Or a woman for that matter. Someone suggested she keeps a few chained in the basement and sucks their blood when she gets hungry. That's the song that popped into my head. Dumb, but effective."

He chuckled. "Sick, man. Sick."

"If Dale isn't going to be home for a while, I'll fill him in another time. I found a roommate."

"Someone will be taking the last bedroom upstairs? Cool. I hope you're charging them more since that bedroom has an ensuite."

I shook my head. "Not exactly. Cheyenne, the contestant you mentioned, is moving in with me. She'll be sharing my room."

"Oh man, my big mouth got me in trouble again. I'm sorry, bro. I didn't mean to make fun of her outfits."

I held up my hand. "No offense taken. All of us wore wardrobe. She didn't have a choice. Everyone else dressed casually and I perceived it as a bit humiliating, with her being the only female contestant. She joked about it, though. We're going to use my prize winnings and current media popularity to open a restaurant together with Zach."

"That's cool! I take it you won?"

"Yeah, spoiler alert. And I'll be looking for competent wait staff, if you know anyone who's interested. You included."

Avery nodded. "Congrats, man. I'm happy for you. And I will keep your offer in mind."

I knocked on Venus's doorframe. She waved me in, even though it appeared she was talking to someone on her computer. She rose from her seat.

"Austin, I've been talking to our client. I'm going to find some decent coffee. Have a seat and chat. I'll be back in a flash." She gestured to her comfy office chair.

I walked around the desk and faced the screen. Sydney.

"Hi, Austin," she murmured.

I think my mind spazzed. I stared and blinked multiple times, unsure if I was hallucinating. She appeared a bit disheveled in an oversize sweatshirt and with her hair askew in a messy bun.

"I'm sure you weren't prepared to see me today," she said. "I wanted to meet with you in person, but this is the next best thing."

My mouth opened, but no sound came out.

"I suppose you wonder why I'm talking to you."

I found my voice. "That might be an ideal place to begin. You disappeared over a year ago. It punched me in the gut, leaving the way you did. Why are you talking to me now? That letter was the most hurtful thing that's been done to me in a long time. Bar none."

Fuck. I didn't know how angry I was.

How *fucking* angry.

She lowered her gaze into her lap. "I realize I left abruptly and didn't give you a chance. I lost myself behind all this glitz and glamour. You seemed so happy living that life. You still are. But I didn't recognize myself anymore. I forgot my own dreams and had to find them again. I didn't mean to hurt you ... even though I get that I did. For that, I am truly sorry."

I rallied and started adding bricks to my wall. She wouldn't hurt me again. When I didn't say anything, she continued.

"That last night.... I think about it all the time. I wanted to give you one perfect memory of us. A way to remember me. I never came alive with anyone else like I did with you. And now I have a piece of that to keep with me."

She leaned to the left off camera, and I thought she was leaving. "Wait! Don't go!" I shouted at the screen. Fucking angry, but also... *Don't go. Please.*

She came back into view holding a baby on her lap.

What the?

Wait. I'm not astute at guessing ages, but he couldn't even be a year old. I started counting backwards—

"Austin, I want you to meet Austin James. I named him after his daddy. But I call him AJ for short."

The room spun and I held onto the edge of the desk to keep from falling on the floor. Venus came in a flash. She kneeled next to me and took my hand. "Deep breaths. In, two, three, four. Hold. And out, two, three, four." She repeated this several times with me and I actually did it. I mean, what else was I going to do?

Finally: "I'm okay." I pulled my hand away and narrowed my eyes at her. "You knew about this, didn't you?"

"Austin, you're upset and I understand that. But I am still your boss. Tread carefully."

I breathed through my teeth and gaped at Sydney. She bounced the baby on her knee and he giggled. Two tiny teeth poked through his bottom gums. Venus sat across the desk from me. I wanted her to leave but I didn't trust myself to ask politely.

I couldn't believe what I witnessed on the screen. "How old is he?" I wanted to be sure.

"He's six months. Happy and healthy. Ten fingers, ten toes, and thinks it's funny when he squirts me."

I tried unsuccessfully not to laugh. "Serves you right."

He was adorable. He was... my son.

The anger was gone now, completely.

She was chewing her lower lip as I processed. Then she said, "There's something else. This is why I didn't tell you right away. AJ is a twin."

Now I felt dizzy. Twins!

She leaned over and put AJ down. Then she bent to the right and picked up another baby. A black baby. He sucked on a pacifier and grabbed Sydney's hair in his little fist. "This is Andre Marcus. I think you know his father."

My jaw dropped open. "Is this some sort of joke? I don't get it."

She shook her head. "No, Austin. It's not a joke. I had sex with Marcus three days before I had sex with you. In all the excitement for the Oscars, getting assaulted by Jason, and you coming home from rehab, I forgot to change my birth control. You each fertilized a separate egg. My OB says it happens in about one out of four hundred twin births."

I tried to make all of this make sense, but my brain stayed stuck on tilt.

She continued. "I imagine this is a lot to process all at once. It's a lot for me, too. I'm telling you for informational purposes only. If you want to be involved, we can discuss that. If you don't want to be involved, that's up to you. I don't expect anything from you. I listed you as AJ's father on the birth certificate. I have the means to take care of him, from the royalties."

Sure, sure. That song still put food on my table. Right. Yeah. *Me, a father-that thought terrifies me to my bones* Now I had that title and the duties that went along with it. This falls under the Southern Gentleman Code: Own up to your actions and take care of your responsibilities.

Sydney interrupted my thoughts. "I have settled here in Indiana. We have an amazing group of friends who love and support us. I do not intend to move back to L.A."

Ok. No L.A. I guess that made sense.

"I welcome you in whatever capacity you wish to participate."

I shook my head, attempting to achieve some form of clarity. So many details. So much... everything. "Can I have some time to think about this?"

"Of course. I wouldn't expect any less. My phone number is the same. Venus can give it to you, if needed."

As in, if I'd deleted her completely.

I confessed, "I still have your info in my phone. I didn't want to give up hope you would contact me someday. However, this is nowhere near what I imagined would happen when you did. Have you told Marcus?"

"He's my next meeting. Feel free to contact me when you're ready. I know this is a lot and I've had time to process these changes in my life. It was good to see you, Austin." With the click of a mouse, she was gone. I sat there, numb, attempting to digest everything. I blinked at Venus.

She scanned my face. "Are you all right?"

I set my expression in neutral and added some more bricks to my wall. "I'm fine. Shocked but fine. I will see myself out now."

I drove around aimlessly, trying to wrap my head around the news.

I'm a dad.

I have a son.

I never intended to be a father. The best way to stop a vicious cycle of toxic behavior is to not repeat it. Yet here I was, and I didn't like it one bit. I replayed the events in Venus's office over and over. How did I miss this? It was easy since Sydney had abandoned me. She remained an enigma for over a year. This wasn't the direction I envisioned my life going.

I had plans. I had things in the works.

My immediate goals involved getting Cheyenne to move in with me and setting up a restaurant.

Sydney's baby surprise didn't change that.

Unless I was supposed to be a co-parent or something. Was that what Sydney wanted? She didn't say anything about it. Was that what I wanted?

I wasn't father material, not as far as I was concerned. What I wanted was what I'd planned. I had strong feelings for Cheyenne and wanted to be with her.

But...now I'm a dad.

Holy shit, how does a person process something like this?

The timing certainly couldn't have been worse. I would have to start financially supporting this child before Sydney took me to court. Would she do something like that? I didn't understand her as well as I thought I did, and I didn't like taking chances.

When I got home, Avery was still commandeering the couch, reading his script.

He set it face down on his lap. "Hey, brother! How'd it go with your new client?"

I shook my head. "I don't want to talk about it."

"That well, huh?"

"Yeah." I clomped downstairs to my room and collapsed on my bed, staring at the ceiling fan. I needed some time to figure out this monkey wrench. I pulled out my phone and texted Sydney.

> I heard every word you said. Our son is beautiful. You shocked me to the core today on several levels. I need some time to think about this.

She responded right away.

> Take all the time you need, Austin. I didn't expect my life to go the way it has either. Sometimes you just have to go along for the ride regardless of the circumstances. AJ is a miracle and I'd like you to appreciate him the way I do. You aren't doomed to follow in your father's footsteps unless you want to be. This might be what you need to lay those demons to rest.

I laid the phone on my bed and rested my arms behind my head. Being a father was never part of my plan. The horrors in my mind haunted me. I didn't want to become my father, and not having kids was the easiest way to stop the cycle of nightmares.

I didn't expect my life to go the way it has either, she'd said. For the first time since talking with her, I wondered what it must have been like for her. Finding out she was pregnant. Have the baby—both babies. Twins. Shit. That must've been a lot.

But why didn't she tell me? What happened to us? She was my best friend. But then she left, cutting me off.

I'd started the video call so angry with her. But seeing that baby—our son.... Anger wasn't in me anymore. What I wanted to do was wrap her in my arms and take care of her. But she always had to show me how strong she is. As if needing help was the worst thing she imagined. Why did she do that? It only hurt us.

I wondered how Marcus fared with his news. I almost texted him to give him a heads up but decided not to. He deserved to be as shocked as I was.

I caught up with him the next day in the parking lot on our way to work.

"Hey, Marcus! Can we talk?"

He slowed his pace to let me catch up to him. "Let me guess. You spoke to Sydney yesterday, too."

"She completely blindsided me. I had no idea. I haven't heard from her since she left LA."

"That makes two of us, but for vastly different reasons."

"Have you decided what you're going to do about it?"

He stopped and turned towards me. "You mean about being a father? No. I haven't. Sydney's had quite a bit of time to think about the situation. I have not. Neither have you. This is not even close to the way I Imagined being a father. I can't be a father from thousands of miles away. I don't know what she expects from me. From you." He growled in frustration. "I don't want to discuss it."

"I'm not trying to upset you, Marcus. No one else is in the same situation that we are. I'm sorry I mentioned it."

He stared over my shoulder into the distance. "I loved her. But with you in the picture I never stood a chance. I fooled myself into thinking that I did." He locked eyes with me. "We may work together, Austin, but we are not the same. Don't mistake my professional courtesy as a colleague for friendship."

He turned away and left me standing there with my mouth gaping. That encounter was awkward, but what exactly did I expect?

Whenever I'd had a problem, Sydney had been my sounding board. I hadn't had that this past year, but then, I hadn't had many problems. I was working toward my dreams; things were falling into place. And now my sounding board was the one who blew that all up.

I wanted to talk to my mom, but how would she react? This could go either way. I scrolled through my phone and found the next best thing.

"Well, look what the cat dragged in! How ya doin', brother?"

I could count on Danny. "Oh, you know. Living the glamourous life."

"I'm surprised you called me. I figured you'd be living in a mansion in Beverly Hills by now, with a handful of staff to fulfill your every wish."

"Hardly. I don't think my roommates would like to be referred to as my staff."

"Yeah, that might not go over well. What can I do you for? You don't call just to shoot the breeze. Lay it on me."

"Can't a guy just call his buddy for no reason?"

"Yeah, unless we're talking about you. Give it to me straight."

I filled Danny in about Sydney. He listened without interrupting. When I finished, he replied. "That's intense. I understand why you're rattled. Daddy territory is not your strong suit. No offense."

"I'm not offended. She blindsided me. I almost passed out from the shock."

"Wish I could've seen your face hearing the news. You realize what you must do now. It's part of the Southern Gentleman's Code."

"Say what?"

"It's not written down, bro. But it's something we all know."

"And what is it I'm supposed to know, Danny?"

"If you knock her up, you marry her."

I gulped. "That had not occurred to me. I don't think she's going to go for it. And she's not going to move back to L.A. She told me as much."

"Then you're going to have to fall on your sword, brother. You aren't the first and you sure won't be the last. At least it wasn't a one-night stand."

I winced. "I didn't intend it to be that way."

Danny busted out laughing. "I'm sorry, man. I had no idea. You should call more often."

"Gee, I wonder why I don't."

He rallied. "Okay. Seriously. You need to offer to marry her, even if she's not going to go for it. Honestly, I'm surprised it took this long. I thought you would knock someone up in the first six months you were in California. Or got Renee pregnant in college. But she had your number on Day One. Teenage guys aren't mysterious."

"I knew what you were going to say before I called. But I had to hear it for myself."

"Listen, it's only an eighteen-year sentence. You might enjoy it."

"Doubtful. Having a kid terrifies me. I don't want to become my father."

"Then you should have gotten a vasectomy. Your dick has been in charge since you hit puberty." He chuckled at his own joke.

"All right. I think I've taken enough abuse. I'll send you a wedding invitation."

"Hey man, in all seriousness, I'm glad you called. It's not going to be as bad as you think. Tell me where you're registered for gifts."

"Thanks, Danny."

He was right. Why hadn't I thought of that? My brain hurt from overload. I stood in the shower and let the hot water run over me. Not moving. Not thinking. Listening to the water and breathing in the steam. I poured some body wash onto a puff and scrubbed off the day. Thank goodness it was a poker night. Exactly the medicine I needed to unwind from this intense day. *Bring it on, boys. Austin's coming to play.*

Twenty-Eight
Vinnie - Fresh Perspective

Whenever I go on a work trip, I stop at Tony and Micky's on the way home. I catch up on what's going on with everyone, and Micky is a better search engine than Google for gossip. This time, I had been out in Los Angeles for two weeks on a consultation job. In two months, I would go back to observe the implementation of my strategy. For now, I managed the project from my home office.

When I pulled into the driveway, Ainsley was outside throwing the ball to Duke. He wasn't as quick as he used to be, but he still loved chasing a tennis ball. Ainsley ran to greet me.

"Uncle Vinnie! You're back!" I bent over and scooped her into my arms.

Of course, I am! How could I ever stay away from you, you silly monster!"

She giggled. "I'm not a monster. I'm a monkey. Daddy's a monster."

I flipped her over and held her by her ankles as she laughed. "Maybe I'm a monster too!" I swung her back and forth, then laid her down on the grass.

She scrambled to her feet. "Did you bring me something?"

I put my finger to my lips. "Hmm. I might have something in my travel bag for you. Let me look." I opened the back seat and unzipped my black duffle bag. Two pairs of Barbie™ pink sunglasses with rhinestones all around the rims sat right on top in a plastic bag.

"Look what I found!" I held up the bag up just out of reach. "Let's put these on and go show your momma."

She squealed with delight when I opened the bag. "They're so sparkly! I feel like a movie star!" She put them on and sashayed to the house with her nose in the air.

"Hello!" I shouted as we entered through the front door.

"In the kitchen!" Micky responded.

Ainsley ran ahead of me. "Mommy! Look what Uncle Vinnie brought me!" She tugged on Micky's skirt while she stood at the sink washing dishes.

She turned and gasped. "Vinnie, you didn't tell me you were bringing a movie star home!"

She said to me, "How was your trip? Are you staying for dinner? We're having crocodile stew tonight." She winked at me.

"Yum! Crocodile stew is my favorite!" I had no idea where Micky was going with this, but I was willing to play along.

"We got a book from the library about crocodile stew and we made some earlier today. Right, Ainsley?"

"Yes, Mommy. It smells yum! When is dinner?"

Micky looked at the clock. "Your father should be in soon. Do you need a snack?"

"Yes please. Do we have graham crackers?"

Micky reached into a cupboard and grabbed the box. She put several squares in a bowl. "Please go eat these at the table. Uncle Vinnie, do you need a snack, too?"

"Nope. I'm going to grab a beer out of the fridge in the garage, if you don't mind. Would you like one?"

Micky clucked at me. "No thank you. Help yourself." She returned to the dishes in the sink.

When I came back inside, I set the bag on the counter. "I got a pair for Zoey, too. I don't think she's ready for them yet."

Micky smiled at me. "You. Are spoiling these girls rotten."

I puffed out my chest. "That's what fun uncles do."

Tony came in from the back door. "What do fun uncles do?"

"Spoil your kids, knucklehead." I laughed. "I dare you to try and stop me. I'd buy them a pony if you'd let me."

Ainsley perked up. "A pony? Are we getting a pony, Daddy?"

Tony gave me the stink eye. "No, princess. Uncle Vinnie is just kidding." He elbowed me.

"Ouch! Yes, Ainsley, I'm just kidding." I rubbed my side. "Your daddy has enough animals to take care of." Then I remembered. "Micky, I got something for Sydney's boys. I couldn't resist. I was taking a walk one day after work and the mannequins in the window of a children's clothing store wore them. Would you mind giving them to her?"

Tony interrupted. "Why can't you give them to her? She's probably in her room taking care of the twins."

Micky agreed. "Go knock on her door, chicken."

I shook my head. "I'm not sure that's a good idea. I don't think she likes me very much."

"What makes you say that? What's not to like?" Tony asked.

"When we took Ainsley to the park, I made an insensitive remark about single moms, and she took offense right away. I didn't know she was pregnant at the time. I don't think she's gotten over that."

"What a better time than now to take a peace offering?" Micky suggested. "Go talk to her. How can she resist a present for the boys?"

I stood dumbfounded.

Micky rapped her wooden spoon on the spoon rest. "Then it's settled. Go tell Sydney and the boys dinner is ready."

I crept toward her door with my stomach churning and my mind blank as to what I should say. I knocked and heard Samson's deep woof.

"Coming!" Sydney opened the door with Andre on her hip and Samson standing right in front of her in a defensive pose.

"It's all right, Sam. It's Vinnie. Go lay down." He trotted off to his dog bed keeping his eye on me every step of the way.

She waved her arm. "Come in. Have a seat. The boys are just waking up from their afternoon nap." She deposited Andre in the playpen and disappeared back into the bedroom, then returned with AJ and added him to the playpen.

I sat down on the edge of the couch. "Micky said dinner is ready. We're having crocodile stew. I'm not sure how I feel about that."

Sydney explained. "It's actually beef stew, but she mentioned something about a library book she read to Ainsley. I've never seen that child excited about eating stew, so it worked. Micky's teaching me all her tricks. I'm going to need it with these two hooligans, for sure." She rolled her eyes towards the playpen.

"I'm glad she sent me over. I've been wanting to talk to you for a while but we never seem to have any time one on one."

She nodded. "You have my attention. What's on your mind?"

I swallowed hard. "I think we got off on the wrong foot. I wanted a chance to explain myself from that day at the park. What I said about single moms was insensitive and out of line. I admire what you're doing, Sydney. The number of single moms far outweighs single dads, and there's a reason for that. I'm quite certain I couldn't do what you do daily without help. Men like to think we are the stronger sex, but most of the time we're just fooling ourselves."

She wiped Andre's face with a cloth. "I appreciate you saying that. I don't consider myself a hero by any stretch of the imagination, but I do work hard every day to keep these little faces happy, healthy and well fed. This isn't something I thought I'd ever sign up for, but here I am. I accept your apology. I was hard on you, and I apologize for that."

"Thank you. Not necessary, though. Bianca chewed me a new one when I told her what happened."

She chuckled. "Lessons on Not Crossing an Italian Woman."

"That could be a show for sure." I joined her laughter. "I found something while on my latest trip that I picked up for the boys. I saw these in a shop window and thought it was hilarious." I held the bag out to her.

She eyed me warily. "It's not a puppy, is it?"

"Nope. A puppy is the last thing I'd bring a mom with two babies already."

She reached into the bag and pulled out the tiny t-shirts. They were red, with *Thing 1* and *Thing 2* written on them. She laughed. Score!

"This is a hoot! Thank you, Vinnie!" She hugged me. Her skin felt soft against my cheek, and I caught a whiff of a floral scent on her neck.

I stood up, feeling awkward and warm and fuzzy all at the same time. Tony's words echoed in my ears, *What's not to like?* Her sense of humor, kind nature, and ability to forgive me so quickly impressed me. I decided to take a chance. "We should probably head into the dining room for dinner. But I have to ask you one thing."

"What's that?"

"Can I take you out to dinner tomorrow night?"

"Oh. That does sound lovely. But I can't ask Micky to take care of the boys like that."

I had to think quickly to overcome her objection. "I'll bring the sitter—someone owes me a favor. Make sure you wear a dress. We're not going to Burger Burger."

"Duly noted. Great. I can't wait. In the meantime, let's go eat some crocodile stew."

I could hardly wait myself.

Twenty-Nine
Sydney - Bistro 501

A dress? The last time I wore a fancy dress was during my baby shower. The canary dress gave me sexy vibes, and it would fit better now that I wasn't carrying around two watermelons in my mid-section. Thank goodness for stretchy fabrics. I tried it on and stood in front of the mirror on my closet door. It would have to do, especially since I didn't know where we were going.

During naptime for the twins, I took a long shower, scrubbing my skin and shaving my legs. Shaving took two passes as I had not shaved in at least a year. Pregnant women receive an automatic pass in my book. I towel-dried my curls, added some frizz-taming lotion, and let it air dry. The one thing I did miss about my job in L.A. was the glam squad. My hair and makeup always appeared a thousand times better when a professional took care of me. When I tried to copy their handiwork, I came off as if a five-year-old had gotten into her mother's makeup.

It had been a long time since I'd been on a date. Taking care of the boys and helping out around the farm took up all of my time. I hadn't had much of a social life since my evening with Corey. That seemed like an eternity ago. Now I felt nervous, excited and nauseous all at once. Was that weird? Maybe. Because while it was sweet of Vinnie to ask me out to dinner, I wasn't convinced he liked me in a romantic sense.

Vinnie arrived at six o' clock on the dot. He wore a navy sport coat, light blue dress shirt and a blue striped tie. Dress pants and shiny dress shoes completed his outfit. I wasn't used to seeing him like this. Whenever I saw him at Micky's, he wore a polo shirt and khakis or jeans. Bianca came with him to stay with the twins.

He saw me and exclaimed, "You are gorgeous! These are for you." He held out a bouquet of Gerber daisies.

"How did you know these are my favorite? Oh right—Micky. I love them! Let me go put them in water. Bianca, the twins are in their playpen. If you want, I'll show you where to find all the important things."

She followed me into the kitchen. I got out a quart Mason jar and assembled the flowers in some water and a little bit of Sprite from a can. Something about the Sprite makes the flowers last. Bianca listened as I rattled off the locations of food, diapers and emergency numbers.

Before we returned to the living room, I grabbed her hand and stopped her. "Thank you for doing this. Can you tell I haven't been on a date in ages? What does your brother have planned?"

"No clue. He changed the subject when I asked. Which means you're going to have a fantastic time. If not, he gets to answer to me and Sofia." She smiled sweetly, but I knew she meant it.

We came back into the living room and, at the risk of soiling my only dress, I picked up Andre, then AJ, and left lipstick marks on their cheeks. "Behave for Miss Bianca," I told each of them. Vinnie took my hand and we departed into the night.

Bistro 501 reminded me of the fancy restaurants they use for episodes of *The Bachelor*. Crisp, clean table linens, candles, mood lighting, and strategic seating to give the illusion you are the only guests. Our server, Leo, was efficient and friendly without being too solicitous. He recognized Vinnie, meaning he had been a patron many times. I wondered how many other women he'd brought here to impress.

The number of offerings on the menu were minimal and I thanked my lucky stars we weren't at The Cheesecake Factory. It's always so difficult to decide with thirty plus cheesecakes alone.

Vinnie peeked up at me over his menu. "Do you mind if I order for us? As you can tell from Leo recognizing me, I've come here often enough. Everything is superbly delicious, I promise."

It caught me off guard. "As long as you avoid Brussel sprouts or raw meat, you've got a deal." I couldn't ever remember a guy offering to order for me. This restaurant reached a level of fancy I enjoyed on occasion with Venus, but at lunchtime when the dress code is a little more relaxed and so are the prices.

Leo appeared and Vinnie ordered all our courses, including a bottle of wine.

"Do you prefer a sweeter or a drier wine?" he asked me. "I want to select appropriately."

"Sweeter, please. I've tried dry wines but they're not appetizing to my palette at all."

Leo chimed in. "I recommend Paradise Ridge 2017. It's a balance of both and affordable."

"Sounds perfect. We'll have that." Leo returned with the bottle of wine and Vinnie gave it his approval before Leo poured it for both of us. It was delicious and I sipped it.

"I've been meaning to ask you about your life out in L.A. I worked out there on a consulting job these past two weeks, and I found it fascinating. How did you handle the traffic? It was the worst part, in my opinion. Six lanes of traffic in each direction going nowhere. That's nuts anywhere except L.A. Maybe Washington DC, too."

"We didn't always work the standard nine to five, so we avoided the biggest snarls of the day. Austin and I rode together to work, and having a commuting buddy to pass the time with makes a world of difference. When you're living somewhere, you adjust to the environment."

"I suppose that's true."

"Now, it's my turn. Why aren't you married? Are you a George Clooney?"

Vinnie raised his eyebrows. "What's a George Clooney?"

"A man who plays the field and stays single until he's fifty or older."

"Not on purpose. I've had two serious relationships in the past ten years. Up until the pandemic, I was gone for business quite a bit. Taking a girlfriend on a work trip is frowned upon, and both said I was married to my job. They weren't wrong. I love what I do. I like working with companies that are struggling to strengthen their place in the market. If a company invests in its employees first, that's half the battle. People want to be appreciated and acknowledged for their contributions. When a company loses sight of that, their business goes downhill. Some of them take longer to sink than the Titanic."

"Speaking of the Titanic," I interjected. "Austin and I wrote a song for a movie a few years ago. Not *Titanic*, though."

"Micky tells me you won an Oscar and a Grammy."

"It's still like a dream when I think about it. Sitting in the same theater with Meryl Streep, Tom Hanks, Lady Gaga, and Robert DeNiro—and now I'm on the invitation list every year since I won one."

We enjoyed some pâté first, followed by French Onion soup. The cheese melted to a golden perfection, reminding me of the marshmallows we roasted around the fire when we first met. Vinnie ordered strip steaks for us with Yukon potatoes and creamed spinach. My mouth drooled from the exquisite flavors—a joygasm for my tastebuds.

"Can I ask you something important? You don't have to answer me if it makes you uncomfortable."

It might have been the wine talking but I said, "Sure. Shoot."

"Are you involved with either one of the twins' fathers? I don't want to step on claimed territory, if you'll excuse the expression."

I nodded. "You're not making me uncomfortable. I am not involved with either one. They are aware they have a child, and they have decided how involved they want to be. Since they aren't sitting here, you can guess their level of involvement."

"I appreciate your honesty." His demeanor changed and he seemed more relaxed. But again, maybe the wine was talking.

Leo brought us two forks and a piece of layered coconut cake with a side of fudge sauce for dessert. I decided if I only got to eat one kind of cake for the rest of my life, this would win in a heartbeat. I enjoyed spending time with Vinnie and discovering more about him. I didn't want the evening to end.

After dinner, we took a drive around Purdue's campus and ended up on Slayter Hill. We got out of the car and walked down towards the stage of the outdoor amphitheater, shining with soft lighting. Thank goodness I'd opted for flats instead of heels.

"I've never been here," I confessed.

"Really? My dad used to bring us here to go sled riding, and I've seen some amazing concerts and plays here over the years."

"I can imagine this would draw sled riders. This is a perfect outdoor space for a venue like this."

"There haven't been any performances here since the beginning of the pandemic. I hope they start having events here again. Otherwise, it's going to waste."

I thought about that. "I don't think our world is ever going to go back to what it was before the pandemic. It scared people. My dad's brother died from Covid. I still see folks wearing masks out in public, and they require them at the doctor's office."

Vinnie checked his watch. "Oh my, I better take you home. Bianca's going to think I kidnapped you."

I turned to start back up the hill, but he grabbed my hand and pulled me close. "I've been dying to ask you this all evening. Can I kiss you?"

I nodded up at him. He leaned towards me and I closed my eyes as our lips found each other. I tasted the coconut and fudge that lingered from dessert. He wrapped his arms behind my back, pulling me even closer. It was gentle and sensual at the same time. My toes curled with delight.

When I opened my eyes, he scanned them for my reaction. "I'd like to try that again."

"Mmm. Me too," I murmured. The first kiss always comes with so many butterflies and uncertainty. This second one took it up a notch with a boost of confidence behind it. I hadn't felt like this in quite a while.

When we arrived back at the farm, he opened the car door for me and walked me to the front door.

"I had a wonderful time. Can I see you again?"

I blushed and kissed him on the cheek. "I'd like that. Thank you for getting me out of the house tonight. It was pleasantly unexpected." I opened the door and slipped inside.

Bianca sat in the rocking chair in my sitting room reading a book. "You look like the Cheshire Cat. I guess things went well this evening. The boys have been down since nine. They're delightful and I will babysit any time. I better catch my ride home before he forgets he brought me. See you soon." She picked up her sweater and closed the door behind her.

I floated to bed on a cloud of endorphins and had the best night of sleep in a long time.

Journal entry

Vinnie apologized for the awful things he said about single moms when we were at the park with Ainsley months ago. He was sincere and I forgave him. How could I not? He and Tony put together the cribs for the boys, and he didn't have to do that. It showed me he was a stand-up type of man who didn't let one hot-headed pregnant woman deter him from being a nice guy.

It did surprise me that he asked me out. He's right, I don't venture out much these days. The twins consume every waking moment I have. I haven't sent Venus a song in several months. She's been patient with me, calling it "extended maternity leave." Even though we're friends, I suspect she'll need to give me some tough love if I don't send her something soon. It's hard to be creative when I change diapers and feed babies nonstop.

Samson adjusted to playing third fiddle with only an occasional minor tantrum. Sometimes I'm too tired to take an evening walk with him. I let him out and he sits in a chair on the patio with his back to me. He makes me call him multiple times to come back in, acting as if he didn't hear me all ten times. But at bedtime, he still expects me to hold up the side of the covers so he can climb underneath them. I suppose all first-born children get upset when they're upstaged by the new baby. I can and will only feel so guilty.

That kiss! It's so sexy when a man asks permission to kiss me. This kiss with Vinnie felt different than any other kiss I've had. It's difficult to put into words: mature, confident, and a bit trepidatious. And then he asked to see me again!

This could be the start of something. But I don't want to get ahead of myself. Try to take this one step at a time, Sydney. You can't just think about yourself now. Your boys deserve to come first. <u>Remember that.</u>

Thirty
Vinnie - Confession

The ride home with Bianca was quiet for the first few minutes. I was lost in thought, replaying the events of the evening in my head. I thought things went well, and I wanted to take Sydney out again.

Bianca spoke up. "Are you going to tell me about your evening, or do I have to beat it out of you?" She glared at me.

"I'm sorry. What can I tell you?" I stammered.

"Where did you go? What did you do? Are you going to ask her out again? That's for starters."

"I took her to Bistro 501 for dinner. You know that's one of my favorite places."

She nodded. "Of course. Excellent choice."

"Leo was our server, and I ordered for us. We had a delicious bottle of red wine, pate with crackers, French Onion soup…"

"Mmm. I love their French Onion soup!"

"It's delectable. Just the right ratio of melty cheese, soggy croutons and onions. Then we had strip steak with potatoes and creamed spinach. Of course, coconut cake for dessert. We split a piece."

"Their food is so yummy. You didn't bring me a piece of cake, did you?"

I smiled. "I asked Leo to put a piece in a take-out box. It's behind my seat."

She clapped with excitement. "Thanks, brother. My mouth is watering already. Now. Back to the date. Do you like her? Do you want to go out again? Did you kiss her?"

"Yes."

"Yes what?" she demanded. "Vinnie, I want details."

"Hang on. I'm telling you." I chuckled. "Yes, I like her a lot. Of course, I want to take her out again. And yes, I did kiss her. That's all I will say. In the words of Guy Patterson, '*It would be ungentlemanly of me to elaborate.*'[8]

"You were gone a long time for dinner. What did you do after that?"

"Sometimes you're too smart. We drove up to Slayter Hill and took a little walk around the amphitheater. It's always so magical when it's lit up."

"All of this sounds wonderful. I'm impressed. Have you considered how things might go if you and Sydney become serious? She does have two babies. That's a huge package deal to take on, Vinnie. I'm not saying you shouldn't, but it should be on your radar. You're a fun uncle, but fatherhood is a whole different ballgame."

"I realize there's a significant difference when they're your own children, but it doesn't have to be that way. You're right, it's a lot to take on, but I think she's worth it. I've never met anyone like her."

"Those are dangerous words. I think you're falling for her." Bianca pinched me on my arm.

"Ow! What's that for?"

"I wanted to make sure you're awake and not still on cloud nine."

"That hurt, Bianca." I rubbed the spot where she pinched me.

"What are you going to do when one of these little angels kicks you in the nuts?"

"That's not funny." I turned the tables on her. "Did you enjoy the twins?"

She smiled. "They are adorable. I'd babysit them again."

I knew I had her. "How about tomorrow?"

She turned towards me. "Did you ask her out again already?"

"No. I wanted to make sure I had a sitter first. I was going to call her in the morning. I don't want to behave like a stalker."

A grin crept across her face. "Let me check my schedule, but I might be able to manage that. Vinnie's got a girlfriend. Who knew?"

I couldn't help blushing at her comments. Thank goodness it was dark.

Because yes, Vinnie's got a girlfriend—if she felt that way, too.

My phone rang at 8:01AM. Micky.

"I can't believe you waited this long to call. You're slipping."

"I was making breakfast for a handful of little people. I already spoke to Bianca. Spill."

"Okay, okay. I like her. I'm going to ask her to go out again tonight. But you knew that already, didn't you?"

"I wanted to get it straight from you. That's fantastic, Vinnie. I'm so happy for you both."

"Hey now, Sis. Don't get ahead of things now. I'd like to go on a few dates before you marry us off." I knew how Micky's mind worked. She and my mother were probably planning the wedding already; they were practically the same person. That's why Tony loved her so much.

"I just want you to be happy, Vinnie. You deserve that."

"I am happy, Micky. I will be happier if you keep your nose out of this. Understand?"

I heard her sigh. "I'll do my best. Just promise me one thing."

"What's that?"

"Sydney's been through a lot. Be gentle with her heart."

"Cross my heart." Mine needed that, too.

Thirty-One
Austin - Teamwork
(explicit scene)

Opening a restaurant is a major undertaking. Between leasing a building space, getting permits, designing the setup, purchasing fixtures and equipment, and hiring staff, my brain was swimming in deep waters. My SCORE mentor, David, kept me in line. He checked in with me several times a week to make sure I stayed on the right track.

Cheyenne took charge of the design aspect. I communicated with her regarding the general ambiance I wanted, and she took the ball. She came back from shopping trips showing me fabrics and fixtures. I trusted her judgment, but she wanted my stamp of approval first. We worked well together and I was glad to have her here with me.

Avery and Dale both liked Cheyenne a lot, and they stayed home more often, although it might have been my imagination. We used them as guinea pigs to test out dishes for the restaurant, and neither one of them complained about free food. I took dishes to work and poker nights for additional feedback.

Life felt perfect with Cheyenne. She made me want to be a better person, and I wanted to do anything I could to make her happy. For now, that meant keeping AJ a secret. I wasn't sure how she would react and I wanted to keep the ship upright and moving in the right direction.

I sent Sydney a check once a month, and she cashed them. I thought about AJ a lot, but how do you be a real father from so far away? I couldn't figure that out. My life was here. My career was here. My business was here. Danny told me to fall on my sword, but moving to Indiana wasn't in the cards for me. I wanted to ask Sydney about AJ, but I didn't want her to get false hope that I would play a more active role in his life. I'm sure this was one more way for me to disappoint her, but I didn't see any point in sharing custody. I knew she could handle this without me.

The restaurant was scheduled to open in two weeks, and the one snarl standing in our path was not having our liquor license.

I sat on the couch and called David. "I at least wanted to serve beer on tap when we open," I said.

"Austin, relax. You filed the paperwork in plenty of time. Give it a couple more days before you go bananas. Trust me."

"I can't place an order without a license. How am I—"

Cheyenne grabbed the phone out of my hand, having reached from behind me. "Hi, David! It's Cheyenne. Have you talked this knucklehead off the ledge? It's not time to panic yet...he's a hard nut to crack...Of course. Talk to you later." She hung up.

I took the phone back—with more force than intended. "Don't do it again," I growled.

Her eyes grew wide. "Oh, give it a rest. It's not like I caught you on the phone with your side chick. Don't talk to me like that. I'm only teasing you."

Ugh. What am I doing? I wrapped her in my arms. "I'm sorry, sweetie. I'm so stressed out over this nonsense. I didn't mean to take it out on you." I kissed her on the top of her head and bent to kiss her lips. I started out soft and gentle, but I amped it up as my dick stirred. I pressed against her and grabbed her ass.

"Oh my! Is someone in the mood to play naked games?" She stared up at me in a dare.

"I might be. Are you?"

She blushed. "Maybe." She let go of my hand and took off for the stairs down to our bedroom.

I followed on her heels as I pulled my t-shirt over my head—and nearly tripped on her blouse as I rounded the corner to our room. She lay on the bed. *Good god, she's gorgeous.* I dove on top of her, and she squealed with delight and wrapped her arms around my neck, drawing me in for more passionate kisses.

Her red lacy bra and short black skirt were too much to handle. "You are so sexy. I can't get enough of you." I murmured. "How did I end up with such a sexy woman?" I rolled us over so she was on top of me. She straddled my hips and pressed her wet heat into my crotch, making my cock even harder and ready to dive into her sweetness. I cupped her pert, small breasts with my hands, then reached around and unhooked her bra to give myself full access.

She moaned as soon as I had one breast in my mouth, teasing the nipple with my tongue and nipping it into a hard point. I rolled her over again to give her other nipple the same attention. She squirmed and lifted her hips to maintain contact with my straining cock. I slid my hand up under her skirt to pull down her panties, but I couldn't find them.

"What are you looking for, stud?"

I couldn't hide the confusion on my face. "What did you do with your panties?" I stopped and lifted her skirt all the way.

She giggled from behind her skirt. "I'm not wearing any, genius. How hot is that?" She smacked me on my ass. "Now take your pants off so we can play together."

I could have beaten Superman's time for my quick change. "Slide yourself down on the bed and bend over. You're going to get it. Hard and fast."

She licked her lips and followed my command. She wiggled her bottom in the air, teasing me. I picked up a tube of lube she set on the bed. Squirting a dollop on two fingers and spread it over the head of my penis.

"Are you ready? You've been naughty and I'm going to teach you a lesson." I positioned myself at her entrance.

"Are you going to spank me? I have been a bad girl." She glanced over her shoulder at me. "I'm ready for my punishment."

Placing my hands on her hips, I pushed into her with full force. She gasped. "Oh my! I have been naughty. I need some more discipline."

I backed out as she whimpered. I entered again, pushing hard and holding her hips in place.

"Fuck! You're so hard! Can I have some more?" She panted in anticipation.

I repeated my thrusting and smacked her ass cheek. "You want some more? I've got more where that came from." I slapped her again and she yelped.

I got a little concerned. "Tell me if it's too hard for you."

Her words came in gasps. "Keep going. Harder. Faster. Make me come, baby."

I obliged, working my pelvic muscles sliding in and out of her moist peach. I didn't want to stop.

"Oh god! You're hitting my g-spot! Oh my god! Don't stop, babe."

My cock tingled, signaling my impending orgasm. "That's it! Tell me how much you love it!"

Her moans and gasps became more intense. I grabbed a handful of her hair and pulled at it. "Yes! Oh god! Yes, Austin! Yes! I'm coming!" She gasped and her body shook all over. I'd never seen a woman have an orgasm this intense and I shot my cum inside her before she finished coming down from her high.

We fell back onto the bed together, waiting for our breathing to return to normal.

"What possessed you to go commando? That was so hot!" I stared at her. "Just when I think I have you figured out, you surprise me again. I like it when you don't wear panties. One less thing to take off."

"It's a turn-on for me. I know I'm not wearing any panties, but no one else does. It's titillating, and it lets my naughty bits breathe from time to time. You enjoyed it, right?"

"Of course, I did. I'm going to start checking when you wear a skirt."

"That's cute you think I only do that if I'm wearing a skirt." She winked at me. "Let the games begin."

Thirty-Two
Vinnie - Next Level

The more time I spent with Sydney, the more I fell for her. I found excuses to stop by the house and visit her, and I ate with the family whenever I could. When I wasn't on a trip for work, we went out at least twice a week. Bianca made bank babysitting thanks to my love life.

AJ and Andre stole my heart. They crawled now and tested out standing up. Sydney changed wet bibs from their teething drool multiple times per day. Sometimes Samson laid in the middle of a blanket on the floor and let them pull on his ears and tug at his tail. He got up and moved when he had enough.

We'd been out on at least a dozen dates and I had only kissed her. I didn't ask her to come in at the end of a date, and so far, she hasn't invited me. I wanted to take things at her pace so she wouldn't think of me as a horny toad. Every time I breathed in her perfume, though, I wanted to ravish her. She always smelled like lilacs and vanilla. It could bring a man to his knees.

Last night, on the way home from a movie, I had to say what was on my mind.

"Can I talk to you about something?" I glanced at her.

"Of course. What's on your mind?" She held her gaze on me, making me nervous. I'm typically articulate, but this time was different; the stakes were higher.

"I want to tell you I've enjoyed all the time we've spent together. You make me happy, and I hope I make you happy, too."

"Yes, you make me happy. I guess I've never said that out loud."

"I'd like to take our relationship to the next level, but only if you're ready." I waited for her response, with the butterflies in my stomach throwing a rave.

"I think I understand, but I need an explanation."

I exhaled through my mouth. "I don't want this to come out the wrong way. I am completely smitten by you. I've never met anyone like you, and I want to keep you all to myself and not share you with anyone. Take off all your clothes and worship your body from head to toe. Make love. Leave you begging for more."

"That's a pretty full explanation."

I waited for the rest of her response.

"I must admit, I've thought about it. It's not as simple as inviting you inside. I mean, are you going to make Bianca wait in the living room? I'm not comfortable with that scenario. We could go somewhere close to a bed and breakfast, but I don't want to impose the twins on anyone overnight. They're a handful. If you have any other suggestions, I'm all ears."

I sighed. "I hadn't thought of either one of those scenarios, but finding solutions for problems is what I do. Let me think about this for a little while. If I can bribe, I mean convince, Bianca to stay over with the boys, would you consider going away for the night with me? She's been babysitting since she was twelve and has CPR and first aid certification."

"I'm not trying to complicate things. It's just, my life isn't simple anymore."

"I understand. All I want is to be with you. If we need to wait a bit, that's okay." I reached over and took her hand. "I'm not going to leave you over one little hiccup."

She laughed. "I think this is a little bigger than a hiccup. But I'm sure we can figure it out together." She leaned towards me and kissed me on the cheek. Then her soft lips met mine in a gentle kiss. She pulled on the door handle before I could come over and open it for her. "Good night, handsome. I'll send Bianca out."

Her skirt swished back and forth as she climbed the steps to the front door. I needed some time to regroup and strategize my next move. That hadn't gone according to plan.

The next day Tony and I dug holes for new fencing out in the pasture. That blasted alpaca Larry had discovered another way to get loose and we worked to seal off his latest escape hatch.

"You've been quiet today," Tony said after a few minutes of shoveling. "What's going on in the dark cloud above your head?"

I glanced upward. "Where? I don't see anything."

He set down his shovel and leaned against the fence. "You're not fooling me. I know something's bothering you. You might as well tell me now."

I sighed. "I want to take things to the next level with Sydney. But it's complicated when there are two babies and a babysitter in the equation."

Tony coughed to stifle a laugh. "I see. That might present a challenge. Let me call in reinforcements." He whipped out his phone and started typing.

"Who are you texting?"

"Who do you think? My wife considers herself the queen of matchmaking. She'll figure something out to push you two in the right direction. Lighten up." His phone pinged mere seconds later. He clicked his tongue as he read the response. "My wife is a genius." He slid his phone into his back pocket and picked up his shovel.

So, he was going to play with me. "Tony? Hello? What did she say?"

"Oh. You wanna hear it? It's a good one."

"Yes, I want to hear it! Don't make me beat you."

He dumped a shovelful of dirt before answering. *This guy...*

Finally. "Your mom is going to invite all four of the children for a sleepover and pillow fort party. This way there will be two adults and four hands to wrangle everyone." He chuckled. "I could her excitement in the text." She was so excited!" His phone pinged again and he glanced at his smart watch. "Micky said your hormones can thank her later."

Indeed. I picked up my shovel and got back to work.

Thirty-Three
Sydney - Bed and Breakfast
(explicit scene)

Then we had our weekend away. I was so ready for it. I knew it would deepen our relationship.

Nearly as soon as we checked into our room, we were on the bed naked, working our way to some hot love making. "God, Sydney, you're so sexy." He turned me over on my stomach and laid on top of me. Suddenly I felt claustrophobic and had a flashback of Jason pinning me to the ground.

"Get off of me!" I shouted. I squirmed underneath him, trying to break free.

"Sydney, what's wrong?" Vinnie held still.

"Get off me! Stop! Don't hurt me!"

He rolled off me and pulled me to a sitting position. "Sydney, what's wrong? What did I do? I would never hurt you!" He searched my eyes for the meaning of my outburst.

I breathed through clenched teeth. My whole body shook with adrenaline. I stared at him, but I didn't see him.

He rubbed my back in slow circles. "Take some deep breaths. I'm right here. I'm not going anywhere. You're okay. No one is going to hurt you." He sat there, waiting for me to come around.

I leaned against his shoulder and began to weep. Full out waterworks and snotty nose. It was embarrassing, but I couldn't help myself. We sat together, staring out the window, while my breathing returned to normal.

I turned to him. "I am so sorry. That's never happened to me before."

"What's never happened before? Are you okay? I'm concerned about you."

"I'm concerned about me, too. I didn't realize how deeply my past affected me. When I was working in LA, someone I worked with and trusted tried to rape me. It was scary, but someone stopped him before he had a chance to have his way with me."

Vinnie stammered. "Sydney, I had no idea. I'm so sorry."

"I thought I'd buried it in the past. Apparently, not well enough. I've never talked to anyone about it. Maybe I should get some help with this."

Vinnie pulled me back onto the bed and laid my head down on my pillow. He laid beside me and pulled the covers up to our chests. He turned on his side and tucked himself against me. "Let's cuddle. We've got lots of time to light the world on fire with our sexcapades."

It made me relieved to have the pressure off me. It meant a lot to have him hold me and not expect anything. If he was disappointed, he didn't show it. I lay there, musing over the whole episode. My heart burst thinking about how much I loved this man, for putting my needs above his, and for caring for my boys like he was their father. His steadfast presence made me all warm and fuzzy.

The next thing I knew, sunlight streamed in the window, signaling the start of another day. Vinnie still had his arm wrapped over my waist. I turned to face him and kissed him on the lips. He started to stir, and I kissed him again. This time he kissed me back, hot with desire. I climbed on top of him and pressed my hips against his pelvis. He responded, probing my mouth with his tongue, and putting his hands on my ass, kneading the juicy flesh.

He pulled back and smiled at me. "I could make a habit of waking up like this. Are you in the mood for some hot sex this morning?"

Crossing my arms, I drew my silky gown over my head.

"That's a view I love seeing. Yummy." He reached up and held a breast in each hand. "So soft and tender. Delicious."

"I aim to please. You. Often." I purred. "What would you like to do to me?" I licked my lips to tease him.

"I want to suck on your breasts, cover you with kisses, and lick your warm, juicy pussy. Once I have you begging for more, I'll use my dick to pleasure you on the inside. How does that sound?"

"Yes, please! That sounds like heaven." I bent towards him and our lips met again, causing sensations in my body I'd almost forgotten. Almost.

Vinnie flipped me over on my back and began worshipping my breasts. "Tell me if I need to stop. I want us both to enjoy this."

His genuine concern for my well-being put a lump in my throat. I closed my eyes and focused on my body. I moaned and gasped with pleasure as he worked his way from my breasts to my soft belly. He rubbed his hands all over and kissed it repeatedly.

He moved down to my wild and untamed bush. I never shaved, and I'd never had anyone complain. Vinnie licked my wet lips and kissed on the insides of my thighs. "Delicious!" I heard him mumble from between my legs.

"Yes, more!" I wriggled with pleasure under his touch. His tongue touched my swollen clitoris and I made a sound somewhere between a cry and a gasp. "Oh fuck! Yes!"

He continued licking and sucking, driving me to the brink of ecstasy. "I'm coming! I'm coming!" Vinnie didn't stop, and my orgasm came rolling in, hard and fast. I let myself go and cried out with pleasure. "Yes! Oh god yes!" I shook from head to toe, releasing all my pent-up tension.

Vinnie came back up and lay beside me. "It sounds like you needed that." He kissed me on the lips.

"Indeed. We're not finished, are we?"

"I can continue, but I don't want to pressure you."

"You're not. I want you to squeal, too." I smirked at him. "Take me, baby. Make me come again."

"You asked for it." He rolled on top of me and started kissing me fiercely.

His hard cock pressed against my wetness. "I want you inside me. Now," I whispered in his ear.

"Your wish is my command." He rolled on a condom, positioned himself, and dove between my legs.

I cried out. "That's it! Yes! Give it to me, baby!"

He quickened his pace, and I savored each thrust. His breathing became heavy. "I'm going to come. Gawd, your pussy feels amazing!" His face contorted and he shouted out, "Yes! Oh yes! So hot!" I rode his wave with him and held him when he collapsed on top of me.

"That was something," he murmured. He kissed me and I nuzzled against his chest. We fell back asleep and missed breakfast. But it was worth it.

From then on, Bianca drove herself to babysit. This way Vinnie could come in if he wanted. And he did. But I never let him stay overnight. The twins got up early, and I didn't want an awkward situation in the morning. They were too little to understand, but it made me feel better. Again, he never complained, and he never tried to talk me into letting him stay.

One day, while on the phone with Micky, she asked me the question. "Do you love him? I'm asking because you give off happiness vibes and I've never seen you like this."

"I keep taking things one day at a time, and I didn't realize I developed all these feelings for him. He's so wonderful to me and the boys. Yes, I'm in love with him. I didn't think it would ever happen to me again."

"Maybe you should tell him that. He's waiting for you to say it out loud."

One night, a week later, we lay in bed after sex, gazing at each other. Vinnie kissed me and rolled over to sit up on the edge of the bed, his back turned to me.

I reached out and brushed his arm. "Don't go."

He glanced over his shoulder and sighed. "I know the rules. I respect that, Sydney." He reached for his dress pants.

I tried again. This time I held on. "Don't go. I want you to stay."

"Okay. I'll take the bait. What are you planning to tell the boys when I'm eating cereal with them in the morning?" He raised his left eyebrow.

"That I love you and I want you to stay." I met his eyes and held his gaze.

His puzzled face morphed into a humongous grin. "What did you say? Can you repeat that, please?"

I sat up. "I love you and I want you to stay. Did I stutter?"

He pounced on top of me, both of us falling onto the mattress. "You love me, is that right?" he growled and buried his lips in my neck.

I shrieked in surprise. "Yes! Yes! Is that so difficult to believe?" I wrapped my arms around him.

His face popped back into view. "I've been waiting to hear you say that. I love you. So much. You don't know how happy you made me in this moment." His eyes welled up.

I grabbed his butt cheek. "Why don't you show me how happy you are, stud?"

He licked his lips. "Challenge accepted."

And boy, did he show me.

Journal entry

Our overnight getaway was a key turning point for Vinnie and me. I had feelings for him, but I got stuck trying to figure out how to take things to the next level. I'm glad he came up with a solution to benefit both of us.

I feel bad about my PTSD/panic attack at the B&B. But Vinnie handled it like a champ. He didn't pressure me, and he didn't pry, which meant so much to me. I started talking about what happened to me with a therapist. I don't want one incident to ruin me for genuine love and affection.

Vinnie and I are more in synch now, and our relationship has deepened. We text constantly, even when he's away on business. We go out a few times a week when he's home. Sometimes he even joins me when I take the boys to the toddler-friendly play area at the mall. He grabs us both a coffee—iced for me—and we chat while the boys practice climbing on surfaces other than Samson.

I'm glad Micky said what she did. When I told him I love him, Vinnie's reaction was everything. I love him so much and feel like the luckiest woman in the world. I don't want this feeling to end.

Thirty-Four
Cheyenne - That One Time

The grand opening for the restaurant loomed on the horizon. It promised to be a huge blowout, and the three of us were excited to see our hard work come to fruition. Austin and I spent so much time at the restaurant, we should have pitched a tent in the corner of the dining room and slept there.

Today I had other plans. I made appointments for my hair and nails since the opening was only a few days away. In addition, I made an appointment with a new OB/GYN to get back on birth control. Austin never complained, but condoms were not his style.

At the doctor's office, I filled out the requisite forms, provided a urine sample, and waited my turn. They called me back to an exam room about as warm and inviting as any table with stirrups could be. I put on my paper gown and someone knocked on the door.

"Come in."

"Hello, Cheyenne. What a beautiful name. I'm Dr. Miller." We shook hands and she skimmed over my chart. "You're new here. What made you move to this fabulous city?"

"Who. My boyfriend. We're opening a restaurant together. The grand opening is on Friday. ACZ BBQ. Please come by, if you like."

"I do love ribs. We don't have a lot of authentic barbeques here. Splendid choice."

"My boyfriend won the Barbeque Championship on TV, and decided this was a logical next step."

"Congratulations!" She stopped her finger midway down my chart and tapped on it. "It says you came in for birth control."

"That's right. I'm in a monogamous relationship, but my boyfriend doesn't care for condoms."

She frowned. "I don't think I can help you with that today."

I tilted my head. "Why not?"

She sat down, getting her eyes level to mine. "Your urine specimen indicates you're pregnant, Cheyenne. Birth control isn't going to change that."

"What? I'm pregnant? I can't be pregnant. I, I, I can't have a baby!"

She put her hand on mine. "I have some colleagues that still perform abortions if you need a referral. When they overturned Roe vs. Wade, everything went to shit. Pardon my French."

I blinked and looked around the room like I was looking for... I don't even know what. "I can't be pregnant. We use a condom every ti..." I stopped myself. Oh fuck. That one time. We were both drunk. The conversation went something like this:

He said, "Do we need a condom?"

I said, "We're two mature adults. What's the worst that could happen?"

We didn't use a condom. I think we're at worst case scenario now.

I gaped at Dr. Miller. "I'm sorry. I think I just hallucinated. No birth control?"

"How about some prenatal vitamins?" She smiled as she wrote out a prescription on her pad.

While I sat at the salon, I concocted a plan to tell Austin the amazing news. At least I hoped. It wasn't ideal timing with the restaurant opening and the work it will entail. We never talked about anything in the future, and now it concerned me more than a little. I also understood he wasn't an open book.

He wouldn't be home until at least dinnertime. When I finished at the salon, I went to the quick print shop and ordered a banner. Then I went to the dollar store and picked up some balloons. Once at home, I hung the banner over the window from the dining room into the kitchen. The balloons got spread out in bunches of threes.

I texted him.

> When are you coming home?

> On my way out the door now.

That meant I had fifteen minutes to rethink my decision. Getting pregnant wasn't something we'd planned, but I hoped he would react positively. Time passed so slowly. It was poker night so he didn't pull in the garage. He tromped up the front steps and opened the door, focused on the mail in his hands.

"Hi Sweetie. How was your day?" I asked from my chair.

He looked up from the mail and his jaw dropped open. I sat directly under the banner that read "We're pregnant!" waiting for him to process it. His face turned serious. He came over and grabbed my hand. "We need to talk. Now."

Thirty-Five
Austin - The Whole Truth

"I have tried so many times to talk about this with you, but the timing never felt right. I should be jumping up and down with joy right now, but I can't. I have a secret I never told you. Please hear me out before you decide I'm an asshole."

She nodded numbly and waited for me to tell her the awful truth.

"In the simplest terms, I am a father already. No, it wasn't planned, and I never intended to share it with anyone. Until I met you. I should have told you a long time ago. Part of me was afraid you would leave me, and that was the worst thing I could think of happening. The more time passed, the less important telling you was to me. At least that's what I told myself so I wouldn't feel so guilty."

"Can I ask you a question?" she interrupted.

"Go ahead."

"How old is your child?"

"I think he will be one here shortly."

"Have you ever met your child?"

"Not in person. I saw him on a Zoom call when I spoke with his mother."

"I'm assuming this would be your writing partner. What's her name again?"

"Her name is Sydney. Yes, she's the mother. How this happened is a long story I don't want to elaborate on for personal reasons."

Cheyenne bristled. "Be that as it may, you will now have two children to support. Are you giving Sydney any money for your son?"

"I give her a thousand dollars every month. She said she's putting it in a college fund."

She sat at the table, tapping the ends of her fingers together. "I wish you'd told me this before I moved out here. But since you didn't, I have to deal with my feelings now. I'm not thrilled, let's acknowledge that. Not to mention how my pregnancy announcement didn't quite go as planned."

I knelt in front of her. I took her hands and gazed into her eyes. "I am beyond thrilled you're pregnant. We're pregnant. I'm here for every moment: foot rubs, funny cravings, cranky pants, taking extra naps. I'm your guy. Rub cocoa butter on your belly, read to the baby, put a crib in the office at the restaurant. Whatever makes you happy. Look no further." My eyes got misty. This was amazing news! We would have at least six months establishing the restaurant before Cheyenne would take a hiatus.

I laid my head in her lap. "There is nothing I want more than to share my life with you. I recognize I'm not the easiest nut to crack. Please know I'm crazy about you, first and foremost. Whatever life brings us, we can handle it together. I can't wait to meet our little sweetheart and start a family with you." I placed my hand on her abdomen, picturing the life growing inside her.

She traced her fingers around my forehead and back over my ear. "I hope you mean that, cause you're stuck with me, bucko." She stroked my hair, and I could have stayed there. But my phone rang, and I reached around my belt to put it on silent. I leaned in and kissed her stomach. "Is it too early to start talking to the baby?"

She swatted my head. "It might be a little too early for that."

"In that case, I'm going to ravish you instead. Can't knock you up twice." I rose up and pulled her over my shoulder as she shrieked in surprise. I took my woman to our bedroom and gave her what she deserved.

Thirty-Six
Sydney - Surprise Party

It's true what they say: parties only grow bigger as you plan them. That held true for the twins' first birthday. Thanksgiving weekend temperatures in Indiana aren't suited for outdoor festivities. Between Vinnie's family and mine, Micky's house would have been bursting at the seams. I ended up renting a conference space at the local hotel. The hotel offered catering and a block of discounted rooms for out-of-town guests, which made my life a whole lot easier. I ended up spending more money than I originally considered reasonable, but the tradeoff is that someone else sets up, takes care of things during the party, and cleans up afterward. Yes, please!

The most important thing was providing entertainment for the kids. I decided on face painting and balloon animals. The boys didn't have any favorite cartoon characters yet, so I chose Mickey Mouse décor. All my Amazon deliveries for the party sat stacked in the dining room.

Vinnie came over to help me load up the minivan and dress the boys in their co-ordinating birthday outfits. Even though everyone can tell them apart, I never dressed them exactly alike. Today, they wore different-colored sneakers and shirts and the cutest jean overalls. Dressing them had been easier as infants. Now they wiggled and squirmed, making things more challenging. I pulled my favorite yellow dress out of the closet. Vinnie wore a dress shirt, tie and sport coat despite my protestations that no one else would be dressed that formally.

My parents, Brooke, Abby, Tori, and Venus all had rooms at the hotel, making their trip to the party easy. The entire Patterson clan and Allegro family would be in attendance. It surprised me that my parents made the trip, but I suspect my dad finally put his foot down about something. When I told my parents about the boys having two different fathers, and Andre being bi-racial, my mother went off the deep end. I got an earful about my slut behavior and how that affected her precious reputation.

I've always been the first to admit our relationship is complicated and messy. It really made me happy to watch them interact with their grandsons. My mom did her best to hold her tongue and keep her face in neutral, and my dad seemed to get a kick out of them. The twins stood now and tested their legs for walking. We brought their little baby walkers so they could roam around the room.

Everyone talked, ate, and mingled. The smash cakes stole the show. We stripped the boys down to their diapers and set them in their highchairs next to each other. Abby and I each held out a cake with one candle on it while we sang "Happy Birthday." The boys gawked around the room as we sang. Abby and I blew out the candles and set the cakes in front of the boys.

They stared at the cakes. Andre reached out with one hand and put it in the cake, then immediately pulled his hand back covered in white frosting. AJ scanned the roomful of people staring at him.

"I have an idea," said Abby. "Put them facing each other. Then there aren't as many distractions." We came up behind them and turned them towards each other.

Andre examined his hand. He pulled it towards his mouth and stuffed a couple of fingers inside. His face exuded delight and he promptly stuck the rest of his fingers in his mouth. Then he plopped his other hand right into the middle of the cake and grabbed a huge handful. He switched hands and got half his face covered trying to fit it all in his mouth.

AJ saw his brother shove a fistful of cake in his mouth and was clearly inspired: he stuck his whole face in the frosting. We laughed and cheered for them, and I let them make a mess. I'd thought ahead and put a plastic tablecloth down to catch anything that fell from the highchairs. Abby had been assigned baby cleanup duty helper—she had two towels at the ready, and when the joyful mess was over, she and I wrapped up the boys and carried them to her room for quick baths.

As we dried and redressed them, Abby took this opportunity to talk to me.

"I like Vinnie. I can tell he likes you, too."

"It's been refreshing to have someone around to have adult conversations with. I didn't like him at first, but he's grown on me. The boys love him. He gets down on the floor and plays with them. He treats me like a goddess. The sex is hot, too."

Abby laughed. "That's a bonus I can handle. He makes you happy?"

"Yes. And I never thought I'd be able to say that about anyone. I didn't think I would ever find someone with the boys. We're a package deal, and Vinnie understands."

Abby put Andre down and sat on the edge of the bed. "If he ticks all of your boxes, he's a keeper."

I thought about it. "I'm so wrapped up in the daily minutia of chores and taking care of the boys and don't think much beyond today. I think Vinnie's a keeper. For as long as he'll put up with me."

Abby shook her head. "He's totally smitten with you. Sydney, you are an amazing woman and mother. Any guy would be lucky to have you."

I wrinkled my nose. "I'm not special." I finished dressing AJ and put him down with Andre.

Abby came over and hugged me, refusing to let go. "You are so much more than you give yourself credit for. You deserve to be happy, Sissy."

"I am happy. Now let's rejoin the party."

I ran into Katie, the balloon artist, in the hallway. "How's it going with the kids?"

"Everything is great. I appreciate the gig. I'll leave a few business cards in case anyone else wants to book me. Your boyfriend gave me a generous tip for the balloon I made for him."

"That's cute Vinnie wanted a balloon. He's a kid at heart. I better take the birthday boys back inside. Thanks again, Katie!"

I spotted Vinnie and handed AJ off to him. "I'm going to find my wallet and pay the balloon artist and face painter so they can take off."

"Okay. Do you want them to open a few presents, or were you going to wait until after they got home?"

"Let me think about it for a second. I'll be right back."

I paid Katie and Molly and thanked them for their services. It made me feel good to help young entrepreneurs like them.

When I returned to the party room, everyone was in a semi-circle with Vinnie and the twins in the center. The boys sat inside a giant balloon in the shape of a circle, and Vinnie held a bouquet of red roses in his hand. I came towards them, unsure what was happening. After a few steps, I figured it out. The circle wasn't a circle at all. It was a gigantic diamond ring made from balloons. I froze in place.

Vinnie spoke to me. "Sydney, the boys and I have something we want to ask you."

I started to cry. I wasn't expecting this. I came a few steps closer and Vinnie reached for my hand. I took it. Tony brought out a chair and set it next to the boys. Vinnie directed me to the seat and I sat down. He handed me the bouquet.

"Andre and AJ had a chat with me a few weeks ago while you were getting dressed for our date. They asked me if I loved you, and I said yes. They asked me if I wanted to marry you, and I said yes. They asked me if I would be a good father to them, and I said yes. Then they gave me their blessing."

He knelt on one knee. "I couldn't think of a more perfect time to declare, in front of all our family and friends, that I am completely smitten by you. I love everything about you and I want to be with you for the rest of my life. Will you make me the happiest man alive and say you will be my wife, and my partner in Life?"

I nodded, tears falling down my face and onto the bouquet of roses in my arms. "Yes," I finally managed. Vinnie pulled a small box from his pocket and opened it facing me. The ring was gorgeous! The brilliant cut made it sparkle and shine. It looked like a whole caret, surrounded by a ring of tiny diamonds. Abby took my flowers. He put the ring on my finger and we kissed. Everyone clapped and whistled. I wrapped my arms around Vinnie and kissed him again.

"Save it for the honeymoon!" I heard Tony shout. We all laughed. I still couldn't quite believe what just happened. But now there was a ring on my finger that made it real.

Journal Entry

I had no idea the boys' birthday party would turn into an engagement party. Vinnie took me by surprise with his romantic proposal in front of both of our families. And the ring! Holy carets, Batman! I think I might need sunglasses to protect my eyes, or a sling to hold up my hand with this gigantic rock. It's so beautiful! I'm a little afraid to wear it.

Vinnie and I never discussed getting married. Including AJ and Andre in his proposal sealed the deal for me. I know I love him, and he meant every word. He included my boys in his declaration, and it means more to me than I can express. A lot of men want the woman but don't give a rip about the kids that come with her. Vinnie comprehends we're a package deal. He made sure I knew he was more than okay with taking on the role of their father.

Austin and Marcus have not indicated they want to be active father figures for their sons. I receive a check for each boy every month, and I put the money in their savings accounts. It will be a sizable nest egg for them down the road.

Now planning a wedding is on the agenda. It's still so fresh, and we haven't picked a date yet. I don't want to wait two years like some brides. I want us to start our lives together sooner than later. More to come...

Thirty-Seven
Austin - Grand Opening

For the past three days, we had been putting our new staff through their paces, learning the menu, serving routine, and the location of important items like wine glasses, silverware and napkins. We incorporated a tasting dinner so everyone would be able to speak to the menu when patrons had questions. Dale became our in-house sommelier. His experience in other upscale restaurants gave him street cred, even if he didn't have a fancy certificate. Avery committed to joining us when we needed extra staff for events. His recurring TV gig extended past his three-episode arc, and he milked the shit out of it.

For our Grand Opening, we decided to focus on dinner. Cheyenne ran the show, making sure all the vendors delivered on time to make this opening fantastic. Zach and I holed up in the kitchen all day, smoking dozens of racks of ribs, roasts, and whole chickens. The rest of the kitchen staff arrived at four to begin chopping and prepping for orders. We chose our top three menu items to keep things simple for the first night.

I anticipated us being busy. Cheyenne purchased some ads to run on radio and Spotify. She gave the local radio stations coupons for free dinners to use in giveaways. We took out a half-page ad in the Sunday paper and she mailed fancy invitations to national and local food critics. With my status as the winner of the American Barbeque Championship, I made the circuit of morning talk shows and late-night shows to announce our opening.

Yesterday I stopped by the Drew Barrymore show with pulled pork sandwiches for the whole audience. Drew is such a sweetheart in person, just like she is on her show. She took one bite of my sandwich and whispered it was better than In-N-Out Burger. My head and chest grew three sizes bigger. I told her I would be thrilled to cater for her any time.

At five, the wait staff arrived, and I kicked it into fourth gear. Once I made it to fifth gear, I would be on fire. Zach and I had a natural rhythm between us from working together all those weekends on the food truck. I tuned the rest of the world out and concentrated only on the food.

Cheyenne came and tapped my elbow. "It's time, sweetheart."

I glanced at her and wiped my hands on a dish towel. "Okay." I kissed her on the cheek. "Here we go! Zach, let's move!" It reminded me a little of the makeover reveal moment in an episode of *Bar Rescue*, but we were just getting started.

We opened the door and stepped out into the crowd of people gathered around the entrance. I hopped up on a curb for a better view.

"Wow! Thank you for coming to our grand opening this evening. We are excited to have you try our menu and become barbeque fans, if you aren't already. Never in a million years would I have thought a scraggly kid from Kansas City would come this far. I especially want to thank my lovely lady Cheyenne for her talents in creating an inviting atmosphere, and for supporting me in this gigantic adventure. Also, my friend and business partner Zach. He helped me slug it out in my food truck and is equally responsible for our success. We have a special menu this evening and I hope you enjoy yourselves. Welcome to ACZ (pronounced ACE) Barbecue!"

The evening flew by in a blur. I got pulled out to the dining room multiple times to meet important people: the mayor and his wife, Shaquille O'Neal, "Fluffy" Gabriel Iglesias, and some movie producers I'd never heard of. Cheyenne escorted me to each table, whispering their names in my ear like Andi in *The Devil Wears Prada* so I didn't appear stupid.[9] Alton Brown and Bobby Flay made appearances. Guy Fieri tweeted congratulations and mused that we were a little too classy for an episode of *Diners, Drive-ins and Dives*.

When we finally closed the doors shortly after midnight, I slumped into a booth at the back of the dining room. I ached in places I didn't know I had muscles. Zach came over and sat across from me. Cheyenne scooched me over and joined us. I put my hand on her not-yet-noticable baby bump.

"Are you all right, honey? Too much?"

She sighed. "I'm tired. But happy. I think overall we had a fantastic evening. Do you want to say something to the staff before I let them go?"

I turned to Zach. "I think you should do it. You're the head man in the kitchen. I'm going to be the dancing chicken around here."

Zach nodded, and Cheyenne came back with the kitchen and wait staff. Zach stood to address them. "Please have a seat. I'm going to make this short since I know most of us have been on our feet all evening. We think everything went well tonight. A few hiccups, but nothing problematic. This is a testament to your skills and professionalism in your jobs. Austin, Cheyenne and I are thankful you have chosen to work for us. I'm not trying to shoot sunshine at you; it's the truth. What issues or questions do you have right now?" Silence. "The office door is always open if you want to discuss anything, offer suggestions, or say hello. You should be proud of your efforts tonight. Go home, rest, and come back to do all of this again tomorrow."

OUR MEAT BELONGS IN YOUR MOUTH

Thirty-Eight
Cheyenne - A Hundred Roses

The day after our grand opening, Austin and I drove to work separately. He had a meeting with one of our meat suppliers, and I didn't want to wait for him. Pregnancy took a lot out of me. Making another human used up so much of my energy. We wanted to keep it a secret for a little while. I said that was fine while I could still fit in my pants.

On the way home, all I could think about was taking a nap under my electric blanket. That would leave me refreshed for Austin. On top of being tired, my breasts were sore and tender, and my hormones were stuck in horny teenager mode. I could not get enough sex. At least I knew why.

I pulled in the driveway and noticed a thin, red line going all the way up the front steps. When I got closer, I realized they were rose petals. I walked around them and opened the front door. Our living room had been transformed. The floral scent of dozens of roses around the room hung in the air. Our retro Formica table sat in the middle of the living room, covered with a white linen tablecloth. China place settings and a rose centerpiece decorated the table, and a candelabra of white candles burned next to it. The couch and coffee table had disappeared.

I couldn't speak. Dale appeared from the kitchen wearing a server's uniform.

"Good evening, madame. Welcome to Chez L'Amour. May I take your coat? I assume the rest of your party will be joining you shortly."

"Yes?" *The rest of my party?*

He pulled out a chair for me, and I sat.

"May I offer you a beverage? Iced tea, perhaps? We lost our liquor license yesterday or I could offer you some wine. We do have a lovely sparkling grape juice chilled."

"I'll have water with lemon slices if you have them."

"Of course, right away." He vanished into the kitchen.

I surveyed the room. I guessed there were at least a hundred roses in vases, placed around the room. I deduced what might be happening, and it made my heart skip rope in my chest. This was over the top to apologize for his reaction to my pregnancy announcement, but I wasn't going to protest. Footsteps echoed behind me, and a hand rested on my shoulder.

"Is this seat taken?" Austin came around to stand in front of me. He wore a tuxedo and I could smell his favorite cologne waft around him.

"Be my guest," I replied. "Do I need to change into something more appropriate?"

"Completely unnecessary. If it makes you more comfortable, then that's fine, too."

"I'll be right back." I raced downstairs to our room and pawed through my side of the closet. I pulled out a silver dress with fringe all over it that I'd never worn. It still had the tag on it, but the scissors made short work of it. The dress stretched a little snugly across my swollen breasts and expanding abdomen. Standing in front of the mirror, I ran my hands through my hair in an attempt to minimize the frizz. I added some sparkly sandals and my favorite long, silver drop earrings. That would have to do.

Austin stood as I came upstairs. "Wow! You look gorgeous!" He kissed me on the cheek and pulled my chair out for me. Dale came out with salads and set them in front of us. Mixed greens with apples, grapes and pecans. Feta cheese garnished the top and it was drizzled with a light dressing that was tangy but sweet. He followed those with a basket of knotted rolls and a butter spread.

"Who catered this wonderful meal?" I wondered.

Austin cocked his head. "Yours truly. I do know my way around a kitchen."

I blushed. "I know you do. How did you have time to do all of this?" I gestured around the room.

He shook his head. "Fort Knox, babe. I'm entitled to my secrets."

"I am sufficiently impressed. Did you hire a violinist, too?"

"I knew I forgot something!" He slapped his hand on the table. "Waiter! Waiter! Where is my violinist?"

Dale hurried out and pushed a few buttons on the TV remote. Soft instrumental music came wafting out of the TV. He whisked our empty salad plates away and returned with a soup course. At first, I thought it was tomato soup, but it looked pink. It also had a white swirl in the middle. It was cold and sweet. I snapped my face up towards Austin in a question.

"Strawberry soup. It's supposed to be cold. Do you like it? They serve it at some of the restaurants in Disney."

"It's delicious. But I was expecting warm."

He dabbed his mouth with his napkin. "This is where I need to leave you for a few minutes. Steak is better when it's hot, and I didn't want to keep it in a warmer. Excuse me." He stepped into the kitchen.

I saw Dale trying to slip by behind me. "Come here," I whispered. "Sit," I hissed. He sat in Austin's seat. "What is going on here?"

He blinked at me. "Ma'am? I was hired to serve dinner this evening. Is dinner satisfactory?" He stood back up.

"Yes, dinner is delicious. Thank you for your assistance." I waved my hand to dismiss him. As he passed, he whispered in my ear. "He's giving me a free month of rent for this. I'm not going to blow it." He kissed my cheek and went to assist Austin. I sat listening to classical music and eating my soup.

Austin returned, and Dale carried out our entrees. Filet mignon, twice-baked potatoes, and a zucchini medley.

I cut a bite of my steak, and it melted in my mouth. "Oh my. This steak is mind-blowing. I'm sorry, but I may have to run away with the chef."

Austin put his fork down. He got up from his chair and knelt in front of me. *This is not happening! He's going to propose! It all makes sense now. Geez, Cheyenne, you're pretty clueless.*

He took my hand and looked up at me. "The other day, you turned my world upside down. I was not prepared for your news, and I didn't handle it properly. It only seemed right to show you how I feel. You have made me happier than I ever thought possible. I'm so glad that not only are we business partners, but we're going to be parents together. I want us to be a family. I want you to be my wife. I'm not perfect, but I will spend the rest of my life making sure you and our children are taken care of. Cheyenne, will you marry me?"

Everything happened in slow motion. Tears spilled down my cheeks and he wiped them away. "Are these happy tears?"

I nodded because I couldn't speak. His sincere words overwhelmed me and my heart burst with happiness. He pulled out a ring from his pocket and slid it on my finger. The large diamond in the center must have been at least half a caret. The band around it held smaller round diamonds. It was perfect. Until it wasn't.

"Wait a minute. Are you only marrying me because I'm pregnant? I don't want to be accused of trapping you into a marriage."

Austin bristled. "That scenario had not occurred to me until now. Yes, the chivalrous Southern gentleman owns up to his responsibilities. That's not what this is. This is me, saying I love you and I want to be with you forever. The baby is a bonus. I was planning on asking you once the restaurant got off the ground. I've had this ring in my sock drawer for weeks."

He rose to his feet and pulled me up with him. "Cheyenne. I have never met anyone like you, and you have stolen my heart. I would be honored to be your husband and partner, if you let me." He tilted his head towards me and kissed me softly.

"Okay," I managed to say. "I can do that."

He swept me up in his arms and hollered into the kitchen. "Waiter! You're going to have to put dessert back in the fridge for now. Dinner was delicious!"

He carried me downstairs and kicked open our door. The room had been transformed into another rose-covered oasis, complete with candles and soft music. It didn't look like this when I was down here earlier. *How did he...?* I had no idea.

He laid me on a bed of rose petals in the shape of a heart. Then he joined me. He brushed my hair back from my face with his hand. He gazed into my eyes and traced his finger around my lips. He followed it with a kiss and nuzzled into my neck.

"You smell amazing! What are you wearing?" he breathed in deeply.

"Juicy Couture. It's one of my favorites. You smell amazing, too! Hugo Boss?"

"Mmm hmm. I heard a rumor you like that on me."

I breathed in his scent. "Yes, yes I do."

He pulled back to see my face. "Tonight, I want to concentrate on you. I have drawn a bubble bath and I will rub your feet while you sip on sparkling grape juice and relax. I'm going to moisturize every inch of you with cocoa butter. And I might practice knocking you up again. What do you think?"

I licked my lips. "That sounds fantastic. But it shouldn't be all about me."

"I won't hear of such nonsense. Are you ready?"

I nodded.

"Let's begin."

Thirty-Nine
Sydney - An Invitation

"Hi, Mom! It's Sydney."

Silence emanated from the other end of the line.

"How are you?" I tried again.

"I'm well. To what do I owe the honor of your call?" I thought we were in a good place at the boys' birthday party, but her icy tone made me want to hang up and forget this whole charade.

"I wanted to invite you to come wedding dress shopping with Abby and me. She made an appointment at Kleinfeld's for me, and we're going to make a weekend out of it."

More silence. "I will discuss this with your father, but it's a long way to come to look at dresses."

My heart sunk. My mom wasn't one for sentimentality, but in the back of my mind, I'd hoped she would agree to come. Tears spilled down my cheeks as my emotions got the best of me.

"Who is going to care for your children while you are off frolicking in New York City?"

"Micky. Her two girls love it when the boys come over to play. It will be like an extended slumber party."

"I see. I don't think I would recognize my own grandchildren in a lineup." *Is she serious? She was at their birthday party mere weeks ago. What a drama queen!* She twisted the screw just right and I fell for her hijinks every time.

"Mom, I have mentioned you are welcome to visit the boys any time you like. I send you pictures every month. It's a lot easier for you to fly than it is for me." The lengths this woman would go to play the victim astounded me. I have spent so many hours in therapy, and I try hard to establish boundaries with her. It doesn't always work as well as I would like. My self-esteem and sanity always ended up lying in the dirt by the time I got off the phone.

"Clearly, you don't need me. I might as well check myself into the old folks home now."

Lord, she's exhausting. "Mom, you're not old enough for the old folks home." What I wanted to say was, *I agree completely as long as it will get you out of my hair.* It's the same thing, right? But I chose the first response because it was the only way to pacify her.

"Did you invite Brooke?"

"Of course, Abby invited Brooke. But she doesn't have the greatest track record when it comes to showing up."

"Your sister has an important job. It's difficult for her to take time off on short notice." Except for when Brooke vacationed in Europe or took an African safari. Noted.

"I wouldn't count on her coming is all I'm saying."

"Sydney, I don't know what to say to you. We tried our best to raise all three of you with exemplary values and morals. Yet you insist on doing everything you can to go the opposite way. You have twins who don't have the same father, and now you're marrying a third man. That's not how you were raised."

"Would you have preferred I got an abortion? Would it have made things easier for you? If I'm such an embarrassment to you, then you're right not to come."

"Here we go. You're being so dramatic. I don't know where you get that trait. I need to leave for my quilting club. Your father and I will discuss this and I will tell you what we decide."

"Okay, Mom. I need to tell you one more thing before you pick out your dress. We're asking everyone to dress in black for the wedding."

"Black? Sydney, that's for funerals, not weddings. What are you thinking?"

"I've seen it in some wedding magazines and it makes the photos so sharp."

"I'm not sure I could bring myself to wear black to a wedding."

"That's okay, Mom. It was just an idea. Enjoy your quilting group. Bye."

I shook my head as I ended the call. Who's the dramatic one? I knew she wouldn't come, and it was for the best. Abby would be disappointed, but it would be easier to decide on a dress without her criticisms.

Journal Entry

Mom called me back and declined to participate in dress shopping. I'm not surprised. But I am disappointed. Moms are supposed to help their daughters plan their wedding and pick out a dress. Not my mom. If this was Brooke getting married... But it's not.

I'm thankful Abby and Micky share my enthusiasm. Micky declared herself the official wedding planner. Let's hope we can keep this shindig at a minimum $$$. It's only one day, after all.

My dad called me and told me he would be sending me a check for $20,000 towards the wedding expenses. I tried to decline since Vinnie and I have the means to pay for the wedding on our own. But he insisted and I caved. I didn't want to hurt his feelings when he and Mom had spent a lifetime saving for this blessed event.

I am excited to have an appointment at Kleinfeld's. I've been watching their show Say Yes to the Dress *for years. It will be cool to see the store in person. Maybe I'll fall in love with one of Randy's creations. I hope I find one they can make in my size.*

Forty
Cheyenne - Vegas, Baby
(explicit scene)

With all the work we needed to do for the restaurant and preparing for a baby, a fancy wedding was not high on our list of priorities. We settled on eloping to Las Vegas in two weeks and having a celebration with friends and family later.

I booked a ceremony at The Little Vegas Chapel, a hotel room at the Bellagio since we're both fans of *Ocean's Eleven*, and a helicopter ride over the Strip that landed in the middle of the Grand Canyon. Neither one of us had ever flown in a helicopter. I called my doctor to verify that it was safe for me. A honeymoon adventure!

We got in late after driving four hours from L.A. Our helicopter ride was scheduled for 9:30AM the following morning, so we skipped gambling to go right to bed. The helicopter ride was pricy, but it turned out to be worth every penny. Seeing the Strip from above gave it a whole different perspective. Standing in the middle of the floor of the Grand Canyon took my breath away. I took tons of pictures, but they paled in comparison to seeing it with my own eyes.

I took a nap when we returned to the hotel, and Austin did some exploring in the casino. The wedding time was coming on fast and I wanted to be fresh and all bride. No tired mom-to-be today! Austin owned his own tuxedo from going to Hollywood parties, but I didn't have a suitable dress. I shopped three times until I found the perfect tea length, pale pink dress. It reminded me of the 1950s, with a tulle skirt that flared out and made me feel fancy. The sweetheart neckline emphasized my swollen breasts, but they were partially obscured by an illusion neckline of tiny, appliqued flowers and cap sleeves. I finished off my look with slingback heels and my favorite rhinestone dangle earrings.

When I came out of the bathroom, Austin's jaw hit his chest. "Good lord, Cheyenne, you look gorgeous! I want to ravish you right now."

I blushed. "I'm glad you like it. You clean up well, too, handsome."

He kissed me on the cheek. "You ready?"

I nodded. He put on his favorite black Stetson and took my hand. As we walked through the lobby, people stopped and stared at us, and a few offered congratulations. When I booked the chapel, I'd read that over a hundred and fifty marriages are performed daily in Las Vegas, but I suppose I would've done the same thing seeing a bride and groom[10]. It made me a little self-conscious, but Austin squeezed my hand and I relaxed.

The limo took us to the courthouse to purchase our marriage license before heading to the chapel. We chose their outdoor courtyard for our ceremony. It was a wonderland of green plants, colorful flowers, and beautiful fountains. Neither one of us has strong religious beliefs, and that option suited us best.

Our ceremony lasted all of five minutes, but it was still beautiful. As I walked down the cobblestone path towards Austin, my heart swelled with emotion. I knew I loved him, and I held high hopes for our future together. Even though he'd already seen me, he wiped away a tear from his face as I approached. We clasped hands and listened to the officiant talk about love. Austin said his vows first.

"Cheyenne, you are the most amazing woman. You're kind, passionate, and feisty as hell. I need someone to give me a run for my money and make me a better man. You are that woman for me. Every moment with you is an adventure, and I can't wait to grow old with you by my side. I promise to take care of you and our family. I love you more than words can say."

"Austin, when I met you, I wasn't looking for love. Your charm and sincerity melted my heart and I fell for you. I want to spend every moment with you. I promise to stand beside you as your partner and your lover. I'm honored to share this adventure called Life with you, and I can't wait to see what happens next. I love you with all my heart."

The officiant asked, "Do you have rings to exchange?"

"Yes, we do." Austin removed both rings from his pants pocket and gave his to me.

"Cheyenne, with this ring, I thee wed."

"Austin, with this ring, I thee wed."

"By the power vested in me by the state of Nevada, I now pronounce you husband and wife. You may kiss the bride."

Austin dipped me and kissed me behind his black Stetson. The photographer caught it on camera, and it's my favorite picture from our perfect day. We capped off our whirlwind trip with dinner on the terrace at Picasso. The view of the Bellagio fountains couldn't be beat.

We swung by the casino on the way back to our room. Austin wanted to play some blackjack, so we took five hundred dollars out in chips for him to try his luck. He picked a twenty-five-dollar table. He lost his first few hands, then won a few hands, boosting his confidence. I was never a gambler. Seeing the money come and go so easily was strange—scary, thrilling. This weekend was about adventure and we'd budgeted for loss if it happened, so I decided to lean into the thrill. And oh the thrill when he hit two thousand! He kept going—but he handed me half of the chips so he wouldn't lose everything. It reminded me of being on the game show *Press Your Luck*. How much can you win before the house takes it all back with one whammy?

When we walked away, my tiny clutch purse bulged with chips. We cashed them in and ended up with over five *thousand* dollars—and a tax return slip to go with it, which cracked me up. It was like fantasy and reality packaged together. Austin's winnings paid for our weekend with a little left over. Sweet!

When we got back to our room, all jacked up on winning and wedding, I started stripping him down the second the door shut. Then I stopped myself—I had my plans for this weekend, and lust would *not* derail them. I asked him to unzip me then scooted into the bathroom. I came out wearing a white silky slip of lingerie held up by two spaghetti straps that barely covered. Austin sat against the headboard wearing nothing but his boxer briefs.

He patted the bed next to him. "Come over here, my beautiful bride."

I straddled him, sitting on his crotch with my knees tucked behind me. His penis grew hard below my thin slip of panties. Wrapping my arms around his neck, I leaned in and started licking it. He grabbed my breasts over my slip and I gasped. They were tender, but the sensation aroused me. He rubbed my nipples through the fabric, waking them up. I continued licking and sucking on his neck, while he moaned and laughed when I hit a sensitive spot.

"Careful, woman. You might hit the wrong spot and turn me into a horny toad."

"I thought that's what I married. What's the return policy for faulty merchandise?"

"Final sale. No exchanges. No refunds. You're stuck with me, like it or not." He pulled down my straps and exposed my breasts. "How did I get so lucky? You are so sexy. These pregnant breasts are irresistible." Taking a nipple in his mouth, he continued to tease the other one with his fingers. I arched my back and savored the feeling. I shifted my pelvis back and forth over his crotch, increasing the heat coming from his cock.

"Easy, baby. Easy." He held my hips. "I don't want to rush this."

"My hormones will not let me behave. You made me this way."

"Indeed. And I'm enjoying every moment of your torture." He wrapped his arms around me and rolled us over so he was on top. He took one of my arms and then the other and placed my hands over my head. "Can I trust you to keep your hands there? Or do I need to tie you up?" He winked at me.

"I will do my best to keep them here." I shuddered in anticipation.

"Hang onto the rungs of the headboard if you lose your cool."

Bending towards me, he drew me into a passionate kiss. My breasts and my pussy pulsed for attention and I struggled not to wiggle. His lips and tongue danced with mine. He trailed kisses down the side of my neck and made his way to my waiting breasts. I gasped as he swallowed my tit in his mouth, using his tongue to drive me crazy. His other hand massaged and nipped at my exposed breast.

"Oh yes! Do that some more!" I closed my eyes and concentrated on the way he touched me and turned me on. He moved south and kissed all over my belly. No one had ever done that to me, and it felt so decadent and sensual. After he covered my belly with kisses, he parted my thighs and began kissing them. He came so close to my wet lips but didn't touch them. I moaned and writhed under his touch. I didn't want him to stop, and my desire to have him inside me grew with each passing moment.

I couldn't take it anymore. I reached down and grabbed him by the hair. "I want you. Inside of me. Now."

He removed my hand. "I'm not done yet. And you will be coming more than once. Let go. It turns me on."

I came the second his tongue touched my throbbing clitoris. The endorphin release as he licked my most sensitive spot overpowered me. I cried out. "Yes! Yes! Oh God! Fuck me, baby!" I didn't care if our hotel neighbors heard us. He continued with his mission until I started coming down from my high. Grinning at me from between my thighs, he came up and kissed me. My juices lingered on his lips and tongue. He wiped his chin with the back of his hand and lay down next to me. He reached his hand over and laid it on my bump.

"This is going to sound strange, but I'm afraid I'm going to hurt the baby." Austin confessed. "I figured I could still pleasure you orally."

I propped my head on my hand, staring at him. "Sweetie, it's safe to have intercourse during pregnancy. It's encouraged. My OB said to enjoy it as much as I'm comfortable."

He looked relieved. "That's good news. Are you ready for Round Two?" He raised his eyebrows at me. Someone knocked on our door. Good god, security was coming to tell us to pipe down with my vocal acrobatics.

"Room service," someone announced.

I looked at Austin. "Did you order room service?"

He hopped off the bed and put his boxers back on. "I might have. Let me check."

He opened the door and a server wheeled in a cart. Austin signed for it and the server left.

"What did you do, Mister Mitchell?" My curiosity got the better of me.

"I ordered some chocolate-covered strawberries, five-layer chocolate cake, and a carafe of milk. No champagne for us, Mrs. Mitchell."

"We ate that scrumptious dinner earlier, but I am kind of hungry again. It might be me or the baby, but I could eat."

"Then I timed it right. Let's grab some forks and dig in." He brought over the plate of strawberries and two slices of cake. We lay side by side, propped up on our elbows, watching the spectacle of the Vegas Strip and devouring our late-night snack. He poured our milk into two champagne glasses and we toasted to our new life as husband and wife.

And I came two more times that night.

Forty-One
Austin - Melody

True to my word, I doted on Cheyenne every step of the way through her pregnancy. The restaurant demanded our constant attention, and we both spent long days working. The office didn't have much room, but I managed to fit a small recliner in the corner for her.

"Anytime you're tired, or your feet are sore, come in here and rest. Take a nap. I'll bring in a blanket tomorrow."

"Austin, you shouldn't have!" She hugged me and devoured my mouth with hers. "But I probably will nap from time to time."

"That's what it's here for. And then we'll trade it for a playpen when the time comes."

"You thought of everything. I have the best husband ever!"

I picked her up and she wrapped her arms and legs around me. I squeezed her juicy ass and kissed her hard. "I'm going to ravish you when we get home," I rasped in her ear.

"Can I play, too?" Zach appeared in the doorway. "Newlyweds, geez."

I laughed. "Sorry, Zach." I set her down. "What's up?"

Zach held up an envelope. "We received our permanent liquor license. And by permanent, I mean as long as we are on their good humor."

"That's a relief. We only had a couple more days on our temporary license. It needs to be hung up behind the bar for the Liquor Board. Put it in the lower left corner of the mirror."

"I'm on it." Zach disappeared around the corner.

"I better go put some meat in the smoker or we will be serving pb & j for dinner." She smacked my ass on the way out. "You're all mine later, hot stuff."

Time flew by and we sat at Cheyenne's appointment for her thirty-second week. Her baby bump kept growing and rivaled a small watermelon. Dr. Miller measured everything and declared our baby was developing as expected. Cheyenne's hormones stayed set on "horny teenager" these days—we had hot sex before bed almost every night. *No complaints from me!* After we finished, she laid her head on my chest and clutched her giant body pillow in between us and everything felt perfect.

Tonight, I fell asleep while listening to her breathing but startled awake when she shook me. "What? Do you need some ice cream?" I started to roll out of bed, but she grabbed my arm and pulled me back down with a strength I didn't know she possessed.

"Something's wrong. I think I'm in labor. It's too early. I'm scared." It was dark, but I could hear the terror in her voice.

Stay calm, cowboy. She needs you.

"Let's call Dr. Miller first." I picked up my phone from the nightstand and found her emergency number. I spoke to her answering service and they assured me she'd call me back. It seemed like forever, even if it was only five minutes.

"Hello, Dr. Miller. Cheyenne thinks she's in labor. Should I take her to the hospital? It's too early."

"It is too early. How far apart are her contractions?"

"Between three to five minutes, and they are getting stronger."

"She needs to come into the hospital. We have drugs to stop labor, and we can better monitor her here. I'll meet you."

I sighed with relief. "Thank you. We're on our way."

"Tell me." Cheyenne sat on the edge of the bed, trying to breathe through another contraction.

"Dr. Miller wants us to go to the hospital. They may be able to stop your labor."

I stood up and picked up my jeans from the floor. I tossed Cheyenne her pajama bottoms. "Do you need me to bring anything? I don't think we'll be staying long."

She shook her head. "I can't think of anything. Let's go."

I didn't drive like a maniac, but I did run a couple of red lights. I pulled right in front of the Emergency Room entrance and raced into the lobby. "I need some help! My wife is in labor." Two nurses came out with a gurney and transferred Cheyenne to it. One of them grabbed my arm. "We're going to take care of her. Park and register her." They rolled her through the doors and disappeared around a corner. I found a parking spot.

The nurse at the registration desk waved me off. "Go be with your wife. They're in curtain number three."

When I pulled the curtain back, Dr. Miller was examining Cheyenne. "I need a baby monitor and a shot of terbutaline, stat." A nurse scurried off to retrieve them.

Stat wasn't good. I heard it in a million movies and shows. My stomach flipped.

Dr. Miller put Cheyenne in stirrups, and I came up next to her head to hold her hand. She squeezed hard. Neither one of us spoke.

"You're five centimeters dilated. I'm going to give you a shot of terbutaline to attempt to stop the contractions. It takes fifteen to thirty minutes to take effect. It's hard but concentrate on breathing. Slowly." The nurse returned with the shot and monitor. Dr. Miller administered it in Cheyenne's shoulder. "Let's put you on the monitor so we can keep track of your baby. I'll be back to check on you both."

Once the nurses left, I waited with Cheyenne among a lot of beeping machines. I rubbed her hand. "You're so brave, sweetie. Dr. Miller is going to take good care of you."

She nodded as the tears flowed down her face. "I don't want to lose our baby."

"Everything is going to be okay. We're in the right place. We need to trust Dr. Miller." I spoke with more confidence than I could muster. I needed to take her mind off her fears and ignore my own. "I thought of something. We haven't settled on a name yet. You're sure we're having a girl?"

"That's what they told me. They aren't always correct, but I can't see what they do on the ultrasound machine."

"What do you think about Emily?"

She wrinkled her nose. "All I can think of is Miranda Priestly calling her poor assistant the wrong name all the time. 'Emily? Emily?' Veto for me."[11]

"What do you like? You've been pouring over those baby name books."

"I like Ophelia. Destiny. Hannah. I don't remember the rest. I had it narrowed down to ten names."

"Only ten? I like Hannah, but not the other two." Then it hit me. "What about Melody? I think it's pretty."

She gritted through another contraction. "Like the ones her daddy writes? I do like it. Melody."

"Then it's settled." I got up and kissed her on the forehead. "Do you want some coffee? I need a cup or five."

"I'm probably not allowed. But bring me back a cup just in case."

I walked down the hall to the lobby, but I didn't buy coffee right away. I sat down in a corner, away from everyone else. My hand shook as I called Zach.

"Hello?" His voice sounded groggy. I realized it was four in the morning and he was still sleeping.

"Oh shit. I'm sorry Zach. I forgot what time it was. I'll call you later."

"Wait, wait. I'm awake. What's going on?"

I gave him the short version. "I'm so scared. I'm trying to be brave for Cheyenne, but I don't have a good feeling about this." I started to sob and I covered my eyes with my hand.

"Oh man, I am so sorry. What can I do? Name it."

"Nothing. She's with the doctors and they're doing the best they can. I don't know if I'll be coming to work today."

"No problem. I've got it covered. Go take care of Cheyenne. I'll be thinking about you both."

I sat with my phone hanging in my hand. At least my hands weren't shaking anymore. I felt more... emotionally exhausted. Depleted.

No. This wasn't the time to crack under the pressure. *Cowboy up*. I bought two coffees and carried them back to our curtain.

"Dr. Miller came back and gave me a second shot. She isn't seeing the results she wanted from the first shot. She didn't want me to have any caffeine, so a nurse is bringing me some ginger ale."

I pulled a folding chair next to her bed. There wasn't anything else for me to do. "Do you want to watch some TV? Might help take our minds off things."

She nodded. I found an episode of *The Big Bang Theory*. We sat in silence for the most part. When a new contraction started, I let her squeeze my hand and breathed through it with her.

After a bit, Dr. Miller came back in to check on Cheyenne. She checked the printout from the baby monitor. "Your baby is doing fine, but your labor has not stopped. Thirty-two weeks is not ideal, but we do have a much better success rate for preterm babies than we did five years ago. I'm going to give it to you straight. My biggest concern is lung development, which is not complete until around thirty-six weeks. I want you to be aware your baby might need to spend some time in the NICU until her lungs develop."

"You can't stop her labor?" I wanted clarification.

"Not at this point. She's too far dilated. We're going to move you to a delivery room. Cheyenne. Austin. Get ready to meet your baby." She patted Cheyenne's knee. "I'll be back when it's time to push."

In another hour, Cheyenne needed to push. Dr. Miller positioned herself at the end of the stirrups and assessed Cheyenne's cervix. She looked up from the sheet. "You're ready to go. Start pushing with the next contraction." She looked at me. "Dad, grab one leg and pull it up for her with each contraction, then let her relax in between."

I stood next to my wife on one side, and a nurse stood on her other side with a leg in her arms. While she pushed, I did my best to encourage her and felt relieved she wasn't screaming at me.

"I see the top of her head. Just a few more pushes and your baby will be here," Dr. Miller announced.

Once the head was out, Cheyenne stopped pushing. Dr. Miller pulled her out and cut the umbilical cord. Then she rushed Melody over to a warming table and began to examine her. I watched them work on her, my heart pounding and stomach clenched.

"She's not crying." Cheyenne panicked. "She's not crying! What's wrong?"

I squeezed her hand. "Sweetie, I don't know. Let Dr. Miller do her job." *Stay calm. Cheyenne needs you to be strong right now.* My head hurt and my knees felt weak. Time moved so slowly as we held our breath, waiting.

Dr. Miller used her stethoscope to listen to Melody's heart and lungs. "I need a chest x-ray." She turned towards us, and her expression looked serious. "I don't want to worry you unnecessarily, but I don't like what I'm hearing in Melody's chest. She's not breathing on her own. We need to intubate. Is that something you want me to do?"

We locked eyes with each other. "What do you think?" I asked Cheyenne.

"Will she survive if you intubate?" she asked Dr. Miller.

"She has a much better chance this way, but I can't tell you for certain."

"What do you mean? Is she going to make it?" My heart clenched in my chest and Cheyenne began to cry.

A nurse came over, holding an x-ray film. Dr. Miller took it over to the lightboard and studied it for a moment. She came back to us, shaking her head. "I was afraid of this. Melody's lungs are not formed. In fact, they aren't as developed as much as most babies at this stage." Her voice shifted, went soft. "Even with intubation her chances of survival are minimal. I am so sorry. I know this is hard."

"You're, you're saying there isn't anything you can do to save our little girl?" My eyes pleaded with her to give us some hope.

"I'm very sorry." Cheyenne was sobbing. I felt woozy. "Would you like to hold her? I can put you in a post-partum room to give you some privacy."

Hold my baby? Yes. God, yes. I nodded. "Thank you. How long does she have?"

"A few hours at best. She'll go to sleep and it won't hurt."

Cheyenne was mumbling words like "isn't happening" during her sobs, and "not real" and "just a dream."

My wife needed every bit of strength and calm I could muster. I leaned close. "It's not a dream, honey. Melody is sick and she's not going to survive. Let's have some time with her before she goes."

A nurse handed Cheyenne a tiny blanket with Melody wrapped in it. I followed them as they wheeled my wife and baby down the hall to a private room. My body went through the motions in a haze. When we were alone, I climbed into bed with them. We both cried while she held Melody against her chest.

"This isn't how things were supposed to be." I punched my fist into the mattress. "The worst part is there isn't anything we can do to save her."

She opened the blanket to look at our daughter. Those tiny eyes were closed, and her wee little mouth formed the letter O. Cheyenne's sobs had turned to something softer, something so much sadder. She held up Melody's hand, and I heard her counting.

"She has ten fingers and ten toes. She's perfect. Do you want to hold her?" She offered Melody to me and I cradled her in my arms, tears streaming down my cheeks. The love for this little person ran through my whole body, making me feel alive and in the deepest pain I could imagine all at once. This precious little being who would never know us or how much she meant to us. Heartbreak, rage... I went back and forth. Cheyenne leaned her head on my shoulder and we watched this miracle slip from our hands. I knew when she passed, and at that instant numbness set in my heart. Time had stopped for us while the rest of the world turned. We stayed in bed together, unmoving.

Dr. Miller used her stethoscope to check for a heartbeat she wouldn't find. She glanced at the clock, writing the time of death on her chart. She had tears in her eyes as she addressed us. "I am so sorry. Take all the time you need with her. I have some paperwork for you to sign and a few decisions to make when you're ready." She left the room.

"What are we going to tell people? The shower is in three weeks," Cheyenne wondered.

I put my arm around her and pulled her in close. "The truth. It hurts like hell, but that's all we have."

We buried Melody at a cemetery nearby.

My mom, Zach, and Cheyenne's parents came to the private funeral. We didn't want to publicly share our pain. It hurt too much. My mom stayed for a week, taking care of the condolences and deliveries from our friends and family. Having her here made me feel better, but most of the time I was a useless zombie.

After a week, I went back to work. Dr. Miller gave strict orders for Cheyenne to recover like any other mother who gave birth and put her on medical leave for six weeks. I did my best to help her, but we were both grieving and I felt so inadequate. I wasn't giving my best at work, but Zach picked up the slack so the restaurant never lost a beat. Me, though? I couldn't find any beat. Nothing made sense, nothing felt routine. I kept waiting for life to go back to normal, but it never did.

Forty-Two
VINNIE - CHANGES

As the wedding approached, Sydney became more and more stressed. Her mother, Gretchen, kept making suggestions about the wedding regarding table settings, food to serve, floral arrangements, and a bevy of other things to drive Sydney crazy. She told her mom she wasn't going to have bridesmaids, and I winced from the kitchen as the woman berated her for excluding Brooke and Abby.

"How will it look when your own sisters are sitting with us instead of standing up next to you? Unacceptable, Sydney."

"Mom, I discussed it with Abby and Brooke and they don't want to be bridesmaids. They will hold AJ and Andre during the ceremony."

"They didn't want to hurt your feelings. Which is more than I can say for you."

"Okay, Mom. I will talk to them again. I have to go. Andre needs changing."

She hung up and counted to twenty. Then she came back to the dining room. I kept filling little fabric bags with colorful M&M'S® with our monogram on them.

"Vinnie, I swear I'm going to throw my phone out the kitchen window and hope one of the goats eats it. This day is supposed to be about you and me. She's turned it into The Gretchen Show. I realize my dad gave us quite a bit of money towards the wedding, but I had no idea it came with so many strings attached."

I nodded. "I understand. Your mother envisions things in a certain way. Take a deep breath. Take five deep breaths. Our wedding is going to be wonderful, no matter how much she attempts to ruin it. If she's like this with you, can you imagine what she will be like when Brooke gets married?"

This made her laugh. "Oh dear! I can picture it now. My dad told the three of us many times that the first one to marry receives financial help with the wedding. The other two get bupkis. How much do you want to bet my mother will make him find money for Brooke, too?"

"I'm so glad my parents aren't that way."

"Your parents are saints. They have their own business, sit on charity boards, and give parolees jobs. My mother nags and insists on getting her way. There's no comparison."

We finished the favors and put them along the wall in the dining room with all the other boxes of decorations for the wedding. I wanted to have our wedding right here on the farm, and Micky and Tony agreed. We selected a large level spot behind the big red barn for the ceremony and rented a gigantic tent for the reception festivities.

Micky came in through the kitchen. "Are you finished counting candy pieces yet? I've been trying to keep the 'id-kays' away so you wouldn't have little beggars around."

I nodded. "Yep. One more thing to check off the list. Right, Sydney?"

She stood. "Yes, sweetie. Thanks for helping me."

"You're not the only one getting married. I want to help. No thanks needed." I wrapped her in my arms. "Two weeks from now. I can hardly wait." I paused. "Sis, how long until dinner?"

Micky checked her watch. "The crockpot will be finished in about an hour."

"Would you mind if I steal Sydney for a few minutes? There's something I want to show her."

"Show me what?" She cocked her head. "What are you up to, Vincent?"

She only called me that when she was serious or angry. But I loved it. "It's a surprise. Do you trust me?"

"I wonder. It better not be a puppy or a motorcycle."

"You have to come with me to find out." I shook my keys in my pocket. "You coming?"

"Do I have a choice?"

"Always. But I hope you choose the right thing."

She held out her hand and I took it. "Excellent choice, my sweet. Let's go so we can get back in time for dinner."

We drove a few miles and then I took a left down a side street.

Sydney perked up. "I never saw this road in all the times I've driven past it."

I maneuvered through a wooded area and then came into a clearing. As we crested the small hill, a house came into view. A Cape Cod with buttery siding and bright blue shutters standing tall in the middle of the meadow. A curved cobblestone walkway led from the driveway to the front porch. The wooden front door was engraved with a border of flowers and leaves circling the oval frosted glass in the middle.

On the left side, a creek bubbled down the hill. It was less than three feet wide, but it had layers of depth along the way. The water flowed over a couple of miniature waterfalls as it descended down the hill. It looked like a Thomas Kinkade painting come to life.

"Wow! Who's the lucky duck that lives here?" Sydney said. "A friend of yours?".

"I guess we'll have to go to the door and knock." I parked the car and we walked up to the front door. I reached out and turned the knob.

Sydney grabbed my wrist. "What are you doing? This isn't an episode of Goldilocks and the Three Bears."

"I'm just going to peek inside. Relax."

"Relax? This is breaking and entering, Vincent."

"I'm not breaking anything. No one will know. They're not even home." I pushed the door open and stepped into the house. I grabbed her hand and pulled her in with me.

The inside of the house was as quaint and charming as the outside. Hardwood floors flowed throughout the living room and dining room, with a staircase separating them. Crown molding framed the tops of the walls. A brick fireplace graced the corner of the living room and an intricate chandelier hung in the dining room. Beadboard lined the walls around the dining room up to a chair rail. The kitchen sat behind an archway at the back of the dining room. It had plenty of cupboards above and below the counters. The sink had a window above it that faced the backyard. Black-and-white checkered tile covered the kitchen floor, reminding me of the 1950s, along with the retro-styled appliances. A turquoise refrigerator, stove, and microwave matched perfectly with the countertops.

"It's so perfect," Sydney gushed. "I would love to live here."

I couldn't help it. A smile creeped up the sides of my cheeks. "I'm so glad you like it. I'm going to sign the papers for it tomorrow."

She gaped up at me. "You're pulling my leg. Is this some kind of joke?"

"No. I made an offer a few days ago. I know you agreed to move into my house, but I wanted us to have a place that belongs to all four of us. A home. With a large fenced in yard for Samson, too."

She shook her head. "I can't believe you did this. But what about your house?"

"I'm going to chop it up and use it for firewood."

"What? Are you serious?" Her shocked face made me laugh.

"No, darling. I'm going to rent it out. Real estate is usually a sound investment." I pulled her into my chest and wrapped her tightly in my arms. "Do you really love it?"

She sighed. "Yes. Of course I love it." Her arms snaked around my waist. We stood like that, not moving. "Can I see the rest of it now?"

Off the kitchen, hidden behind folding closet doors, were hookups for laundry. The next door, on the opposite side, held a powder room. The last door at the end of the short hallway revealed the master bedroom with an ensuite.

We circled back to the stairs. Two bedrooms and a full bath took up the loft space. Each bedroom had a walk-in closet, which would be perfect hiding places for little people playing games.

Inside the fenced in backyard, there was a brick patio with low walls around the perimeter. A small shed and grill stood on the right, next to six steps that led up to the door of the screened porch. Where the patio ended, a large expanse of grass continued through the yard. At the far end of the fence stood a gate that allowed access to the woods beyond it.

As we wandered through the house and the yard, all Sydney kept saying was, "Wow. Wow. Wow."

"I take it you really like it."

"That's an understatement. I could just kiss you!"

"Oh, I think this deserves more than a kiss." I winked at her.

"Well let's start with that, and see what happens from there..." She pulled her t-shirt over her head and raced up the stairs.

I got more than a kiss. And we were late for dinner.

Forty-Three
Austin - Taking a Break
(explicit scene)

When Melody died, Cheyenne and I died, too. But I went through the motions every morning—making us coffee, usually not drinking it, making us eggs, usually not eating them—and I worked at the restaurant. When I came home, I took a shower and sat in front of the TV with some alcohol until I passed out. The will to live had almost left me. Many mornings I would wake up on the couch with a pillow under my head and a blanket covering me. I thought I kept up a brave front for Cheyenne, but the only person I was fooling was myself.

About a month after the funeral, Zach pulled me into our office at the back of the restaurant. We sat down, and he didn't mince words.

"Austin, I'm concerned about you. We, the staff and I, are all concerned about you. You are a zombie when you're here, and you're useless."

I was too exhausted to put up a fight. "What do you want from me? My baby died, Zach. I held her tiny body in my hands as her heart stopped beating. This wasn't supposed to happen. We expected to raise her and watch her grow up. There's no point to all of this anymore." I gestured my hand around the room.

Zach listened as I spilled out my sorrow. "We had all these hopes and dreams for her. That's what you do while you're waiting for this little miracle to arrive. You dream about how things will be for them. Whose nose will they have? Will they be athletic or creative? Will they go to the prom? What will they be like as grownups? It all builds up in your mind.

"Then, when it gets taken away in one breath, it's too much to handle. It's disbelief and shock. You're numb through the funeral. Afterwards, you're in your own personal hell. It's just you and your wife. No one wants to talk about it. You close the door to the nursery and pretend it doesn't exist. It's too horrible to even mention losing a child, one who didn't begin to live. There isn't even a word to describe parents who have lost a child because it's the most horrible thing anyone can imagine. It is. We have a word for children without parents, and we have a word for those who lose their life partner. But all I have left is a hole in my heart that will never be filled."

I felt defeated. "What did you want to talk to me about? Is the restaurant doing well?"

"Yes. I would tell you if it wasn't. We divided the important parts of the daily workload to cover for you."

I believed him. Zach was my right-hand man and he could handle it.

He leaned forward in his chair and rested his elbows on his knees, clasping his hands together. "I want you to take some time off."

I opened my mouth to protest, but he raised his hand to stop me.

"Let me rephrase. I *need* you to take some time off. Cheyenne, too. David and I discussed it at length. Right now, neither one of you is in any shape to run a restaurant. It's understandable and expected. I am treating you like I would treat any of our employees in this situation. You two are on leave effective immediately, for two months. At that time, we will reevaluate the situation. You will remain on the payroll so you keep your health insurance. Use it to go to therapy if nothing else."

I sat, dumbfounded, not believing the words he said. We needed it, but also... my pride. On top of everything, I was failing the business I'd put so much into, and I was being sent home. Damn.

Zach continued. "Text Cheyenne and tell her you're coming home. Go take care of her. And take care of you. Go for a walk together. Binge Netflix shows. Take a pottery class. Have sex. You still have so much to live for, and we are all grieving with you."

He stood up. "Come here." He held out his arms and took me into a gigantic hug. As he squeezed, I started to cry. No, bawl. I made noises I didn't recognize. He held on to me and didn't let go. I was standing but he was the one holding me up. I knew I was a mess. This was the best gift anyone could have given me: the gift of time. When I finished, he offered me a Kleenex.

"I don't want to see or hear rumors of you being anywhere near this restaurant. Are we clear?"

I nodded.

"I mean it, Austin. I will open a can of whoop ass on you."

"Thank you, Zach. This means a lot," I murmured. "You will never know."

"When you need anything, call me. We take care of each other." He clapped me on the back and opened the door for me. "Now, get lost so I can cook the books."

I sat in my car, still in disbelief. I texted Cheyenne and told her I was coming home. On the way, I stopped and picked up a bouquet of flowers for her. Whatever today or tomorrow brings for us, I wanted us to face it together. Hope was the most dangerous four-letter word, but I had to give it a shot. To make Melody's too short life count.

I took the front steps two at a time and swung open the front door. "Honey! I'm home!" I bellowed.

Her voice trickled up the stairs. "I'm down here."

I hung my keys on the hook and took the stairs. Our bedroom door hung open a crack and I pushed it open. Cheyenne lay on her side on the bed, wearing a black lacy bodysuit I hadn't seen before. I stopped in my tracks, my mouth gaping open.

"I brought you some flowers," I croaked and dropped them on the floor.

"Thank you, sweetie. I have something for you, too." She smiled at me and ran her hand along her side. "It didn't come with a bow, but I hope you like the wrapping."

"Yes, ma'am. Very fetching." I gulped.

She put her hand on her ass cheek. "My therapist said we need to return to our regular routine. I thought this would be a start."

We hadn't had sex since Melody died. When we went to bed, we didn't touch anymore. I missed her soft lips and juicy ass more than I realized in this moment. I wasted no time pulling my t-shirt over my head and diving onto the bed next to her. And we got back in the game.

Forty-Four
Austin - One Good Punch

While we were on a forced hiatus from the restaurant, I took over grocery duties and most of the cooking. It was easiest to fill up my cart online and go pick it up in the parking lot at the store. I bypassed awkward encounters with acquaintances this way. I knew they meant well with sincere condolences, but I wanted to avoid them. I parked my car and texted my arrival in the app. Listening to the radio, I waited and watched people coming and going from the store entrance.

And then I saw him. Jason Cooper.

You fucking animal! I started to hop out of my car, but the store associate was suddenly there in my face with my groceries and I got distracted, losing sight of Cooper. My blood boiled and my fists clenched. He'd been going into the store. Once they filled up my trunk, I sat in my car to wait.

Twenty minutes went by without a second sighting. My ice cream wouldn't last long with the top down on my convertible. Just when I reached to turn the key, my luck improved. He walked back across the lot with two bags of groceries. I got out of my car and followed him.

He put his bags in the back seat and turned to get in his SUV.

"How are you doing, Jason? I haven't seen you in ages. Someone told me you started working across the street."

He turned towards me. "Austin. Hi. Yeah, I left that company a while ago. I got a raise and a promotion out of it, so it was a beneficial move."

"Sounds like you took advantage of an opportunity. Good for you. Did your promotion also come with a restraining order?"

"I beg your pardon. What?" The douchebag had the nerve to look shocked.

I leaned in and put my hand on the roof of his car, next to his shoulder. "Did I stutter? Did your promotion come with a restraining order? Sydney told me about your slimeball attempt to rape her. You are the lowest scum on the planet. They should put you on a shock collar so you can't do that to another woman."

"Wait." He put his hands up in front of him. "I don't know what you heard, but it was a huge miscommunication. It was consensual."

I leaned in until my face was only a few inches from his. "You and I have a different definition of what constitutes consensual. When a woman is crying and screaming, that's called rape. If I hear about you bothering Sydney or any other woman ever again, you will be digging your own shallow grave in the desert. Are we clear?"

He blinked at me. "Crystal. Can I go now?"

I backed away from him. "Be my guest." Then I punched him with a right hook to the nose. He cried out in pain and crumpled to the asphalt. I whistled as I walked back to my car and drove home with a smile on my face.

Forty-Five
CHEYENNE - CALLING IT QUITS
(explicit scene)

I could not have prepared for what it felt like to lose Melody. I spent all this time rubbing my belly and talking to her, waiting for her arrival. And then she was ripped away from me in an instant. The worst part was when I woke up in the morning. For just a moment, everything was fine, and then I remembered it wasn't, and I swear to god it felt like losing her a second time. I slept. A lot. It was easier than facing the hard truth when I was awake.

Austin threw away all the work he'd done on staying sober. His days and nights passed in levels of an alcohol-induced haze. I knew he wasn't going to meetings. Even if he'd tried to deny it, the amount of glass bottles in the recycling bin told the real story. His coffee might have been black, but he wasn't drinking it straight. Sometimes I woke up in the middle of the night to find him watching old music videos in the living room. Other times, he would be fast asleep, so I covered him up and turned off the TV.

While we were on our forced hiatus from work, Austin and I tried to reconnect with each other. We took walks, cooked together, had sex, and binged on shows on Netflix. There was no easy road to recovery. Not that it's possible. Recovery implies that you go back to normal. That option didn't exist.

One morning, I awoke to the smell of bacon. Austin stood in front of the griddle on the counter. He flipped pancakes over one by one. He gestured for me to come sit on a stool on the other side of the island. My favorite mug sat next to the coffee pot, and he filled it three quarters full. He filled the rest of it with creamer and handed it to me.

"Thank you, sweetie. What's all this for?"

He smiled. "I felt like making us breakfast. Did I wake you?"

"No. The bacon woke me. Where is it?" I sniffed the air.

He waved his spatula at me. "Not so fast, not so fast. I wanted to finish the pancakes first. Would you mind getting the syrup from the pantry?"

I found it. Austin plated two servings of pancakes and then added the bacon, which he kept warm in the oven. He set a plate down in front of me and came around to sit next to me. He seemed like his old self; his eyes were bright and he'd shaved off his unkempt beard.

"Bon appetite!" He raised his coffee mug and took a sip. "Ah. That's the way I like it."

I dug into my pancakes. "These are so yummy! Thank you."

He nodded with his mouth full and held up a finger. "I want to take you somewhere today, if that's okay. Did you have any plans?"

My curiosity nagged at me. "Where are we going?"

He shook his head. "Top Secret. Can't tell you."

"What should I wear? Can I go like this?"

He assessed my wardrobe. "I suppose. It's okay by me."

I couldn't help but laugh. "I'm not going anywhere in public in my pajamas. I need a shower first and foremost."

An hour later, we were driving in silence, listening to the country station on the radio. We turned off the highway and drove down a two-lane road for a few miles. I always loved riding in his car. Mustangs make a unique sound, and I love to watch him work through the gears as he winds her up on the highway. It's a real turn-on for me.

"Can I tell you something?" I said.

"Sure. Shoot."

"It is such a turn-on watching you shift gears. It's hella hot."

He smirked. "You never told me. How hot are you?"

"About a four. Aroused but manageable."

"Do you want to do something about it?" He wagged his eyebrows at me.

"Do you?" I countered.

"Never ask a man if he's horny. I'm not going to turn down sex if you're offering."

"Then find a place to park." I reached my hand over and started rubbing his crotch on top of his tight jeans. His dick started getting warmer and larger, making them even tighter. He pulled off into a gravel patch at the end of an empty field and pushed the button to close the top of the convertible.

"Pull your seat all the way back. I want to sit on your cock and make you come." I shimmied out of my jeans. He noticed I wasn't wearing any panties.

"Good god, Cheyenne! You're going to give me a heart attack one of these days with your no-panties antics."

I smiled at him and licked my lips to tease him. "Now, lay the seat down. I want full access."

As he lay back, I took his hard cock in my hand and leaned over it. I exhaled my warm breath on the head of his penis and slid it into my mouth. He groaned and put his hands on my head. I pulled back, and used my tongue to tease the head, then licked his frenum from bottom to top. He continued to moan, and I quickened my pace, sliding my mouth up and down his shaft. His breathing became heavy, and I sat back up to change position, which is not easy to do when you must hurdle a stick shift.

I positioned myself over his throbbing, exposed dick, and sat down on it.

"Fuck, Cheyenne! You're the devil!"

I laughed. "Is that right? Fuck me, baby. Let me have it."

My pelvis rocked back and forth. He smacked my ass with his hand, spurring me on.

"That's right. Fuck, you're so wet." He shuddered. Then he reached his fingers between my lips and rubbed my clitoris. I gasped and moaned but did not slow down. He groaned, grasped my hips and filled me with his cum.

"Keep rubbing my knob, baby." I shook and gasped, then laid my head on his chest. His heart beat fast, and we lay together, not moving.

Someone knocked on our steamy window. Fuck. I rolled off Austin and struggled to put on my jeans.

"Just a minute." Austin called to the person outside. He zipped up his jeans and returned his seat to an upright position. He looked at me. "Do you have your pants on?"

I zipped up my jeans and gave him a thumbs-up. He rolled down the window a few inches.

A police officer wearing sunglasses stood outside. He leaned down and peered into the car. "Are you folks all right? I thought perhaps this was an abandoned car."

Austin replied. "No, sir. We were tired and pulled over here to take a short nap."

"Your windows are fogged up."

"Yes, sir. I snore something awful and it caused the windows to fog."

"Can I see your license and registration, please?"

Austin nodded. He leaned over and opened the glove box. He pulled out an envelope and handed it to the officer. Then he reached into his back pocket for his wallet to retrieve his license.

"I'll be right back." He marched back to his patrol car.

"Are we in trouble?" I whispered.

He shrugged. "Why are we whispering?"

"I'm just nervous. I've only been pulled over once. For speeding."

He patted my knee. "Trust me. We'll be fine."

It seemed like we waited a long time, but the officer returned. He handed Austin his papers and leaned on the soft top of the convertible, looking in at us. "I'm going to let you two off with a warning. However, the next time you decide to *take a nap*, do it at home. Drive safely and enjoy your day."

He marched back to his squad car.

"Do you think he would have arrested us?"

"Not likely. I'm embarrassed to say I've had this happen before. If you cooperate and keep your mouth shut, it's not worth the paperwork for them. But if I was a cop, it would be fun to bust people."

"I suppose. Where were we going before all of this happened? Can I have a clue?"

He thought for a moment. "I can't think of anything to say that wouldn't give it away. You're too clever at puzzles and trivia. So, nope. Besides, we're almost there."

Up ahead, I noticed a small wooden sign with white lettering nailed to an overhanging tree branch. It read "Cat Sanctuary" and had an arrow pointing left. Austin turned the car into the drive, and I gasped. "Kitties? Can we play with them?" I felt like my five-year-old self. I squealed with delight.

Austin parked the car in front of a giant sky-blue barn. He covered his ears, feigning pain. "Woman, pipe down. You're going to break my eardrums."

I couldn't help it. I bounced up and down in my seat. Austin put his hand on my knee.

"I stumbled upon a reel on TikTok one night, and they showed a short video of this place. They give a home to cats who have physical issues, are too old to be adopted, or come from kill shelters. It might be beneficial for you to have a furry companion. Since I am in my own grief, I'm inadequate to help you, too. I know how much you love all kinds of animals. If you find one you connect with, we can adopt today."

Tears spilled down my cheeks. "This is the nicest thing anyone has ever done for me."

He reached over and smothered me in his arms. "This is what I mean. You're going to make me cry, too."

He didn't let go. He let me have my feelings and didn't rush me. I pulled myself together and checked my eye makeup in the mirror. "Okay, I'm ready."

I got down on the floor in one of the cat rooms, and a friendly black cat greeted me right away. She had some distinctive white markings. The tips of her ears were white, she had a little triangle patch of white on her chest, and her tail was white, too. Austin strolled around the perimeter, observing the cats in baskets and hammocks, pausing to pet ones who were awake.

One of the volunteers came over to me. "I see you met Flower. Isn't she a sweetie?"

I nodded as she wound around my hand for affection.

"She's part of a bonded pair. Her brother, Socks, is laying on the hammock by the window, soaking up the sun. He's laid back, and she's active. They're senior cats who've lived together their whole lives and should go to a home together. Their owner died, and no one in the family wanted to take them. We rescued them from a kill shelter. Take your time. There is no pressure to adopt."

I looked over at Austin, who was within hearing range. He nodded at me and went over to pet Socks. I could hear him murmuring to the cat but couldn't make out what he said. The number of cats in the room made me sad. How could so many animals end up without loving families? I wanted to take them all home, and I think that's the hardest part. They all deserved to have a warm spot in the sun to call their own.

Austin came over and sat down next to me. "You like Flower, don't you?"

I nodded. "I think it's fascinating her tail is white instead of black. I've never seen anything like it."

Flower moved in front of Austin, rubbing herself along his leg. He reached out and stroked her back. She stood there, letting him pet her, and I could hear her purring. Socks observed the scene from his perch but didn't come over to join his sister.

"We had lots of barn cats at my grandparent's farm," Austin said. "In my experience, outdoor cats are often feral and not affectionate unless you're feeding them. My mom has one indoor cat, Oliver. He's so old now. She said he camps out on my bed most of the time. She thinks he's waiting for me to come home." He waved and one of the volunteers came over to us. "What do we have to do to adopt this pair?" He gestured at Flower and Socks.

"Let me grab their folders and paperwork. I'll be right back." She scooted off towards the office, I presumed. I turned to Austin. "Are you sure you want to adopt two cats?"

"We have enough room in the townhouse. They'll have each other when we're working. Avery and Dale said they don't care one way or another." Avery and Dale had started looking for a new living situation when they learned about Melody coming. But finding an acceptable living situation in L.A. can be challenging and takes time. When she died, they decided to stay, and I'm glad they did. Their support meant a lot to both of us.

"They knew what was happening before I did? What traitors!"

He laughed. "I was excited and had to share with someone. It makes sense to adopt them together. Let's do it."

On the way home from the sanctuary, we stopped at the local pet store. We each carried one meowing cardboard box. The cats got their own shopping cart, and we grabbed a second one for the necessities. We must have looked and sounded like two kids in a candy store to other people, gushing over toys and food bowls. Our cart overflowed with cat supplies by the time we made it to the checkout.

Flower stuck near me all the time, following me around from room to room. She sat right next to me or on my lap. Her purrs could be heard across the room when she got someone to pet her. Socks and Flower each had their own fluffy beds in the living room, but Flower always snuck into our bedroom in the middle of the night. I would wake up to find her sleeping in between our heads.

Socks took a while to warm up to us. He spent most of his day sitting on the windowsill perch Austin installed to charge his solar power. When the sun disappeared, he moved to his cat bed. Socks liked the little fabric mice with catnip and hoarded them in his bed. They had a bunch of cat toys, a tall scratching post with multiple perches, and a giant tunnel toy. It looked like our living room belonged in the pet store.

Even with the cats taking up so much of my time and attention, I could not shake the cloud of sadness wrapped around my heart. I joined a grief group at the hospital. It helped me feel less alone, but it didn't take away my pain. I suggested to Austin that he join me, but he declined. He went with me to couples therapy, where we attempted to return to some semblance of normalcy in our relationship. Our therapist suggested we start trying to have another baby, but it was too fresh, too raw for either one of us.

My mom called me every day to check in with me. I didn't always answer because I couldn't hide my pain from her. She told me multiple times she wanted me to come home so she could take care of her baby. My two closest cousins, Kennedy and Sierra, sent me funny memes and cute cat videos daily to cheer me up. Bubba texted me and revealed that he lost one of his brothers when they were kids. He told me he's never recovered and he would listen to me any time. It didn't help me feel better, but I appreciated his heartfelt gesture.

Austin tried. But his own grief over Melody, and not being a father for AJ, took a toll. We lived like two zombies separated by an invisible wall. We could see each other but we couldn't connect unless we were having hot sex. His gesture in adopting Flower and Socks meant so much. But it wasn't enough. He continued to drink himself into oblivion most days and I *did not* have the strength to confront him.

I gathered my courage and called my mom.

"Is it okay if I come home for a little while?"

"Of course, sweetheart. Your dad and I miss you and want you to come home. I might have mentioned that a time or two or ten."

"I wanted to make sure you meant it. I need to bring the cats with me. Is that okay?"

"I will make room for the litter box in the laundry room and your dad can install a kitty door. Done. Anything else?"

Tears leaked out of my eyes. "No. That's perfect. I'll be home in a few days."

"We love you sweetheart and can't wait to have you come home."

Now I had to tell Austin.

A week before we were scheduled to go back to work, I asked Austin to come talk to me in the living room. He sat next to me on the couch and reached for my hand. I shook my head.

"I have something to say, and you're not going to like it. I've been thinking about it for a few weeks, and I've decided I'm going back to Texas. I miss my family. I don't have any friends here. I'm lonely most of the time, and now with losing our baby girl, I can't take it. I need to be around people who support me."

I could barely look at Austin. The pain on his face was clear.

"Why didn't you talk to me about this? We can figure something out. I love you, Cheyenne. We had this horrible thing happen to us, but don't you think our relationship is worth saving? This turn of events has left me in a hell I never imagined and all I want to do is drown myself in a bottle of Jack. I'll go to a meeting right now. I don't want us to be over. *Please Cheyenne.* Stay."

I didn't doubt his sincerity about this for a second. But that didn't change anything. "Our relationship is worth saving, absolutely—but I don't have the capacity. If I stayed, I'd just end up in this emotional place again, wanting to go home. I don't want to play this elaborate charade only to be right back here in a month or two or six. It's not fair to either one of us. Do you understand?"

"No. I don't accept this, Cheyenne." He exhaled. "I promised to love you and stand by you, and that's what I intend to do. That's what marriage is. I don't want to lose you, too." Tears streamed down his face and he put his hand on my knee. "I'm begging you, don't do this to us."

The lump in my throat made it difficult to breathe. I knew this would be hard, but not like this. I cleared my throat. "I'm leaving tomorrow."

His wounded pleas turned to anger. "Let me get this straight. You've been thinking about this for weeks but couldn't talk to me about it? You never mentioned this in therapy. This is bullshit, Cheyenne and you know it." He stood up. "I need some air. I'm going for a drive."

His footsteps echoed down the stairs and the garage door opened. He revved the engine more than necessary and peeled out of the driveway. I sat on the couch, replaying the whole conversation in my mind and processing my decision. I grabbed a couple of boxes I'd stashed in the garage and started putting my clothes in them. Most of the furniture and other items in the house belonged to Austin. It didn't take long to pack and load the boxes in my Jeep.

When I went to bed around eleven, Austin still wasn't home. I thought about texting him, but I wanted to give him some space. The next thing I knew, the doorbell rang and someone pounded on the front door. The clock on the nightstand read 2:42AM. I threw on one of Austin's t-shirts and hustled upstairs to the door.

"Who is it?" I asked.

"It's Austin. Let me in." He slurred his words.

I opened the door. He slumped against the railing on the porch. I leaned over and helped him into the house.

"Did you know my no-good wife is leaving me?" he shouted.

"Yes, I am that wife. Let's go inside so you can sleep this off."

"You're a nice lady. Do you want to marry me?" He giggled. "Don't tell Cheyenne. She might get upset."

"Where's your car? It's not in the driveway."

"I took an Uber. I lost it in a poker game. Oops!"

At least he'd had the sense to Uber home. I rolled my eyes as I dropped him onto the couch. "You can't be serious, Austin."

He put a finger to his lips. "Shh, you'll wake up Cheyenne."

"I'm certain she's already awake." I pulled his legs up onto the couch and removed his boots. I covered him with a blanket. "Go to sleep. We can talk in the morning." I trudged back down to bed and fell asleep.

In the morning, I gathered the cats and walked through the house one final time. Austin snored on the couch. I told myself it was better to leave this way than have another dramatic scene. It was too exhausting. I made my exit through the garage and pointed my Jeep south.

Forty-Six
Austin - Wake Up Call

My phone rang. Danny.

"Hey man! How's it going?"

Silence.

"Danny, did you butt dial me?" I chuckled.

"No, Austin."

His somber tone caught me off guard and I switched gears. "What's wrong?"

More silence. I waited, giving him space to speak his mind.

"My dad died."

Holy shit. This was not what I expected at all.

"Wow. I'm so sorry, Danny. What happened?"

"Heart attack. Mom said he went to take a nap after the football game. She left to get groceries and when she came home, he was gone."

"I'm on the next plane."

"Not necessary. I know you have your restaurant and your big Hollywood life, but I wanted to let you know. He always liked you."

"Seriously, Danny. I'm on the next plane. You are still my best friend. I have the scar on my abdomen to prove it."

More silence. Then, "Thanks Austin. That means a lot."

"I will text you my flight info. I'm here. Whatever you need."

"Mom?"

"I know. You don't have to say anything. Just tell me when to pick you up at the airport."

I could always count on my mom, even though I knew she had every right to give me a hard time. Or not pick up the phone. I hadn't been the most dedicated son recently.

"Can I stay with you?"

"No, I rented out your room as promised."

"Oh. Well in that case..."

"Sweetheart, I'm kidding. You don't even have to ask me."

"I'm sorry. My head isn't in the right space right now."

"I know Mr. Rockwell was special to you. He always considered you a second son and I felt grateful for that. I did my best as your mom, but sometimes I know you needed a man's perspective."

A lump formed in my throat and I couldn't speak.

"Just text me your flight details, Love Bug. I will pick you up. Everything will be okay."

Even though I knew it wasn't.

It was the next phone call that I really didn't want to make.

"Venus. It's Austin."

"I know. What can I do for you?" All business as usual.

"I realize this timing is not ideal but I need another week off work."

"Why is that?"

"I've had a death in my family. Another one. My best friend's dad died unexpectedly. He was a father figure to me."

A pause. "I acknowledge that you are upset right now. So am I, but for vastly different reasons. I was planning on having this conversation with you on Monday but we will have it now instead. I know you've had a rough go of things recently. Your focus has not been on your work, and the quality of your creative output has suffered significantly. If that does not improve rapidly then I will have no choice but to let you go. Is this clear?"

"Yes. Crystal. I realize my personal life has taken a toll on the rest of my life as well. I appreciate you giving me this last chance."

"You have two weeks to return to work, Austin. I hope for your sake you can pull yourself together by then."

A military funeral is not like a regular funeral. Even in death there are procedures and protocols that must be followed. There's no room for outward display of emotion in this matter. I'd never seen Danny in his pristine dress whites. He displayed three medals on his left chest, two ribbons on his right, and a black armband on his right bicep. He sat stiff and stoic next to his mom and two sisters in the front row.

It must have been difficult to hold his outward composure; he and his dad were close. They both loved Star Wars, the Miami Dolphins (despite living in Chiefs country), and beating each other at chess. They went fishing often when Danny was still at home, and they let me tag along from time to time. Mr. Rockwell had passed his sense of humor on to Danny, and they loved nothing more than getting Danny's sisters riled up with their teasing.

The gunfire towards the end of the service startled me. The soldiers removed the flag from the casket, folded it, and presented it to Mrs. Rockwell. It's a very moving gesture. That lonely Taps call almost did me in, and I bit my tongue to keep myself in check. If Danny wasn't allowed to cry then neither was I.

Danny's dad would have been proud.

I sat on the tractor, mowing the back five acres for my mom. My earbuds had died after finishing the front yard, leaving me with my own wandering thoughts. Mom gave me some tough love last night and her words lingered in my head.

She knew the moment she saw me at the airport that I wasn't well. I couldn't hide from her. Cheyenne leaving me still hurt in ways I never imagined. But I knew she wasn't coming back.

"I'm so sorry about Cheyenne. I liked her a lot. Why did she leave?"

"I don't know."

"Yes, you do. Don't you lie to me. You're drinking again, aren't you? Oh, Austin." She shook her head. "I have something I need to show you. I'll be right back."

When she returned, she laid a small metallic coin on the table. It had the number 30 in the middle with words surrounding it. She pushed it over in my direction.

"Do you know what this is?"

"It doesn't belong to me."

"I know that. It belonged to your grandfather."

"Pop was an alcoholic? No way. I don't believe you."

She sighed. "You don't have to believe me Austin, but it's true nonetheless."

I attempted to wrap my head around this news. "Would you care to elaborate?"

She locked her eyes with mine. "It was a long time ago. By the time you were born he had been sober for almost twenty years. When he died, I didn't think it was important to tell you. It was mostly a part of his past after so much time had passed. I'm telling you now because I know how much you've been struggling. It was a struggle for your pop as well. But this little coin is evidence that you can overcome this disease. And it is a disease."

I reached out and picked up the coin, holding it in my hand, inspecting it on both sides. I never knew my grandfather had the same issue I was having myself. It made me wish that I could talk with him about it.

She continued. "It's a choice you have to make every day, sometimes one hour at a time. The good news is that you have fought and won that battle many days already. That means it's possible for you to win again. And keep on winning.

"I'm not saying it's easy. My dad didn't talk about it much, but I know he had moments where he battled with himself. There's so much you'll miss out on if you choose this self-destructive path."

I glanced up at her but went back to focusing on the coin. "Can I keep it?"

She put her hand over mine. "Absolutely. One day you'll get one of your own."

I'd been sober since Danny called about his dad. I knew he needed me to be present for him in a way I couldn't when I was wasted. But Mom made me realize that I needed to be that present for myself as well. If I chose to drown my sorrow and feelings then I would miss out on many things. Important things. It was time to wake up and move on. *Cowboy up, Austin.*

Forty-Seven
Austin - Aligning the Stars

I spent my two weeks of extended hiatus in Kansas City. My mom couldn't keep the farm maintained by herself, but I didn't want to suggest a retirement community. Wendy wouldn't have agreed to that. Instead, I hired a lawn care company to mow and a handyman who would take care of minor upkeep projects weekly. It was the least I could do for my momma.

I didn't want Miss Cherry sitting in the extended parking lot at the airport, so I'd taken an Uber. When I arrived home, the garage door was open and Dale's car sat in the driveway. I dropped my suitcase in my room and started upstairs but stopped as I heard the conversation in the kitchen.

Avery said, "I'm so happy for her. Any time I talk to her it's 'Vinnie this' and 'Vinnie that.'"

Dale replied, "I know. And I completely understand about not being invited to the wedding. The size of his extended family alone barely caps at a hundred. And she's never been one for holding court in the spotlight."

"Does Austin know about this?"

"I don't think so. I don't want to be the one to have to tell him, do you?"

That was my cue. I reached the top of the stairs and headed for the kitchen. "Tell me what?"

Avery and Dale gaped at me with their mouths open.

"You two look like a couple of kids who got caught with their hands in the candy jar." I chuckled. "What do you know? I'm going to find out anyway, so you might as well tell me now."

Avery looked down at the counter. Dale inspected the ceiling. *Then I knew. Sydney.* "Sydney's getting married." I stared at them, unflinching.

Dale sighed. "Yes. We didn't want to be the ones to tell you. For obvious reasons."

"When?" I waited.

Avery sucked his lips inside his mouth.

"When?" I repeated with more force.

"Saturday," Dale confessed.

It's already Thursday. "One of you is driving me back to the airport. Now."

I missed the turn the first time and had to turn around. I crept up the driveway with my heart in my chest. *Cowboy up.* I didn't care about Venus's ultimatum. I needed to do this or I would lose her forever. As I crested the hill, I saw Sydney's old pickup sitting next to two minivans. The gigantic white tent in the backyard caught my attention.

I strode to the door with my stomach churning. Swallowing hard, I pressed the doorbell. Samson woofed from somewhere in the house. Footsteps approached and the door swung open.

She had her head turned, talking to someone behind her. "It's probably another delivery I've forgotten about. My UPS man has been getting a workout these past few weeks." She turned towards me and stopped. Her mouth hung open like she was about to say something, but no words came out. Her balance faltered and she caught herself against the doorjamb to stop herself.

"Austin, what are you doing here?" She stepped onto the porch and shut the door behind her.

"I came for you. I love you. I need you. My life is not the same without you." I got down on one knee. "I'm willing to beg if I have to."

She stared at me, not speaking. Standing barefoot in cutoff jeans and a stained tank top, she was the most beautiful creature. I forgot how gorgeous she was, even without any makeup. "Get up, for crying out loud. You couldn't have worse timing. Stay here. I'll be right back."

I waited. Her little bungalow sat in the most perfect spot at the crest of the hill. A creek ran off to one side, and the forest surrounding them gave her complete privacy. Footsteps approached and I turned around. She came out of the house wearing sunglasses and sandals, holding her purse and keys in her hand.

"Walk." She gestured towards the cars. I followed her down the steps. "There is a coffee shop about five minutes from here. We can talk there." She hopped into her old trusty pickup and backed down the driveway like a boss. She showed off, but it was impressive. She waited at the end of the driveway while I made my three-point turnaround to follow her.

The bass pulsed out of her speakers and I noticed her in her rearview working her jaw on some fast lyrics. I couldn't read her lips, but whatever it was, I'm certain it wasn't a love song. I found a parking spot but waited a beat before following her into the café. She sat in the last booth, facing away from the rest of the patrons. I slid in across from her. She stared at me, lips pursed in a thin line, hands clasped together on the table.

"Okay, I'll go first," I said. "Did you know you're not easy to find?"

"That's strange. My cell number has been the same since college. Venus would have told you where I was. I never asked her to keep it a secret." She spit her words in my direction. "I don't plan on making this," she gestured her hand in the air, "easy on you. Try again."

"You left without saying goodbye," I countered. "But I'm not here looking for a fight. God knows I don't want to fight with you."

"That makes two of us."

A waitress paused in front of our booth, snapping her gum. "What can I get you?" she deadpanned.

"Black coffee, please. The darker the roast, the better."

"I'll have a mocha iced coffee. Four creamers," Sydney said. The waitress departed.

"I meant what I said. I came for you. I love you. I need you." I reached out and touched her hand, and she pulled away, crossing her arms. "I don't know where to begin."

"I do. I'm getting married tomorrow." She waited for a reaction.

I saw the tent in the backyard. She wasn't bluffing. I was the last batter in the bottom of the ninth inning. There are only two possible outcomes: you win the game or lose it for the whole team. I raised my gaze to meet hers. "Then I still have a chance."

"I don't think you understand. I'm. Getting. Married. Tomorrow."

"Do you love him?"

"You gave up the right to ask me that question a long time ago."

"But if you don't love him, then you shouldn't marry him." I tried to read her face, but it was stuck in neutral. The waitress set our drinks on the table and disappeared.

"And who should I marry instead? You?"

"Yes." I raised my mug and took a sip of coffee without breaking our stare.

"You can't be serious, Austin. Where are the hidden cameras?" She looked around melodramatically. I remained quiet, waiting for her to process my proposal. Her face changed into a question as she grasped the sincerity of my words. "You are serious, aren't you?"

"I wouldn't have come here if I wasn't," I replied. "I've cleaned up my act and I'm sober. (*Two weeks but who's counting?*) You're the only person left on my 'Make Amends' list, but it's taken me a long time to get up the nerve to do it."

"I'm glad you got the help you needed, Austin."

"I screwed up a lot of things, but you're the one I hurt the most. And I can't forgive myself."

She reached across the table and held my hand. "I've had a lot of time to think about what I would say to you if I ever saw you again. I want you to listen to me. Can you do that?" She waited.

"I think so," I replied.

"I forgive you. We were both young and naïve, and neither one of us was prepared for what happened to us. You hurt me, but I know I hurt you, too. I should have stayed and tried to help you, but I lost myself in the process. I couldn't watch you self-destruct anymore.

"And I couldn't take the industry. You always wanted this; I went along for the ride because everyone told me it was a once in a lifetime opportunity. It was an amazing experience, but it's not me. I hate all the schmoozing and game-playing; I want to be someone I recognize when I look in the mirror. When I summoned the courage to leave, I couldn't tell you because you would've turned on the charm and made me change my mind. I needed to find myself again.

"I spent some time on the road with Samson. I reconnected with a friend from elementary school, and tomorrow I'm marrying her husband's brother. Their whole family embraced me and the boys with open arms. I'm happier now than I've been in a long time, and in some ways, you're responsible. If things had gone differently, I never would have met Vincent."

She paused for a moment, but she wasn't finished. "As for your proposal, I am flattered. I've always loved you, and there was a time when I would have said yes. But I don't want to be that girl. I don't want to wonder where you are or spend my time looking over my shoulder. I deserve to have someone who wants me and puts me first. You may think you want me, but I will never be sure if you're sincere. I want to believe you've changed, but I can't take that risk for my own heart. I must be strong for myself. And for AJ and Andre. I've looked out for you so many times, but this time it's my turn. My life is different now, and I don't want to go backward. I hope you can understand."

"Then say yes," I implored. My hand grasped hers tighter and I gazed at her, memorizing her in this moment. "You said in your letter 'if our stars align again down the road, I will welcome that.' I called in a favor."

"I can't. I won't. You don't know what you're asking me to do." She let go of my hand.

"Don't you think I can change?" I searched her face. "I have, and that's why I'm here. I realize what a schmuck I've been all along, not seeing the one person who loved me despite all my shortcomings. That's you. I can't believe I didn't see what was right in front of my face. I've become the cliché in all those country songs. I hope it's not too late for me to make it right with you."

"You have. It took a lot of guts to come and find me. But I can't go with you. I have met the most amazing man, and I will not hurt him for your sake. I did that to Marcus and I will not do that again. Vincent loves me. He treats me like a queen and makes me feel alive in a way I have never been. He would do anything for me, and he puts me and the boys first in his priorities. I want and deserve to spend the rest of my life being taken care of like that. With Vincent I'm certain my 'happily ever after' has a chance at coming true."

"I came here for you and I'm not leaving without you."

After what seemed like an eternity, I heard her voice respond in a whisper. "You have to let me go." Tears streamed down her face but she didn't wipe them away. "I can't go back, Austin. I don't want that life anymore. I never wanted it in the first place but I did it for you. Because I loved you. If you love me like you say you do, you have to let me go."

"I love you, Sydney. I don't want to lose you."

She reached out and put her hand on my chest. "You have me here, and that's all you need. The rest you can do on your own." She stood up to leave but kissed me on the cheek first. "I forgive you. I love you."

She walked out of the coffee shop. I sat there, holding my coffee mug, trying to understand how my plan went awry. How could she tell me she loved me if she wouldn't go with me? It didn't make any sense. Maybe I should have included AJ in my plea, but that would've been disingenuous. I left a generous tip for the waitress and got back in my rental car.

Forty-Eight
Vinnie - Sydney's Confession

Standing with champagne in my hand, I listened to my dad and Sydney's dad swap military stories. They both were in the Military Police at the beginning of their Army careers, and they laughed at some of the funniest times they pulled people over. My dad never talked to any of us kids about his time in Vietnam, so it was interesting to learn about his experiences.

Sydney stood across the room chatting with two of my aunts. Her beauty took my breath away. It didn't matter if she was wearing a fancy dress or cut-off sweatpants and a tank top with a messy ponytail. I couldn't believe how lucky I was to have this amazing woman spend the rest of my life with me. She turned and caught me staring at her. She winked and continued talking to them. I could not wait to marry her tomorrow.

A few minutes later she tapped me on the elbow and whispered in my ear. "We need to chat before you leave." I nodded.

Later on, we took a short detour around the side of Micky's house and sat on some lawn chairs. Nighttime nature sounds peppered the chilly air. I glanced up at the stars in the darkened sky. This evening had been perfect. "You had something on your mind, buttercup?"

She sat forward on a chair with her elbows on her knees. "Something happened earlier today," she began. "It was unexpected and I handled it, but I want to share it with you for full disclosure. I don't want to have secrets from you."

"What happened?"

"Austin came to see me."

"You're writing partner Austin, correct?"

"Yes, that's the only Austin I know."

"What did he want? Let me guess, he wants you back." I didn't like the way this conversation was going. Not at all. Not today of all days. My anger rose in my chest. That bozo had a lot of nerve showing up here.

"Yes, he came to persuade me to go with him."

"I'm a pretty understanding guy, Sydney, but this is a red flag for me. Do you still want to get married?" I needed to ask the question, but I wasn't sure I was going to like the answer.

"Of course, I want to marry you. I love you. I want to spend the rest of my life with you. I'm telling you this so you're aware of what happened. My life is here, my love is here. There's nowhere else I'd rather be. You know this, right?"

"Up until about a minute ago, but sometimes things don't work out the way you planned. I love you and I want to marry you. I'm not sure how Austin fits into this equation."

"He doesn't. I told him no. I'm guessing he flew back to L.A. or wherever he came from. I agree, his timing couldn't be more inconvenient. I made it clear that you are the person I love and want to be with. Austin is a part of my past. Yes, I love him and I always will. You are my future and the person I want to spend my life with. I don't know what else I can say to make you feel better. It's the honest truth. It's the best I can do."

My mind swirled with thoughts of murdering him. "I'm not sure what to say. I appreciate you telling me. Having open lines of communication is a cornerstone for any lasting relationship. I'm allowed to have feelings about this situation. And they're not good feelings."

"I didn't ask him to come here, Vincent. He did that all by himself. I had no idea he still had feelings for me. We haven't spoken since I left Los Angeles years ago, except when I told him about AJ. Never in a million years would I have imagined this scenario. We talked and I explained my position to him. What else can I do?"

I didn't comprehend what to do or say next. I spent so much time waiting for Sydney and taking things at her pace. To have that wiped away in one fell swoop was more than I could bear. "There's nothing else for you to do. It's difficult to wrap my head around it. I hope he's not here to cause a dramatic scene tomorrow. I'm a nice guy, Sydney, but you can only push me so far."

She exhaled. "I can't put money on it either way. As well as you think you know someone, they can still surprise you."

I stood up. I needed to have some time by myself. "I'm going to go back to the party to say good night to my parents. I will see you tomorrow."

Sydney stood and wrapped her arms around me. "I love you." Our lips met and I savored the moment. Her touch made me melt and I wanted to run off and elope right then. My concerns about Austin lingered, but I knew Sydney loved me and wouldn't desert me. At least that's what my gut told me. As I walked away, I looked over my shoulder. She stood there, watching me. Tomorrow couldn't come soon enough.

Forty-Nine

Sydney - Vows

Micky picked up my dress from her mother's house, where it had been kept since my final fitting. It seemed like the best place to keep it when we returned from NYC. If I had brought it home, the temptation to show Vinnie would have been too hard to resist.

"Sydney?" Brooke beckoned. "We need to dress for pictures. Get your butt out of the car."

Brooke is the one person who can bring me back down to earth faster than the speed of light. I complied as slowly as possible, moving my arm towards the door handle at sloth speed, just to tweak her in the way only a little sister can. I knew it was working by the twisted grimace on her face.

"I realize you're the bride, but could you move it, please?"

"I doubt they'll start without me." I smirked at her, which caused her to sigh with exasperation.

"Okay, Sydney. I'm going to try to forget you're so annoying right now."

The stylist had waved her magic wand and my unruly curls lay in perfect movie star waves. I didn't want a veil, but I still wanted to sparkle. When Abby and I were at Kleinfeld's, Randy selected this gorgeous hair accessory for me: a headband of pearls and rhinestones. It was too expensive to justify, and I walked away. Two weeks later, I got a package in the mail from Abby: the headband.

I closed the door to my bedroom and touched my dress, hanging on the front of my closet. Abby and I love to find a bargain, so we focused on the sale rack when we got to Kleinfeld's. We told our consultant, Diane, the bigger the discount, the better we liked it. Vinnie gave me his credit card but not a limit. I didn't need it, but I didn't want to hurt his feelings.

Abby's eyes grew and her mouth dropped open. "You could wear your own one of a kind Pnina Tourney or Randy Fennolli dress!"

"No problem, if I want my first credit card purchase to make my new husband sick to his stomach. Abby, I'm only wearing this dress for one day. When I watch their show and the brides spend ten thousand dollars or more on a dress, I question their sanity."

"Me too. I understand."

"There are so many expenses for a wedding. Why inflate the budget for one piece of clothing? I'm trying to keep the cost of this dress under three thousand. And that's before alterations."

"I see your point, but I love some of Randy's designs."

We ended up finding a bargain, which thrilled me! Diane found the perfect dress, soft and flowy. Not at all like my body-hugging yellow dress, which I only half joked about wearing. The cream-colored bodice had an overlay of intricate lace with little pale pink flowers all over it with an illusion neckline. At the waist, a band of rhinestones and pearls shimmered and coordinated with my headband. The applique flowers trickled down into my skirt, which had some volume but wasn't a full-blown ballgown. The material shimmered and sparkled like it was filled with magic. The original price tag read four thousand, but since it was discontinued, they marked it down to eighteen hundred. I flew home with it on the empty seat next to me.

We decided to move the wedding location to our new home. The giant tent we rented *in case it rains* took up most of the fenced-in yard. Members of our families milled around the property. On our invitations, we'd requested all guests wear black cocktail attire. My mother was the only nonconformist, wearing a navy-blue sequined gown.

From the kitchen window, I viewed a festive human "ant party" of little black figures swarming around the ceremony site down in front of the creek. Right next to it sat a gigantic oak tree at least a hundred years old. A rope swing dangled from a branch over the creek and a tire swing waited for riders on another branch. It was as if the tree knew where the deep-water hole sat and planted itself in the spot on purpose.

Sofia had worked with Micky to design a flower arch to complement the tree. The beautification of our land and transformation into a celebration station left me in awe. We didn't want more than one hundred guests. With the size of both our families, the challenge appeared daunting, but we managed.

Once dressed, I checked myself in the mirror. *Not too shabby, if I do say so myself.* We decided to do a "first look" photo shoot before the ceremony to have a special moment together. I picked up the front of my skirt and Micky held my short train to escort me down the back steps without tripping.

Micky waved at Tony, and he and Thomas walked Vinnie down to the edge of the creek with the photographer. As I made my way down to join them, I watched him getting his picture taken while approaching them. I stopped a few feet away and waited for the photographer to finish.

She gave Vinnie instructions. "Don't move, which also means don't turn around. I'm going to take a few photos of you together without seeing Sydney. Then we will do the reveal."

"Sydney, come forward and stand here, one step behind Vinnie. Put your hand on his shoulder. Excellent." She gave multiple directions as she kept clicking off shots. She placed us back-to-back and had us hold hands.

"Now, when I count to three, I want you both to turn towards each other. Ready?"

"Of course, I'm ready!" Vinnie howled. "Let's go!"

"One! Two! Three!"

When I turned towards Vinnie, I was speechless. I had seen him in suits plenty of times, but this was next level handsome. He got a very close shave this morning. His skin glowed from the facial products they used on him, and his unruly eyebrows had somehow been tamed.

"You okay, sweetie?"

His eyes grew misty and he pulled back to take in my ensemble. "My god, Sydney. I am the luckiest man on earth today." He turned to Tony. "Eat your heart out, brother."

They both laughed. "You deserve it," Tony said. He clapped him on his shoulder.

Micky checked her phone. "Sydney, we need to take you back into the house before more guests start arriving." She picked up the back of my dress.

Vinnie kissed me on the cheek. "You are so beautiful. I'll wait for you down by the creek."

We stood in front of the officiant and all our family and friends. Brooke and Abby stood to my left, and Tony and Tommy stood next to Vinnie on the right. Samson, wearing a bow tie and doggy cuff links, sat in front of Tony.

The weather cooperated for our outdoor ceremony plans—warm sunshine, with a few clouds and a light breeze. I appreciated not having a long veil blowing around my face. The scent from the flowers in our arch wafted over us. I gazed back towards our guests, and something caught my eye on the edge of the house. A shadowed figure stood there, but when I blinked, they were gone.

The officiant talked about love being a verb. It's not passive. It demands action and constant attention. Vinnie did all that for me. He constantly checked in with me to make sure the boys and I had everything we needed. In this moment, I felt like I was the lucky one by a long shot.

"Sydney and Vinnie have written their own vows. Vinnie, would you like to go first?" He handed Vinnie a notecard with some writing on it. He held the paper at his side and stared into my eyes.

"I never thought a woman could surprise me. The more women I dated, the more they all seemed the same. That's until I met you. You surprise me every day with the little things you do and say. Your kindness to strangers, the loving way you parent your boys. I'm so glad I will spend the rest of my life with you, this amazing creature you are. I promise to care for your boys as if they were my own. They mean the world to me and that's what I intend to give them in return. Thank you for making me the luckiest man alive and agreeing to be my partner in life and in love. I love you so much."

It touched my heart to hear those words, and he included my boys in his commitment. I didn't have time to respond or process it before the officiant handed me my notecard.

"When I met you, my heart was in pieces and I didn't know if I would ever want to love someone again. We didn't get off on the right foot but the more time I spent with you, the more I liked you. Your devotion to your family. The way you help wherever you can even if it's not your responsibility. The way you love Ainsley and Zoey melted my heart. For the first time, I felt like you might be the someone I could love that deeply. You have been patient with me and let me make my own decisions about you and your intentions. I'm so thankful you let me come to you on my own terms. There's nothing I want more in this life than to share it with you. I love you so much."

Vinnie turned towards our guests. "Sis, can you bring the boys up here?"

Sophia and Bianca each carried one boy on their hips. They boys wore miniature tuxedos and looked so adorable.

"Stay here, ladies. We're going to give them back in a minute." He held Andre in one arm and AJ in the other.

"Not all families come together in a typical fashion," he told our family and friends. "It doesn't mean they are any less family because of where they came from. Sydney and I designed a piece of jewelry to present to all members of the Allegro family at the reception. All future members of the Allegro family will also receive one.

"When you blend families, sometimes a new tradition helps bridge the gap between the new and the old. Everyone deserves to be loved and this medallion is a symbol of that belief." I put a necklace on each of my babies as he continued. "I say to you, AJ and Andre, welcome to the Allegro family. We're loud, we're nutty, and we take care of each other no matter what."

Some folks burst out in "Hear, hear!" and soft claps filled the air. Vinnie kissed the boys on both cheeks and handed them back to their aunties.

"Now, Mr. Preacher Man, I think this smoking hot woman and I have one last order of business."

The preacher flustered for a moment but recovered. "Oh yes! The rings!"

We exchanged rings and sealed our vows with a kiss. Then we jogged down the aisle holding hands and laughing, our family and friends all around us.

Journal Entry

I decided to steal a few minutes between wedding and reception to capture my joy in this journal. I've filled it with so many emotions, about so many events, but today is special beyond compare.

I'm now Mrs. Sydney Allegro. I am married to Vincent Allegro, and with AJ and Andre, we are a family within a bigger family. I could not be happier.

I'm still going to use my family name Campbell for professional purposes, but legally I will change my last name.

I wasn't sure I would ever find love in this lifetime. Not a love like this. One where I gained an entire family full of love and support. Where my boys are accepted. And I'm already part of the family. AJ and Andre, too. Micky is thrilled we're sisters-in-law, and I couldn't agree more. It's perfect and I'm bursting with happiness.

The medallion Vinnie and I designed incorporates all the letters in the name Allegro. I discovered the concept in an ad on one of my social media feeds, and we decided it was perfect. It can be worn as a necklace or a bracelet, depending on where the chain slides through the medallion.

I worried about Austin showing up during the ceremony and ruining things. Thankfully, he didn't. I was probably being paranoid, but I still can't believe he had the audacity to show up like he did. There may have been a time for us at one point, but not anymore. I love Vinnie with all my heart and I will not hurt him.

My favorite part of the reception happened when we lit up the fire pit and had a rematch of our marshmallow contest from the first time we met. I think Vinnie let me win this one.

Tomorrow, we leave for our honeymoon. I'm looking forward to some relaxation after these jam-packed weeks of wedding preparations. My husband (I need to get used to that term!) is so hot and I can't wait to be naked in paradise with him.

Fifty
Austin - Uninvited Guest
(explicit scene)

I turned into the driveway and crept towards the house. Two young men assisted with parking on the lawn. I rolled down my window and spoke to the closest one.

"I'm not staying long. Where can I keep this nearby for easy extraction?"

"Park next to the delivery trucks. That should make it easy to leave when you need to."

I pulled up next to a catering truck and got out of the car. If I timed myself right, the ceremony would have already started. I crept along the side of the house and peaked out into the backyard. Down the hill, a group of people were gathered, all dressed in black and sitting in rows of white wooden folding chairs.

A gigantic floral arch stood in front of the creek next to an enormous oak tree. Three people stood underneath the arch. The officiant, dressed in black, stood in the middle. A tall, dark and handsome man in a black tuxedo stood to his right. Vincent, I assumed. On the left was the most beautiful woman I'd ever known. Today was no exception. Her flowing, shimmering dress and the long waves in her hair took my breath away, even from this distance. Her happiness mattered most to me, despite the fact she loved someone else.

As I watched the ceremony, an old George Strait song popped into my head that my grandma used to play over and over on their stereo. A cowboy sees the woman he loves dancing with another man. He can tell by her face that she loves this new man and he wishes that she looked at him the same way.[12] I never understood the way he felt until this very moment, watching the woman I love most in this world give her whole heart to someone. And that someone wasn't me. As I stood there musing, she turned her gaze and I swore she saw me.

I ducked back around the corner and made a beeline towards my rental car. A voice I recognized stopped me.

"You must not want to keep your job that badly. Couldn't stay away, huh? I don't blame you. I might have done the same thing."

I turned on my heel. "Venus. Why aren't you down at the ceremony?" She took a drag on her cigarette and exhaled through her nose. Her black dress hugged every curve, highlighting her ample cleavage and showing off her bare back. I would have bent her over in a hot minute if she wasn't my boss.

"I came up to smoke. I keep trying to quit, but you can see how well that's going. Call me crazy, but I thought I noticed a shady character by the side of the house lurking like Beetlejuice in the cemetery. I came over to check it out."

"Good detective work, Nancy Drew," I deadpanned.

"Calm down. I'm not going to tell her. Vincent and his brothers were ready to rumble if you showed up today."

"I'll bet. I just wanted to see her in her dress. I'm leaving now."

"Where are you going? Want some company?"

I squinted at her. "Shouldn't you stay here for the festivities?"

"With both of their extended families here, I doubt she'll miss me for a little while. Let's go for a drive."

She hopped in the passenger side of the rental car and buckled her seat belt. She patted the driver's seat. "Are you coming?"

I opened the door and got behind the wheel. We made our way down the driveway and out onto the main road. "Where are we going?"

She put her hand on my upper thigh. "Some place private." My brain hit tilt. *Is she attempting to seduce me?* That's what it looked like from my vantage point. She massaged my thigh, throwing any doubts about her intentions out the window.

"I'm not familiar with this area." I gulped. "Is there a park nearby? Or do you want to go back to my hotel room?" This turn of events was not on my radar, leaving me flustered and confused.

"I don't think I can wait. Pull over on a side street, or an empty parking lot."

I swung into a school parking lot and drove around the side so the car couldn't be seen from the road. "Let me make sure I understand what's happening here. You want me to have sex with you, correct?"

"Yes. That is my intention."

"Why now? I mean, I'm willing, but the timing is bizarre."

She looked at me. "I'm not in love with you, but I am in lust with you. I'm in the mood for a physical release and I thought you might be, too. It doesn't have to be complicated unless you make it that way."

She got out of the car and stood in front of it with her legs spread apart. Placing both hands on the hood, she bent over it, giving me visions of hard rock music videos with women crawling on top of cars. She licked her lips at me through the windshield as I sat in the driver's seat. "Come get me."

I hustled around the car and pressed my hard cock, straining against my jeans, into her backside. Sex out in the open is risky and titillating at the same time. *What if someone pulls into the parking lot?* She arched her back and wrapped her arms backward around my neck. "I only have one rule: no kissing." She pushed her juicy cheeks into my crotch, fueling my desire.

"Put your hands back on the hood," I commanded. I pushed her tight skirt up to reveal bare cheeks. Gawd, it turned me on when a woman wasn't wearing any panties. She was expecting to get some action, and I planned to deliver. I knelt behind her and spread her legs further apart. Using my tongue, I licked and flicked around her most sensitive parts. I swallowed her warm juices as I pleasured her. She moaned, pushing her ass towards me, wanting more. I worked her over until I was certain she was on the brink.

I stood, dropped my pants around my ankles and positioned myself to enter her. Then it hit me – fuck! "I know this isn't great timing, but do we need to use protection?"

"I'm fixed," she responded. "Take it away, stud."

I grabbed her hips and thrust my cock all the way into her soft, wet pussy. She cried out. "Yes! That's it! More!"

I withdrew as she mewed in ecstasy. I thrust harder this time, and she got louder. "Fill me up! Yes! Your dick is so hard. I love it!"

"You want some more?" I slapped her ass cheek.

"Yes! More! Harder!" I kept pulling back, then thrusting as fast and hard as I could. "Now faster! Fuck me, stud."

I began rocking back and forth. "I'm close. Are you?"

She gasped. "Yes! Bring me home, stud!" I moaned as my juices pumped into her. She screamed and convulsed with ecstasy. We remained melded together for a moment before I pulled out.

She pushed her skirt back down and smoothed it along her hips. She reached up and kissed me on the cheek. "I knew you wouldn't disappoint." She walked around and got back into the car.

I started the engine and turned toward her. I only had one question.

She beat me to it. "This never happened."

Fifty-One
Vinnie—Honeymoon Suite
(explicit scene)

We flew from Indianapolis to Montego Bay International Airport. A black SUV picked us up and whisked us to the Excellence Resort and Spa. I wanted this to be a memorable experience for both of us, and I splurged on getting a junior suite. We had sparkling wine and fresh fruit waiting for us when we arrived. The porter took our suitcases to the walk-in closet in the bedroom. He pointed out a few things about the suite to acclimate us to this luxurious tropical environment.

Sydney gushed, "I can't believe you did this! I would have been happy with the Hilton and an outdoor pool. Seriously."

I wrapped her in my arms. "Only the best. It is our honeymoon, after all."

"What should we do first? Go for a swim in our private pool?"

"I'm up for that if you are. Let me get my suit."

She laughed as she pulled her sundress over her head. Her pink lacy bra and panties turned me on and I felt myself getting hard at the sight of her. She reached behind her and unhooked her bra, then ran out the door and made a cannonball in the pool.

"Who needs a suit? I've seen you naked, Stud. The water feels fantastic. Come on in!" She tossed her panties onto the deck in an invitation I could not refuse. I hustled out of my clothes and followed her lead with my own cannonball.

"That's more like it!" she said as I surfaced. "This place really is paradise. I may not want to go home." She dove under the water and swam to the far end before coming up for air.

"I didn't know you could hold your breath that long. That's impressive."

She waved me off with her hand. "I wanted to be a mermaid when I grew up. Life had other plans. Good ones, but not underwater, unfortunately."

"I'm certain we wouldn't have met if you'd taken the mermaid route. I'm more of a cabin in the woods kind of guy. Hunting, fishing, fire pits. Being out in nature recharges me and brings me peace."

"I'm game for that kind of adventure, as long as we have a bathroom with plumbing."

I nodded. "Fair enough. I'm getting hungry. How about I bring out that delicious-looking fruit plate I saw on the coffee table?"

"That sounds good. Let me get it." She stepped out of the pool and I watched her walk away. Even dripping wet, she made me ache between my legs. Her ample ass looked so juicy and her thighs rubbed together in a dance, back and forth. I wanted to lick her from head to toe. She had to know what she was doing to me. Good lord, she was going to kill me with that sensuality.

She disappeared for a moment and came back out carrying the plate of fruit. I took it from her and set it on the patio where we could reach it. She took some pineapple and sat on the steps of the pool to eat it. I took a slice of mango. I watched as she licked her fingers, my desire growing. She caught me looking and slowed down to tease me, putting one finger at a time into her mouth and then slowly pulling it back out.

"Do you like that?" she asked me.

I gulped and nodded. "Yes. Very much. Do it again."

She picked up a slice of watermelon and licked the rind. "Do you want to taste my fruit? I have a peach, wet and slippery, just for you." She reached between her legs and started rubbing her lips. My brain shut off as the blood rushed south and my hormones took over completely. I came towards her and threw her over my shoulder before exiting the pool. I dropped her face up onto one of the gigantic sun loungers and leaned over her, my arms balancing on the cushion behind her head, and one knee in between her legs.

"I want your peach." I growled low in her ear. "You belong to me." I reached down in between her legs and covered her wetness with my hand. "I'm the only one who gets to eat this peach." I leaned in and kissed her forcefully. Her body responded by arching towards my touch. Her tongue twisted with mine as the heat grew between us. I could have taken us to the bedroom, but I didn't care. I bent down and took her lips in my mouth. She moaned with pleasure and her hips wriggled with desire.

"Oh God, Vinnie! Yes!" she cried out. "More! Fill me up!" Ignoring her demand, I continued tasting her sweetness.

She moaned and yelped. "Vinnie. I want you. Inside me. Now." She slapped my shoulder to reinforce her message.

I came up for air and kissed her breasts on my way up to her mouth. I reached down and guided my cock into her warm, wet peach. I groaned, the feeling of her sweetness overwhelming me. Pushing in and out of her, our breathing became faster. She grasped my waist and looked at me.

"Keep your eyes open. I want to see your face when you come. Harder, baby. You're not going to hurt me."

I increased the intensity of my strokes and listened as her sounds became more urgent. She shook with her release but held my gaze. I followed right after her, and we stared at each other, caught up in the ecstasy of the moment. I lay down next to Sydney and wrapped her in my arms. "Mrs. Allegro," I whispered in her ear.

"Mr. Allegro," she replied. And we drifted off to sleep, still naked, listening to the ocean.

I would like to say that we took advantage of all the amenities at the resort, but that would not be accurate. We got up late each morning, had a leisurely breakfast on the patio, and decided what to do with our day. Sydney wanted to go snorkeling, and we had an amazing time watching all the fish in their natural habitat. We took a siesta in the late afternoons. Sometimes we had sex then, and sometimes we didn't.

After our nap, we cleaned up and went to dinner. There were ten restaurants to choose from, and we tried out most of them at least once. Sydney had determined that she would try the local cuisine. She selected something different at every place we ate, except for the Lobster House.

After dinner, we sat outside with a cocktail, watching people go by and having our own conversation. I learned a lot about Sydney this week, and I told her things that I hadn't revealed previously. When you have two little people around who need constant attention and supervision, stimulating conversation and personal revelations aren't on the top of the list.

I did get up the courage to talk to her one evening about an issue I had been thinking about since I proposed. "Can I ask you something? I've been thinking about it for a while and want to know where you stand."

"Of course. Ask me anything."

"We probably should have discussed this before we got married, but I'll be satisfied with whatever we decide together. I know you're on birth control right now, but I'm wondering if you see us having any babies together. I love the boys. But I want more than two children. I grew up in a large family and that's important to me."

She reached out and took my hand. "I'm glad you asked about that. It's not something I've thought about much. I'm so busy trying to get through one day at a time with AJ and Andre that I don't think past today or tomorrow. I'm open to growing our family when it's best for us. I think we should be married a little while first."

"How long is a little while? I'm just curious."

"I think a year is a good starting point. Leaving Micky's and moving in together is going to be a big change for the boys. For all of us, really. I want us to have time to gel before we add any more family members."

"That's a fair assessment. I'm glad I asked." I squeezed her hand to let her know that I meant it. "Do you want to go to one of the clubs and listen to some live music?"

She shook her head. "I want to go back to our room and make our own music."

I wasn't going to argue with that. "Lead the way, my bride."

Fifty-Two

Cheyenne – Formulating a Plan

Being back in Houston, around my family, helped my broken heart. My grandpa and I went horseback riding often, our special bonding time. We rode the trails together, not saying much, mostly listening to the birds and absorbing the peacefulness of the natural environment around us. He didn't understand my pain, but he didn't have to. His faithful support sustained me.

Kennedy and Sierra made sure I went shopping and took me on lunch dates. They didn't accept my excuses and would have drug me out in my pajamas—only to buy me new outfits. My mom kept her homemade snickerdoodles (my favorite) in the cookie jar. She doted on Flower and Socks, transforming half of the back deck into a catio for them. Socks thought he was in heaven and rarely came inside, except at dinner time for his wet food.

Despite the love and care surrounding me, I thought about Austin every day. I missed him. When I left, I intended to file for divorce, but I couldn't bring myself to hire a lawyer. He'd been sober for almost two years, but then gave up entirely when Melody died. I didn't blame him for seeking solace in the bottom of a bottle of Jack, but I couldn't watch him self-destruct when my world had crumbled with his.

A couple of months after I left, I received an unexpected phone call.

"Hello?"

"Hi Cheyenne. It's Zach. How are you?"

"I'm okay. Is Austin okay? Are you calling about him?"

"Austin is fine. He's been back at the restaurant for a month now and working on his sobriety faithfully. He goes to a lot of meetings, at least once a day. It must be difficult when there's a fully stocked bar at his fingertips here at the restaurant, but somehow he makes it one more day at a time."

"I'm happy for him. He deserves that." I paused. "So why are you calling, if it's not about Austin?"

"The restaurant is doing well. So well that we've been receiving interest from investors. They want to open several more locations to capitalize on our popularity and profits. David and I discussed it at length, but we won't make a move without you and Austin on board."

"That's fantastic news! I'm glad things are going so well. It's worth consideration. Can you give me more specifics?"

"We set up a meeting with them next week. Would you be able to fly up and meet them with us?"

I hesitated. "What did Austin say? Is he on board?"

Zach sighed. "No. He's not in favor of it. He's concerned about maintaining quality standards across the locations and doesn't think we have enough tenure under our belts to consider it."

"He has a valid point. But I think we need to hear them out regardless. When do you want me to be there?"

"Will next Friday give you enough time? I don't want to pressure you. I know life has been difficult."

He wasn't wrong. These past few months presented me with challenges I never could have imagined. Being able to focus on something outside my internal struggles would help me climb out of this eternal funk of sadness. At least I had to take a chance. For the restaurant. And maybe there was a second chance in it for Austin and me as well.

"I'm on board. Next Friday works for me. There's only one little problem."

"What's that?"

He had to ask, didn't he? "Who's going to break the news to Austin?"

Fifty-Three

Austin - The Next Phase

ACZ BBQ had only been open one year, and we were already talking about adding additional locations. I was skeptical. It mattered to me to keep everything homogenous between locations. We sat around a table in our private event room, having a meeting. Zach and David were here in person, Cheyenne conferenced via video. We'd met with investors last week. Their plan took all of my concerns into account, but I wasn't convinced. We hadn't had enough time yet to fully establish ourselves.

"I'm happy with the way things are right now. We have a steady stream of customers for dinner every night, and we're open for lunch four days a week. This is comfortable. I can keep my eyes on everything. Profits are up. Why mess with a good thing?" I had no intention of spreading myself too thin across multiple restaurants. Venus had officially fired me from the studio, but I knew it was more for show than anything. She hinted at a freelance deal like the one she'd given Sydney and I was considering it.

David replied, "You have reservations, but this type of expansion will be beneficial in the long run. We need to add a few investors in order to pay for this expansion. Trust me. You will thank me later."

"I agree with David," Zach interjected. "It's a challenge, but with the right people, we can manage. I say we go for it."

"What do you think, Cheyenne?" I hoped she would be the voice of reason and back me up on this.

"You can continue with the way things are right now, or you can take a leap and go for it. We have a customer base and potential to grow the business. I'm game for growing."

Damn! I was out-voted. "Can we table this and revisit it in six months? We don't even have a year's worth of hard data. How can we make such a risky move without more concrete evidence?"

David glanced at me. "Austin, everything in business is a risk. Based on the data we have, it's not a foolish consideration."

"I'm not saying it doesn't make sense. But why do we need to open three more locations at the same time? The staff I will need to hire makes my head swim." I hated interviewing candidates. Zach stepped up to the plate when we needed another member of the kitchen crew. Avery and Dale came in to help me hire competent servers. So far, except for one server who never showed up to work, we had a solid crew.

"We can stagger the openings to make it less overwhelming," David explained. "Cheyenne, would you be willing to come here for a few months to work with the designer? We need your expertise to make sure we keep the vibe consistent across the locations. They shouldn't be cookie cutter copies, but we want people to have a sense of familiarity regardless of which one they visit."

"I can do that. When do you need me?"

My brain went on tilt. I didn't want Cheyenne here. She'd stomped on my heart, leaving me like she did. And then I made this impulsive decision to go chasing after Sydney like I thought she would wait for me forever. *Boy, was I stupid.* My renewed commitment to sobriety was still so fresh, and I didn't trust myself to be around her for months while we worked on this expansion. I shook my head. Someone said my name and snapped me back to reality.

"Will that work for you, Austin?"

"What? Sure, not a problem." *What did I agree to?*

"Then it's settled. Cheyenne will stay with Austin while she is here to help. Thank you, Austin."

Oh, sweet Jesus. That was not in my plan. At all.

Avery and Dale acted surprised when I told them the news.

"No kidding? Should we move out to avoid the fireworks?" Avery quipped.

"Ha. Ha. You're hilarious. This was not in my game plan. Trust me." I grabbed a beer from the fridge, cracked open the pull tab, and took a long swig. Sobriety is overrated, especially under these circumstances.

"Are you two getting back together? I have to ask," Dale said.

"I hope that's not why she agreed to come here. She is in for a huge disappointment. I only let someone break my heart once."

"That's the spirit! When will she be arriving? What is the room situation?" Dale peppered me with questions.

"Two weeks. I will give her Sydney's room and stay in the basement. No one needs to move. I'm guessing she's bringing the cats, so keep your doors closed when you aren't here unless you want them to claim your pillow."

"We love Cheyenne and can't wait to see her. You have any other bombshells for us?" Avery joked.

I ran my hand through my hair. "Good lord, I hope not. I didn't realize what I was getting roped into at the time. There's not enough alcohol in the world." I took another swig.

Avery pried the beer can out of my hand. "Let's not go down the rabbit hole again." He poured the remaining elixir down the drain.

I didn't fight him. I pulled my keys out of my pocket. "I'm going to take Miss Cherry for a ride and find a meeting."

Fifty-Four
Cheyenne – Re-Igniting the Flame

Even as I agreed to help with the restaurant expansion, I understood Austin would be a problem for me. I still loved him, but I couldn't look at him after Melody died. The grief was too much to bear. He tried to help me, but his own heartache consumed him just as mine did.

Having the love and support of my family helped a lot. They let me wallow but gave me tough love when I needed it. It took months before I wanted to leave the house, let alone my darkened room. Flower and Socks cuddled with me in bed, steadfast in their companionship. I didn't comprehend how much I needed them. But Austin did. Maybe it was time to let him off the hook. Me too.

My original plan had me driving from Houston to L.A. in two days, driving twelve hours each day. That got amended after I spent two hours sitting still on the interstate outside of Pheonix on the second day. Between the heat and Socks crying incessantly when we stopped moving, I needed a break. The Hampton Inn provided a much-needed respite, including a swim in their outdoor pool. The next morning, I indulged in the breakfast buffet and filled up my travel mug with hot tea before hitting the last six hours. I love my Jeep, but it wasn't the most comfortable vehicle for long haul driving. By far.

The freeway traffic in L.A. pushed my arrival time back another hour. When I pulled up to the townhouse, the garage door hung open but Austin's red convertible was not inside. It was only three in the afternoon, so he was probably still working with the rest of the hive at the studio. I passed Avery's white Dodge Charger in the driveway as I made my way up to the front door. Knocking seemed strange, but I didn't want to surprise anyone by using the door in the basement.

I pushed open the door a foot and called into the house. "Hello! It's me, Cheyenne. Anyone home?"

As I stepped into the foyer, I heard a voice upstairs respond. "Be right down."

Quick footsteps padded across the hall and down the stairs. Avery enveloped me in a huge hug before I could put the cat carrier on the floor.

"Cheyenne! I'm so happy you're home!" He pulled back and looked me over. "You are way too skinny, girl! You look like you need a few decent meals." He turned to the side and stuck out his stomach. "Your husband's cooking is ruining my girlish figure. I have to suck it in when I go for auditions."

I laughed at his silliness. "Give me a break. You spend more time at the gym than any straight man. Or gay man. Are you home alone?"

He slapped his hands to his cheeks and opened his mouth to imitate the kid from *Home Alone*. "Yes, at the moment."

"Where's Dale? His car wasn't in the driveway."

"He's at his boyfriend's. You may glimpse him sporadically, at least until they break up. Again. They are both such drama queens. I lost count of how many times he's come home swearing off men. Two days later they're back together. If you're looking for a good soap opera, look no further."

I reached out and hugged him again. "I've really missed you. I didn't realize how much until this moment."

He squeezed me and didn't let go. "I think about you all the time. But I didn't want to intrude. Both of you have been struggling. It's difficult when I want to help but don't know how."

I nodded into his chest. "It's okay. I'm getting better. How is Austin?"

He took my hand and led me to sit down on the couch with him. "Honey, I'm not going to lie. It's been rough living with him. After you left, I don't think he was sober for a week. Dale put his foot down and dragged him to a meeting. Things started to improve from there. He's in a better place now, although he's still not the same as he was."

I shook my head. "I don't think either one of us will ever be the same. I don't want to forget Melody, and if I try to move on, that's what will happen. Irrational, I know, but still. My heart aches every day. For her. For me. For Austin. For us. For what might have been. It's too much to take. And no one understands unless they've been there. No matter what they say or the lame platitudes coming from their lips."

I got so caught up in my explanation that I didn't hear the garage door. Avery put his hand on my thigh and gestured towards the stairs to the basement. Austin stood halfway up the stairs, frozen in place. His mouth hung open, but he didn't say anything. There's no playbook for this scenario.

Avery made his way up the staircase. "I'm going to give you two some time alone." He vaporized up the stairs faster than a rabbit being chased by a hunting dog.

Austin reached the top and found his voice first. "Hi, Cheyenne," he whispered. "I knew you were coming, but I thought you were going to be here yesterday. I thought maybe you changed your mind." He moved towards me. "Is it all right if I sit here with you?"

I nodded my head in agreement because I couldn't speak.

"I'm glad you're here, and that you agreed to help with the restaurant expansion project. We need your expertise."

"I'm not going to lie. I almost turned around and went home multiple times. Especially after sitting in traffic for two hours in Phoenix." Seeing him in person made my chest tighten. He still made me feel things. "But I'm glad I didn't."

He reached out his hand, and I thought he was going to touch my cheek, but he stopped and lowered his hand back into his lap. "I've missed you. I didn't call because I wasn't sure you wanted me to. I checked my phone constantly, hoping you would send me a text message."

"I'm sorry, Austin. I held my phone in my hand and tried to send you a message multiple times. But I didn't know what to say to you. I figured you were angry with me and I didn't want to be on the receiving end."

He sighed. "I'm not angry. I mean, I was. But more hurt than angry. I still love you. We can't forget Melody, and I don't want to. But I'd like to think she would want us to stay together, no matter what. Don't you think we deserve to give ourselves another chance?"

Tears welled up in my eyes and I wiped them on the back of my hand. I'd had the same thought a million times. But I always backed away from it, too afraid. But here, looking into the eyes of this man I loved... "I'm willing to give it a try if you are."

He took my chin in his hand and pulled me in for a kiss. I closed my eyes and his lips pressed against mine, soft with a hint of hesitation. I kissed him back, giving him the feedback he needed to proceed. He wrapped his arms around me, drawing me into his chest and igniting the flame between us.

We took our time, reconnecting with our mouths and our hands. I didn't realize how much my body ached for him until he was right in front of me. The connection between us still burned, even if we denied it existed. My desire for him increased as we reconnected.

I let go of his lips for a moment and breathed into his ear, "I'm still your wife. Take me to bed, handsome. You know you want to."

He scooped me up in his arms and carried me downstairs to his room. Our room. That fourth bedroom was never going to get used.

Fifty-Five
Sydney - Reality Bites

On the way home from the Caribbean, I reflected on the last two weeks. Our honeymoon was relaxing and filled with passionate moments. Swinging in a hammock with Vinnie, a frozen cocktail in my hand, listening to the sounds of the ocean. Or walking barefoot on the beach, hand in hand, with the crystal blue water lapping at my feet. I wanted to stay there forever.

We indulged in some of the perks at the all-inclusive resort. Snorkeling through the reefs was my favorite activity, and we went twice. Seeing all the colorful fish, coral and other sea creatures was amazing! I took pictures with my phone in a Ziplock bag, attempting to freeze time. When I was a little girl, I'd wanted to be a mermaid when I grew up, and this experience solidified my childhood decision.

Parasailing over the ocean came in at a close second place. I don't enjoy being up so high. I like to keep my feet on the ground or in the water. Vinnie let me squeeze his hand as we ascended high above the resort. The beauty of the island and ocean from this perspective took my breath away. I was too terrified to take pictures or videos, but the memory is etched into my mind.

Every meal we ate impressed me. The local cuisine was incorporated into the menu selections, and every entrée made my tastebuds euphoric. I'd never eaten fruit this fresh! It made the smoothies so much better than the ones I made with frozen fruit at home.

As wonderful as this island paradise was, at the end of two weeks I was ready to come home. I missed my boys, and I missed Samson. I didn't realize how much of a shadow he was until he wasn't there with me. Grandma and Grandpa Allegro were surely ready for the boys to go home, too. They are adorable, but loads of work.

Vinnie dropped me off at the house and then went to his parents' house to retrieve the boys. I dragged my suitcase over to the washing machine and started loading it with dirty clothes. My toiletries went back on their shelves in the bathroom. I opened Ziplock bags and hung our swimsuits over the shower curtain. I was about to put the suitcase in the garage when the doorbell rang.

"Wow! That was fast!" I said as I opened the door. But it wasn't Vinnie on the porch. A short man wearing a button-down shirt with a tie and dress pants stood in front of me.

"I'm sorry. I thought you were my husband coming home. How can I help you?" I smiled.

"Are you Sydney Campbell?" he asked, without smiling back.

I nodded. "Yes, I am."

He held out a manilla envelope and I took it in a reflex.

"You've been served. Have a nice day."

He turned and walked down the porch steps. *What just happened*? I couldn't believe it. *Someone's suing me*? I turned the envelope over and unclasped the opening. The front door hung open as I walked in a trance to sit on one of the dining room chairs.

I skimmed over the front page of the packet, then pulled out my phone and hit speed dial.

"Venus Anderson," she answered.

"V., it's Sydney."

"How was the honeymoon? Didn't I tell you that resort was fabulous?"

"We had a wonderful time; I'll tell you later. That's not why I'm calling."

"Give it to me straight."

I sighed. "I can't believe this, but I just got served papers. One of my former classmates and sorority sister, Jessica, is alleging I didn't write *Our Dance*. She's claiming I stole it out of her diary. It isn't true, Venus. You know that. I know that. Austin knows that. Mr. Nelson knows it. What am I going to do?"

Venus switched into manager mode. "They served papers to me, too. Nuisance lawsuits like this happen all the time. I already have our lawyers on it. I'm so sorry, Sydney. Yes, I know you wrote the song."

"Austin and I have a copyright on it. We registered it before we came out to record the demo. That's at least one point in our favor. I can send a copy of it to you."

"Great. Yes, send it to me, please. Let me assure you this is not a big deal. We will respond with a copy of the copyright and some strong language, and this should go away. I have your back."

"Yes, thank you. Vinnie is bringing in the kids so I have to go. I'll send everything to you today. You're a life saver and a helluva friend. Bye."

The boys ran into the living room and I stooped down to scoop them up in my arms. Vinnie and Samson found me kissing them all over as they giggled and squealed. I put them down and they raced upstairs to their room.

I took Vinnie's hand and walked us to the table. "Sit down. Boy, have I got some news."

THE END

(but not quite yet)

What We Can't Have: Part III

Coming Summer 2025

Acknowledgements
So many people supported me...

Once again, my wonderful editor extraordinaire, Deborah Halverson, assisted me in making this story shine. She pushed me to delve into the depths and pull out the juicy bits to enhance my vision for this story.

My dear friends Jenny, and Joan (posthumously) who patiently waited for more chapters as I plodded through my rough drafts, and provided encouragement to keep me moving towards the finish line.

Professionally, I cannot thank Alexa and the team at Women in Publishing enough. They provide so many valuable resources and education to help indie authors like me.

Thank you to Sarah at Moonchildreams for creating such beautiful illustrations to add depth and flavor to my characters and the story.

Most importantly:

Thanks to you, the readers. Without you, this story, and my author dreams, would be nothing.

About the author

Selina Violet is a writer, entrepreneur, and author. She is passionate about sharing her stories with others. Before establishing Violet Publishing, Inc., Selina honed her skills in the education, banking, and health care industries. She loves 80's music and movies, concert tickets, and Hershey Kisses. When she's not glued to her keyboard, you can find her reading, crafting, or planning her next epic road trip. Selina lives in Pittsburgh, Pennsylvania with her children and a spoiled dog.

Find out more about her on her website: https://selinaviolet.com

On Instagram: @selinavioletauthor

On TikTok: @selinavioletauthor

Endnotes

1. *The Lost Boys*. Directed by Joel Schumacher, Warner Bros, 1987. Film.

2. **shrek** (n): a gag or prank typically pulled on one person. A reverse shrek is when one person pulls a prank on a group of people. *Indian Summer*, 1993. Film

3. *Willy Wonka and the Chocolate Factory*. Directed by Mel Stuart, Paramount, 1971. Film.

4. *My Big Fat Greek Wedding*. Directed by Joel Zwick, Gold Circle Films, 2002. Film.

5. Swift, Taylor. "The Man. *Lover*. Republic Records, 2019.

6. *Hitch*. Directed by Andy Tennant, Columbia Pictures, 2005. Film.

7. Cinderella. Directed by Wilfred Jackson, Hamilton Luske, and Clyde Geromini, Walt Disney Productions, 1950.

8. *That Thing You Do*. Directed by Tom Hanks, Twentieth-Century Fox, 1996. Film.

9. The Devil Wears Prada. 2004. Movie.

10. www.Lasvegasnevada.gov/News/Blog/Detail/getting-married-in-las-vegas

11. *The Devil Wears Prada*. Directed by David Frankel, Fox 2000 Pictures, 2006. Film.

12. Strait, George. "You Look So Good In Love." *Right or Wrong*, MCA, 1983.

Made in the USA
Middletown, DE
18 October 2024

62849272R00189